DARK ALPHA'S AWAKENING

A Reaper Story

Donna Grant

SMP Swerve

www.stmartins.com

Cover: design by Patricia Schmitt; photographs © Fotorince/ Adobe Stock

Author photo © Yvette Michelle Portraits LLC

eISBN 9781250231710 (ebook)

First eBook Edition: February 2019

For Charity
For your dedication, your organization.
But especially for your friendship.

"Move swift as the Wind and closely-formed as the Wood. Attack like the Fire and be still as the Mountain."

-**Sun Tzu,** *The Art of War*

The Beginning . . .

The nothingness was vast. So far-reaching that it never ended. An eternity of stars and solar systems for her to explore.

She didn't know how long she drifted in the darkness, staring at distant stars. It could have been days or eons. Time meant nothing. She didn't even know what time was.

One day, she grew curious about a planet she passed. For the first time, she wanted to leave the ocean of black and see what was on the massive globe.

Once on the ground, she was astounded to find a world of vivid colors so bright, she had to shield her eyes. As she walked, she took in the moist air and the mountains rising around her covered in tall trees and clumps of beautiful blooms that took her breath away.

Then she heard it. A deep trumpet call. Unable to stay away, she followed the sound until she came across the beast. She had no idea what it was, but it was magnificent. Tall, muscular, with giant horns extending outward and upward.

The soulful, dark gaze of the animal met hers. She took a tentative step closer, wanting to touch such a creature. It didn't move, just waited patiently for her.

Suddenly, the animal reared up, a scream of pain bursting from it. She spotted a thin rod sticking out of the animal's neck. The beast tried to run, but its legs buckled, and it fell over, dead.

She stared in absolute horror, trying to understand what had just occurred.

Then, they came.

The beings were enormously tall and thin, their limbs long. They wore animal fur for clothes, and their skin was covered in some kind of yellow paste that had dried and cracked. They held weapons and rushed around the beautiful creature they had brought down. To her dismay, they began to cut into it.

It was then she realized that they planned to use the beast for food, clothing, and weapons.

She listened to their words, and slowly began to understand them. One was talking about being hungry.

Hunger. She didn't know what that meant.

She wondered why none of them had seen her, especially since she stood out in the open field among the tall grass. Yet, not a single one of them looked her way.

As she studied the beings, she noted their lack of hair. She reached up and lifted the long black strand that fell over her shoulder. Then she noticed the three fingers on their hands. She raised hers and counted five digits. But that wasn't the only difference.

Unable to watch the animal slowly destroyed, regardless of the reasons why, she returned to the darkness she knew. Except she couldn't stop thinking of the creature and the beings, of the rich colors and amazing smells.

She began going from planet to planet, trying to find beings who looked similar to her. Surely, she couldn't be the only one. There had to be someone else out there.

She finally found them.

They were beautiful. Each and every one. As was the world. Flowers were everywhere, so many bright and fragrant buds. She spent more time with the plants, admiring the shape of their petals, learning the subtle scents.

But she also absorbed the language of the planet's inhabitants as she did. She walked among them, learning their words, and somehow not surprised that they couldn't see her.

They were Fae. And while the section of land she was in was stunning, apparently, there was another set of Fae. The Dark. Curious, she went to find them, as well.

Dark was an apt name for them. They cared for power and standing. Where the Light world was draped in colors and cheerfulness, the Dark's half of the realm was nefarious and sinister.

The wickedness touched some Dark more than others. At first, she grouped the Fae into Light and Dark. But the more time she spent with them, the more she realized it wasn't so straightforward.

There were Light who ran on the fringes of what some would call Dark. And some Dark who rarely caused harm. But the Fae didn't care. You were one or the other.

She stood by and watched as a civil war erupted. Despite that, she remained. She walked among the Fae, noting the similarities between them and her. And it wasn't long before she realized that she belonged with them.

War and death were all she witnessed, decade after decade. While she was interested in the Fae's magic, it was their weapons that she truly appreciated. So, it was no wonder that she discovered where they were crafted.

There, she watched as the Fae designed and fashioned each blade with expert precision, each a stunning weapon, unlike anything she'd ever seen.

Eventually, she grew bored of surveying. She was lonely. Observing conversations, laughter, arguments, and even lovemaking made her long to find someone who she could interact with.

But that wasn't meant to be. Her mistake was remaining with the Fae during their endless, relentless war. It became ingrained in her. Instead of wanting to make peace or find someone to be her friend, she came to crave one thing—death.

One day, she decided she'd sat on the sidelines long enough. It was time to take action. She made her way to the Fires of Erwar, the secret mountain where special blades were made. There, she forged her own weapon out of beautiful, black metal. Then she clothed herself in the attire of battle. Instead of picking one side of the Fae to join, she went out into the universe again.

It wasn't difficult to find wars. She willed herself to become visible and joined her first skirmish, and soon learned how good it felt to wield a sword. It took her some time to discover how to use the weapon, but once she did, she was unstoppable.

She was soon dubbed the *Mistress of War*. Any army she joined rejoiced, knowing they would defeat their enemies with her by their side.

She bathed in blood, delighted in death.

Celebrated victory.

But she didn't pay attention to how quickly—or violently—her power grew until she destroyed her first realm. She thought it was just a fluke until the second and third realms were demolished.

It wasn't long before the armies that once cheered at the sight of her now ran in fear. Still, she didn't stop. She comprehended then that she didn't need anyone. She had always been on her own. And she always would be.

So she waged war by herself.

For a while, it helped mask the loneliness that consumed her. She didn't know who she was, how she had the power she did, or where she came from. She had no name, no friends. No home. And no family.

For centuries, she visited realm after realm, laying waste to them. Until one day she looked down at the blood that covered her. Once, it had been the very thing she sought. But now, it made her sick to her stomach.

She ran fast and far until she found herself back in the dark nothingness between realms. She cried, holding herself because there was no one else. Once more, she drifted, but this time, she didn't care about realms or the distant stars. She no longer wanted to exist.

That was her last thought as she lowered her lids and willed her heart to stop beating.

When she opened her eyes again, she found herself lying on a soft bed of grass with birds chirping around her. She rolled onto her back and bent a leg. A dragonfly came to land atop her knee, its large eyes staring at her.

She smiled at it. When it flew off, she sat up and looked around in wonder. Amid the mighty forest were animals of all kinds, watching her curiously. She got to her feet and spotted the tranquil, blue waters of a lake.

With the use of just a small bit of magic, she discovered she was the only person on the realm. It was the first time she'd felt at peace. It was contentment the likes of which she had never experienced before. She knew she'd found her home. This was the place she would call her own, somewhere she could be herself.

She looked down at her hand and spied her sword still clutched tightly in her fist. Before she could enjoy this new realm, she needed to set aside who she was. The Mistress of War would have to disappear. And to do that, she needed to return to where she had been fashioned.

When she revisited the Realm of the Fae, she discovered that their war still raged. She attempted to speak to the rulers of the Light and Dark, but neither were interested in peace.

That left her few options. She could easily best both and bring about her own ceasefire, but she had no interest in ruling anyone—much less an entire race. She would have to think of another solution.

She walked aimlessly for days, looking for some kind of inspiration. To her surprise, she found it on a battlefield.

He was utterly resplendent and battled with a fierceness that stole her breath. A natural leader, men followed him, quickly and easily doing as he bade in order to win their battle.

She could have watched him for an eternity. He was a formidable opponent in war, but with his friends, his smile outshone the sun. He was valiant, fearless, and intelligent. He alone could win the war for the Light.

Yet when he looked her way, she hurriedly veiled herself. She might want to talk to him, to touch him, but she couldn't after everything she had done. He fought, not because he liked it, but because he protected his people.

She'd waged war because she enjoyed it. How could he ever want to be around someone like her?

Feeling more alone than ever, she continued onward, intending to forget the handsome Fae. Her mind, however, was still on him when she stumbled across another Light. He was battle-weary.

There was a kindness about him that instantly drew her. She stayed, trying to figure out why she liked him. For two days, she followed him, learning his movements and his acquaintances. He was a fine warrior for the Fae army. Unfortunately, he chose the wrong friends.

They betrayed him, sinking a blade into his back before they deserted their post and headed toward the Dark. She remained with him, easing his passing as his last breath left him.

She touched his hand, and his eyes opened. She smiled at him.

"Are you Death?" he asked.

She gave a nod, an idea suddenly forming. "I am."

"What happens now?"

"I have a proposition for you, Theo. You're dead, and you can remain that way if you wish. But I can bring you back. You will be the first of my Reapers."

Doubt swirled in his silver eyes. "Reapers?"

"I am Death. I will be judge and jury to the Fae. As a Reaper, you would carry out my orders."

He blew out a breath. "You mean kill."

"I mean justice."

"Yes," he replied instantly. "I accept."

She pushed some of her power into him. It not only healed his wound, but it also made his own magic stronger. "You were betrayed by your so-called friends. Hunt them down and bring them to me."

He rose to his feet and bowed his head. "How will I find you?"

"You need only call for me. I will find *you*. Oh," she said and touched his arm before he left. "You'll discover your magic and power increased. No one can best you as a Reaper."

He smiled and left.

"Death," she said to herself and nodded. She now had a purpose. But first, she had to put her sword somewhere that no Fae could ever find it.

With one last look back at the handsome Fae she knew she would never forget, Death left to find a realm to hide her sword. Because today was the start of a new beginning.

And the Fae were about to be delivered a reckoning.

Chapter One

MARCH

INCHMICKERY, SCOTLAND—REAPER STRONGHOLD

He was dying. Cael didn't need to look at his wound or the blood pooling around him to know that his life was coming to an end.

Shite. Everything hurt. He leaned his head back against the fallen tree. He could hear the distant sounds of battle. How could he have been so stupid as to follow two of the weakest, most cowardly Fae into the forest without backup?

He should've known something was wrong the moment he entered the woods, but he'd been too intent on stopping the pair from deserting. It wasn't until the last second that he realized they had been a distraction all along.

The minute the two deserters stopped and faced him, Cael knew things were about to go sideways. And had they ever. He was surrounded by Dark within seconds.

Yet it hadn't been the Dark who killed him. It had been his men.

He coughed, blood running from the corner of his lips.

With a swipe of his once useful arm, he wiped it away. His injuries would keep him immobile and ensure a slow, painful death.

Certainly not the fitting end for a warrior.

Not the passing he'd expected for more years than he could remember.

Cael coughed again. He had to get his mind off the agony of his body. He tried to think of Corla. She had promised herself to him. He had thought he loved her. Would have sworn his heart was Corla's.

Then, he beheld the woman on the battlefield. Even now, he could recall every detail of her. He was in the middle of combat, dodging Dark orbs and using both his magic and his sword to push back the enemy. His focus had been entirely on his foe.

And yet, for reasons that he couldn't explain even now, he'd turned his head to the side, and his gaze landed on her. Beautiful didn't begin to describe her. She stood on the fringes of the battle, unfazed by the carnage as she stared at him—him!—with lavender eyes.

He had to know her, had to find out who she was. But by the time the skirmish was over, she was nowhere to be found. Cael had searched the dead, fearing she had been killed. But he found no trace of her.

Yet, her image lingered in his mind. Blue-black waves of hair, falling freely to her waist. And eyes that knew not only the secrets of the universe but which had seen everything.

He wanted her heart and her body. Because in that millisecond of time, he knew he was meant to be with her.

Knowing it and finding her were two different things, however. Nearly a thousand years passed without a single trace of her. So much for his vow to locate her again. Now, he would likely go to his grave without knowing her name.

The sound of footsteps approaching alerted him that his torture wasn't finished. He looked at his sword. With his teeth clenched, he leaned to the side to reach for his weapon. Blood gushed from his wounds, and pain sliced through him, robbing him of breath.

Sweat beaded his brow as he fought not to make a sound while he struggled to right himself again with only one hand, all the while holding his sword. If he were going to die, he'd do it while wielding his weapon.

The Dark were closing in on him again. He counted six of them. Then, out of nowhere, a petite figure appeared, spinning and turning from one Dark to the other while a sword danced as swiftly as the attacker's feet.

Cael had seen a lot of Fae fight, but he'd never seen one who moved like this. The speed was unlike anything he'd ever witnessed, but it was the way the assailant attacked that was staggering to watch.

Within seconds, the Dark were dead. And all without one finger being laid upon the tiny person. The warrior stood with *their back to him, a helmet on to hide his or her face.*

He wanted to tell them how amazing they were and thank them for the help, but he was fading fast. Cael kept his eyes on the figure as they turned. His heart skipped a beat when the helmet was finally removed, and he found himself looking into the face of the woman he'd been searching for.

The helmet and sword vanished, as did her bloodstained clothes, suddenly replaced by a long, black gown with a full skirt. Her black hair in an intricate braid.

"Hello, Cael," she said.

He had no idea how she knew his name, but it didn't matter. She was with him. He wouldn't die alone.

Cael fought to keep his eyes open. She knelt beside him and took his hand, her lavender gaze locked with his. He couldn't believe that she was there and touching him. The betrayal of his men didn't matter anymore.

"I can offer you another life," she whispered.

He frowned, unsure whether he'd heard her correctly. Then, his lids became too heavy to keep open, and they closed. It became harder to breathe. He wanted to stay with her. He would endure pain for eternity just to be with her. But he no longer had any say in such matters.

Her hand flattened against the side of his face as his life faded. Seconds later, the pain left him, but he could still feel her touch. He opened his eyes once more.

"I'm Death, Cael. I'm here to offer you a position as one of

my Reapers."

~

His eyes snapped open as he sat up in bed. Cael couldn't remember the last time he'd thought about the day he'd become a Reaper. The dream had been so vivid, it was as if he were reliving the entire event.

He swung his legs over the side of the mattress and dropped his chin to his chest. He stayed there only a few minutes before he rose and dressed.

Wind howled outside as a storm lashed the east coast of Scotland. The Reapers had been in Inchmickery for a while now. He hated being so far from Ireland, but they had to keep ahead of their enemy.

He strode through the old, concrete compound that the humans had abandoned years ago. His six Reapers were in residence, as well. Few were up at the early hour, though. This was the time Cael took each morning to think about the day ahead and ruminate on anything that might have gone wrong the day before.

Cael walked through the door and came to stand outside beneath a protective overhang. Waves crashed violently against the rocks and concrete, sending water soaring. The wind drove the rain at an angle, drenching everything—including him. But he didn't care.

"I suppose you're going to stand there brooding all day."

Cael drew in a breath at the sound of Fintan's voice. Once one of the most feared—and infamous—assassins of the Fae, Fintan was an integral part of the Reapers.

A group Cael led.

"What is it?" Fintan asked over the sounds of the storm and the sea.

Cael waited until Fintan moved closer. "Do you remember when you became a Reaper?"

"I do. It's not exactly something you forget."

"I suppose not."

Fintan crossed his arms over his chest, uncaring that the waves drenched him. "Spit it out, Cael. What's bothering you?"

Cael had come outside to be alone. It seemed fitting that there was a storm raging since he'd felt one within himself for some time. He looked into Fintan's red-rimmed, white eyes. "I dreamed of the day I became a Reaper."

Fintan shoved his long, white hair from his face after a wave struck him. "So?" he asked, confusion marring his expression.

"Have you done that?"

"No."

"Why did I?"

Fintan raised a brow. "You ask me things I can't answer."

"The dream meant something."

"About Erith?"

Cael braced himself for the next wave before it hit. As leader of the Reapers, he knew how each of them had been betrayed. It was one of the many gifts given to him by Death.

Death. Erith.

Her.

He'd known her by all three names. The attraction he felt for her hadn't dimmed when he discovered that she was Death. In fact, it increased.

Right on the heels of that was discovering that there could never be anything between them. However, not even the knowledge that he would spend eons near her but never actually have her could have made him refuse her offer.

Being a Reaper meant everything to Cael. He was doing more for the Fae now than he had when he lived among them.

"Cael?"

He swung his head to Fintan, only then realizing that he hadn't answered. "I do think it was about Erith. It's always been about her."

"You're referring to Bran," Fintan said, his lips peeled

back in a sneer.

Bran. The Reaper who had defied Death and not only fell in love but also told the female Fae who he was. Both offenses were grave. Cael still believed that Erith would have ignored Bran falling in love, despite her rule that there be no relationships, but Bran had broken the first rule of being a Reaper: no Fae could know who they were.

Death had had no choice but to carry out her punishment and end the Light Fae's life. Bran had gone mad with grief over the loss. He split the Reapers, forcing them to fight each other.

Cael had been the newest member of the group at the time. He and Eoghan had bonded quickly, both of them looking up to their leader, Theo. So, when Bran and the other Reapers killed Theo, there was no other option for Cael and Eoghan than to fight Bran.

Before either Cael or Eoghan could slay Bran, Erith stepped in and tossed Bran into a realm she'd created just for his punishment.

Who could have guessed that thousands of years later, someone would let Bran loose? Or that Bran would somehow learn how to syphon Death's power and life force?

"We need to end him," Cael said.

Fintan snorted. "That's not something you need to

convince any of us to do. We're all ready."

"There's something you don't know. I saw Death recently. She returned to the O'Byrne land."

Fintan's brow furrowed deeply. "Are you telling me she got the black sword that Ettie used? The one Bran hunted for?"

Cael nodded. "She called for it. It belongs to her. More than that, I saw her clothes change for just a moment into leather and chainmail."

"Fek me," Fintan murmured as he ran a hand down his face. "She's the Mistress of War, isn't she?"

Cael thought back to the day he'd seen her fight. The day he died and was reborn a Reaper. He'd known she was special before learning she was Death. "I think so."

"Why did she stop?" Fintan's surprise gave way to anger. "And why the fek hasn't she gone after Bran before now? Why did she wait? If she's the Mistress of War, there's nothing more powerful than her. She could wipe Bran out with a thought."

"Perhaps at one time, but not now," Cael reminded his friend. "Bran has taken too much of her power."

Fintan turned his back to a wave that slammed into him. "But she has the sword."

"Which means, she's going after Bran."

"Not alone," Fintan stated.

Cael grinned. "No, she won't be alone. Whether she

agrees or not, we'll be there with her."

"Have you told her that?"

"Not yet."

Fintan crossed his arms over his chest. "Do you know where she's at? She did refuse to answer any of us for quite some time."

"I'm not going to look for her. I'm going to look for Bran. He wants to fight me anyway, right?"

Fintan's smile was slow. "Oh, I like this. Shall I tell the others?"

"Aye. We need to come up with a plan."

"What about Eoghan and his Reapers?"

"We're going to need them, as well." Cael still couldn't believe that Eoghan had returned and that there were more Reapers, but he was glad of it. "So far, Bran doesn't know about them. Let's make certain it stays that way until it's time."

Fintan slapped Cael on the back. "Don't worry, brother. Bran's days are numbered."

Cael waited until Fintan had returned inside before he let out a sigh. He hoped they were able to move fast enough to destroy Bran before Erith was past the point of no return.

Because a life without her wasn't a life worth living.

Cael said Eoghan's name and waited for his friend to arrive. It was time they had a talk.

Chapter Two

The crippling weight of eons of decisions rested awkwardly on her shoulders. Erith stood amid the flowers on her realm, hoping to find the calm they usually brought her. Ever since she'd retrieved her sword from Killarney, memories of her time as Mistress of War repeatedly assaulted her.

Like the sword wished to remind her of all the destruction and harm she'd caused around the universe.

As if she could ever forget.

It didn't matter how much good she did, it would never make up for the horrors she'd committed during that dreadful time. And the life she swore to never return to was now her only option if she wanted to save the Reapers.

She didn't care about herself. It was Cael and the others that mattered. Because if she died, Bran would become Death, and he wouldn't hesitate to wipe out the Reapers as sadistically and callously as he could.

The Reapers were her responsibility. She'd given them power and returned their lives to them. No matter how strong they were—and the Reapers were exceedingly powerful—they would never be able to stand against Bran, who now had almost all of her power.

When Erith realized that Bran was taking her magic and that the Reapers wouldn't be able to fight him on their own, Cael and Eoghan wanted a battle. She understood their need after everything they had experienced, but Bran was too strong now. The Reapers could weaken him, but Bran had taken too much of her magic and life force for them to do any real damage.

Which left her to handle him.

She wasn't afraid to face Bran. What he knew was merely a thimbleful of what she had experienced. Yet he had the upper hand after draining her magic.

If only she knew how he'd done it. If only she could stop him before he took it all. Her fear had stopped her from retrieving the sword until now. And it was that same apprehension that would be the end of her.

Erith slid her gaze to where the weapon lay upon a gnarled tree branch that dipped to the ground. The sword itself was truly a work of art. Created of magic in the Fires of Erwar, it was . . . epic. One of the greatest things she'd ever conceived.

From the moment she formed it, she had heard its call. Even when it lay buried beneath miles of earth, she'd always known exactly where it was. There was a connection between them. Because the sword held a part of her.

She looked down at her palm. She could still feel the weight of the weapon, even after holding it for only a few minutes. Her fingers itched to wrap around the pommel and lift the blade, to feel the heft of it.

And to sink it into a body.

No. Not just anybody. Bran.

The second the Fae doorway opened to her world, Erith felt it. No one was supposed to enter, but Cael defied her orders and ventured there at times. Was it him?

Please, no.

She wasn't ready to face him yet. Especially not after realizing that he'd seen her retrieve the sword. He would have questions, and she didn't want to answer them.

With her eyes closed, she listened for the sound of footsteps. It took her but a heartbeat to grasp that it wasn't Cael. The stride was wrong. The only other one who knew where to locate her was Eoghan.

Erith turned as the leader of the second Reaper group emerged from the foliage. Eoghan's long, black hair was loose and hanging down his back. His liquid silver eyes were trained on her.

Eoghan had always been destined to lead, but his wife's betrayal had broken him in ways Erith worried might never be healed. It had never hindered him being a Reaper, however.

When Eoghan was enveloped in a storm of magic to save Cael, no one had known what happened to him. Even Erith had searched for him, to no avail. It was a Halfling and her violin that somehow called Eoghan home. And when he returned, more than just his eyes had changed.

That's when Erith realized that he was ready to take over the second group. And just as she'd always known, he was doing a wonderful job. His team, which had never quite come together before—because they never had a reason to—was becoming a cohesive unit.

Eoghan's gaze moved from Erith to the sword. His chest expanded as he took a breath. "So, it's true."

She didn't need to ask how he knew. There was only one answer—Cael. Erith merely stared at Eoghan, waiting for his next question.

His head turned back to her. "You knew the sword was with Ettie and her sisters all along."

"I did."

"Because you put it there."

She nodded.

There was a long pause, broken only by the songs of the birds around them. Then, Eoghan said, "Cael is worried about you. We all are."

"You don't think I know what I'm doing?"

"We don't know anything," he said with a frown.

"You've not told me or Cael anything."

"You don't need to know."

Eoghan's lips flattened as his look turned hard. "That's bloody nonsense. If you don't want to tell me, at least notify Cael."

"Why?"

Eoghan snorted loudly. "You know why."

"No, I don't."

The Reaper leaned his head to the side as he regarded her for a long minute. "Is it that you really don't know? Or that you just don't want to admit it?"

"I've no idea what you're talking about. I'm Death, Eoghan. I don't need to remind you that I brought all of you back from the dead and gave you added powers. I can take that all away."

"I'm aware."

She took a step toward him. "I make my own decisions. I've never gone to any of you before. I won't do it now."

He inhaled deeply. "Each of us knows exactly how strong you are. You don't need us. You could easily handle everything on your own."

Her heart missed a beat. He was right. So very right. She'd longed for company, which was one of the reasons she'd created the Reapers. But she soon came to comprehend that they meant more to her. So she had made sure to keep distance between herself and them.

All these centuries, Erith believed that she was keeping herself separate from the Reapers. And all the while, they had seen right through the walls she'd attempted to erect.

For so long, she had hidden the fact that she'd created the Reapers because she didn't want to be alone. And all the time, they had known.

"You don't have to do this on your own," Eoghan said. "In fact, you shouldn't. We're your army."

She shook her head. "You can't defeat Bran."

"Do you really think it'll just be the two of you fighting? You know he'll have the Dark he's been recruiting with him. You can't afford to divide your attention between him and the Dark. For you to win, you need to be focused entirely on him."

"And let you and the other Reapers fight his army?"

"Damn right. And, if the opportunity arises, you know both Cael and I will take a shot at Bran. He didn't just betray you. He betrayed us, as well."

She turned and walked a few steps away. "I think you have a valid point."

"It was Cael's idea."

Erith spun around to Eoghan. "Then why didn't he come?"

"He didn't think you'd see him."

She had blocked Cael and all others from entering her realm for a while. Not to mention, she had ignored his repeated calls for her. She hadn't wanted any of the Reapers—but especially Cael—to see her weakened state.

"Your bond with Cael was always strong," Eoghan continued. "You need to repair what's been damaged."

"Perhaps it's better this way."

"That's shite."

She raised a brow in annoyance. "Careful."

"I'm merely stating what needs to be said."

"I've kept my distance from all of you."

"But mostly Cael. Why is that, I wonder?"

It took a Herculean effort for Erith to keep the worry from her face. Had Eoghan seen something? In his vow of silence, had he noticed something that she had accidentally let show?

The longer she looked at him, the more she saw that he had, in fact, seen quite a lot.

Eoghan's lips curved into a soft smile. "Others tend to forget I'm there when I don't speak. It makes it easy to read between their words. Or see stolen glances that others missed in conversations."

Erith looked away, unsure how to reply.

"Your secret is safe with me," Eoghan told her. "I kept it for the last several thousand years, so you don't have to worry that I'll let anything slip now."

She blew out a breath and returned her gaze to him. "Why haven't you said anything before now?"

"I knew why you kept it a secret. It was rather easy to figure out. I also hoped that you might give in and tell him."

"I can't. I won't."

Eoghan smiled sadly. "I know. Can I ask why you changed the rules and allowed the Reapers to fall in love?"

"I never stopped any of you from finding love. I simply knew that when it came down to it, you would follow your heart before you followed the other Reapers."

"Which is why you put in the rule. I'd have done the same in your place."

She put her hand on the bark of a tree, feeling the rough texture scrape against her palm. It always helped for her to touch the plants—almost as if a little magic were exchanged between them.

"I knew after Bran that the odds of one of you falling in love again were great. It was simply a matter of time. And then it happened with Baylon. Except I saw a way for it to work. Jordyn was a Halfling, but more than that, she went out of her way to help the Reapers."

"And by her being half human, she could know of us without having to be killed."

Erith nodded. "I'm glad those of you who have found love are happy. You deserve it."

"And you don't?"

She didn't answer, because she wasn't sure she could.

Eoghan ran a hand down his face. "There's a whole part of your life we don't know about, isn't there?"

"You know very little about me at all."

"You've made sure of that. Yet, before Cael joined us, you spent much more time with the Reapers. That's when I first noticed you treated Cael differently. You kept him at more of a distance, but you were always the first to congratulate him on his successes."

She swallowed, not liking the sinking feeling within her. "I was that transparent?"

"Only to me."

At least, there was that. Erith didn't want to think about what might happen if Cael ever found out. If he didn't return her affection, she'd likely never recover.

And if he did . . . that was a road she couldn't allow herself to go down.

Ever.

"Don't shut him out," Eoghan cautioned. He glanced at the sword. "I don't care who you once were. I know who you are now. I know what you've done—for us and thousands of other Fae. That's what matters."

His words touched her deeply. "Thank you."

"We need to go after Bran together. We need you. Be the force we know you to be."

Erith watched him as he turned and walked away, his words lingering long after he was gone. She couldn't stop thinking about Cael. She should've known that he would come up with the perfect plan. Not that any of the other Reapers weren't capable, but Cael's mind worked differently than the others'. He saw strategies others never even thought of.

Eoghan was right. They did need to work together. It meant that she would have to be around Cael. In her weakened state, the feelings she tamped down and ignored kept returning, stronger each time.

And she kept wondering ... if she were dying, what would it hurt to tell Cael how she felt? Perhaps even kiss him?

Then she imagined what Bran would do to the Reapers. There was no way she was going to stand by and let Bran hurt her family—because that's what the Reapers were. Her family.

The family she'd never had.

The family she'd always wanted.

The family she had never allowed herself to enjoy.

Chapter Three

The waiting was interminable. Cael paced a spot in the grass in front of the doorway to Death's realm until he wore it smooth. Then he finally sat and began to meditate in an effort to calm himself.

Thoughts of Erith clouded his mind so much that it took him several tries before he could focus and find the peace he knew he would need—regardless of what Eoghan said when he finally returned.

Cael's thoughts drifted like a lazy river, winding and rolling. Slowly, his anxiety lessened, and he was able to see the path before him clearly in his mind. Everyone from his friends to his enemies was around him.

He looked at the Reapers, who were at his back as he and Eoghan stood shoulder-to-shoulder. The Reapers were strong and ready, undeterred by what they were about to face. A massive Dark Fae army spread out behind Bran, who looked supremely confident.

If it were simply a numbers game, then Bran would win.

But this was so much more than that. This was about

family and honor. This was about ensuring that Bran's life was taken so he could never harm anyone again.

As Cael looked over the sea of Dark Fae, he did a double-take when he spotted Seamus among them. When had the Fae left Death's realm? Or had she let him go? Cael hated not knowing. Erith was intentionally keeping all the Reapers at arm's length, and it was going to get her killed.

Bran never intended to go up against Death on his own. If Erith were at full power, Bran and his army wouldn't stand a chance. But now... now, anything could happen.

Cael saw two figures standing between the armies. One was Xaneth. The Fae hadn't chosen a side yet. While Cael wasn't sure about him, the one thing he did know was that Xaneth was a fine warrior. They could use him on their side.

Directly across from Xaneth was a Dark Fae. The face was blurred so Cael couldn't make out who it was. But it was another warrior who could go to either side. They needed to figure out who it was and why that Dark was so important.

Cael looked over the entire scene several more times until he was unable to glean anything else from it. Only then did he pull himself from the meditation. When he opened his eyes, Eoghan was sitting on a rock, rolling a long piece of grass between his fingers.

"About fekking time," Eoghan grumbled.

Cael frowned. "How long have you been sitting there?"

"Two bloody hours. You went deep, Cael. You never heard me."

But Cael didn't wish to talk about his meditation now. "Did you see her?"

Eoghan blew out a loud breath. "I did."

"And?" Cael asked irritably.

"The sword was with her, though she wasn't holding it. She looked better than she did the last time I saw her."

"It's the sword." Cael didn't know how he knew, but he would stake his life on it.

Eoghan shrugged. "She wouldn't talk about the weapon. I did tell her the plan. I also told her it was yours."

Cael climbed to his feet. "You shouldn't have done that."

"Don't be stupid."

"What else was said?"

Eoghan shrugged as he stood. "The normal. Now, do you want to tell me what you saw in your meditation?"

"How do you know I saw anything?"

"Because of your determined look when you opened your eyes."

Cael fought not to glance at the doorway behind him, but he gave up and turned his head over his shoulder. "Bran's army is considerable in size. I saw Xaneth. He stood between us and Bran as if he hadn't made a decision yet."

"And you believe we need to recruit him."

"We fought with him before. He'll be a good ally."

"If we can trust him."

Cael considered that for a moment. "Xaneth has walked with the Light and the Dark. He knows both sides and has worked with both. However, Xaneth is also royalty. If he gives his word, we'll be able to trust it."

"You got all of that from your meditation?"

"I got that from fighting with him against Usaeil."

Eoghan grudgingly nodded. "I'll seek him out."

"There was another who hadn't chosen a side."

"Do you know him?"

"No," Cael admitted. "I couldn't see his face either. But he was Dark."

Eoghan crossed his arms over his chest. "Rordan and Cathal are trying to locate someone Xaneth told us about."

"Who?"

"Isoth. Xaneth said he was someone we might be interested in locating."

Cael dragged in a long breath. "Isoth might very well

be the other person in my vision. We need to find out."

Eoghan glanced past Cael's shoulder to the doorway. "What now?"

"Do you remember the story we were told as children of the god or goddess of war who carried a black blade?"

Eoghan nodded. "You think that's Erith?"

"I do, but I want to find out for sure."

"Sometimes, the past is better left buried."

"Are you cautioning me, believing I can't handle the truth?" Cael asked angrily.

Eoghan gave him a flat look. "I know you can handle anything, brother. I'm pointing out the fact that Death has a past, and it might be better for *her* if you left it alone."

He had to admit, Eoghan was right. "Yeah."

"You're going to talk to her, aren't you?"

"I want to." But did he want to find out that she had once more blocked him from entering her realm?

Eoghan put his hand on Cael's shoulder. "The doorway was open for me. It'll be open for you."

"Why now? Why, after keeping us out for so long?"

"Because she made a decision to fight Bran. And whether she admitted it before I went to see her or not, she knows she needs the Reapers. We are her army."

Cael nodded at his closest friend. "We're going to bring Bran down."

"You don't need to tell me that. I'm already convinced." Eoghan dropped his arm as he jerked his chin to the doorway. "Good luck in there."

Before he could reply, Eoghan was gone. Cael turned and faced the doorway that was invisible to everyone but Death, Cael, and Eoghan. He steeled himself, praying that she wouldn't keep him out again.

It felt like a knife twisting in his gut every time she ignored his call or refused to allow him entrance to her realm. She had never shut him out before. The fact that she'd let Eoghan in hurt Cael more than he wanted to admit.

What he felt for her was. . . . He closed his eyes, not wanting to name it even in his thoughts. He had before, and it had been dangerous because it allowed him to daydream of something that could never be.

Cael opened his eyes and took a deep breath. If she blocked him again, he would find another way to get to her. Because he needed to talk to her, to see her.

He lifted a foot and stepped over the threshold. In the next instant, he was in her realm. Cael inhaled and drew in the smells of the various flowers around him.

With his eyes closed, he listened to the chirping of birds. He heard the soft flapping of butterfly wings, followed closely by the intermittent buzz of the dragonflies flitting about him. And, in the background, the constant drone of the bees as they moved from flower to flower before returning to their hives.

Death's realm was alive with life, but there was only one being he wanted to see. He turned his head as his hearing picked up the sounds of a flock of birds. The avians always followed her. All he had to do was walk toward the noise to find her.

Cael opened his eyes and turned toward the birds. As he walked through the maze of flora, he realized how much he'd missed the place.

For thousands of years, he never ventured here, but ever since Bran's return, he'd spent more and more time in the realm. He glanced through the thick foliage to the white tower that was Erith's home.

It didn't take him long to locate Death. The closer he came to her, the more nervous he got. He kept reliving the first time he'd seen her fight as he lay dying. She outshone everyone. There hadn't been a person who could compare to her beauty before—or since.

Cael's pace slowed when he saw Erith standing next to a giant tree. The tree's branches spread out like twisted, gnarled fingers as they reached in all directions, including some that spanned the ground.

That's where he found the sword. The black metal glistened as if newly polished. From the blade to the pommel, every inch of the weapon was ebony.

It was the markings on the curved blade itself that interested him, though. They appeared to be written in some language, but he couldn't read it.

"It says 'Soul Reaper.'"

At the sound of Erith's voice, Cael turned his head to her. The tightness in his chest eased at the sight of her. He hadn't realized how much he'd missed her until that moment. He gazed into her lavender eyes and became lost just as he had the first time he'd seen her, just as he always did. "You made the sword."

Without so much as a smile, she replied, "I did."

"It's a work of art."

She looked away. It gave Cael the opportunity to let his gaze take its fill of her. She was in her usual black gown. There wasn't a speck of another color on the full, tulle skirts or the laced corset that hugged her body. Her shoulders were bare, and her hair was down. How he loved the long, inky tresses. He'd dreamed of sliding his fingers through the thick locks so many times.

"Ask what you want to know," she urged before moving her gaze back to his.

He took in her oval face with her large eyes framed by thick, black lashes before his gaze swept over her high cheekbones and then landed on her lips. By the stars, what a mouth she had. Full and lush. She rarely smiled, but when she did, there was nothing so brilliant or perfect.

Instead of asking about the sword or her past, he decided on something else. "You didn't answer my call."

A small frown formed on her face, one that was hastily wiped away. "I'm dying. You know this. Call it pride or whatever you want, but I didn't want any of you to see that."

"You look stronger now."

"Aye," she whispered, her gaze darting to the weapon.

He took a step closer. "I'm not afraid to fight Bran, no matter how powerful he is."

"And that will be your downfall."

"I vowed to serve you long ago. And if it means I stand between you and Bran to give you the time to gather your power to defeat him, then I will gladly sacrifice myself."

Anger sparked in her eyes. "I've never asked that of you."

"That's the thing about loyalty, Erith. You don't have to ask."

"No. I forbid it," she declared.

Cael grinned. "I know my Reapers, and I'm coming to know Eoghan's. You chose us well. Each of us is a strong fighter, but together, we're a force to be reckoned with. And we are bonded, not just to each other, but to you. Whether you want it or not, we will do whatever it takes to protect you."

"Stop talking like that."

He moved closer, needing to be as near to her as he could. If he couldn't pull her into his arms, he would get as close as he dared. "You can always make more Reapers. You're the one who can't be replaced."

She held his gaze for a long minute before she turned her head away. "It's me Bran wants dead. I killed his woman. By going after the Reapers, he's hurting me. And he knows it."

"We don't die so easily," Cael stated, unaffected by her words.

"But you do die."

The words were whispered before she turned her back to him. Her skirts swung out, brushing against his legs. He lifted his hand, his fingers sliding against her hair. Cael wanted to pull her against him, to hold her. But he didn't.

No one touched Erith.

It wasn't a rule, exactly. But she made sure that she always stood far enough away that none of them accidentally came in contact with her. The only time Cael had felt her touch was the night he'd become a Reaper.

That was the only time any of them had felt Death's hand.

Cael dropped his arm to his side. He needed to remember his place. In his dreams only, did he tell her of his feelings. "I've seen the battle all laid out in a meditation. Bran's Dark army is massive. But there are two who could be pivotal in the battle. Xaneth is one. Eoghan intends to find him."

"And the other?" she asked, turning her head to the side.

He stared at her profile for a heartbeat. "An unknown Dark Fae. I couldn't see his face. Eoghan thinks it might be someone Xaneth sent his Reapers after."

There was a long stretch of silence, then Erith said, "From the first moment I saw you, I knew you were born to lead. Your skills were unlike anything I'd ever seen. You deserved more than just being a Reaper."

"There's nowhere else I'd rather be than by your side."

He'd never spoken truer words. If he couldn't tell Erith how he felt about her, at least he could give her that much.

Chapter Four

There had been a few times when Erith wished to be a normal person. Now was one of those. If she were, then she would be free to follow her heart and see where it might lead her with Cael.

But she wasn't normal. Never had been.

She wasn't exactly sure what she was, but that didn't matter.

Cael stood strong and defiant—just as he had been the first time she'd seen him. Long hair the color of night fell past his shoulders. The front was pulled to the back of his head, where a strip of leather wound down the length to hold it in place to fall among the rest of his ebony locks.

His probing, silver eyes rarely missed anything. But it was his strong jaw and wide lips that always caught her gaze. His impressive shoulders were encased in a white shirt that stretched tightly over his hard sinew. And the dark trousers he wore hung low on his trim hips.

Handsome didn't begin to describe him. Cael was intensity, strength, passion, and determination. In short, he was a force unlike any other.

The connection she'd felt to him that first time had only strengthened over the centuries. She couldn't have him, but at least he was in her life. It was all she could have, but it was more than she'd ever had before.

"There's nowhere else I'd rather be than by your side."

She swallowed at the words that warmed her heart and faced him. "You would stand beside me despite not knowing my past?"

"Aye."

"Why?" she asked in confusion.

He lifted a black brow and snorted. "If you have to ask that, then I've been remiss in letting you know just how much I respect and admire you."

She hated that he'd seen her retrieving her sword, but in a way, it was beneficial that he had. No longer did she have to worry about keeping the truth hidden from him. "You saw me in Killarney."

For a long, silent moment, he simply stared. "I did."

"Ask what you want to know." She could see the questions burning in his eyes. Why wouldn't he let them fall from his lips?

Cael shook his head. "I don't need to know."

"But you want to know."

"And you want to keep it hidden."

She did. In fact, she'd hoped that part of her life would

never have to be thought of again. She should've known better. The past never stayed buried. She would eventually have to deal with everything that she locked away and never faced. Hopefully, she was strong enough to get through it and still be able to confront Bran.

She would be strong enough. Cael and the others were counting on her. She wouldn't let them down.

She wouldn't let him down.

Erith licked her lips. "I do. Because I'm ashamed of it."

"You know everything about my life, don't you?" Cael asked.

She briefly frowned, wondering what he was getting at. "You know I do."

"Do you regret making me a Reaper?"

"Never. But my past is different."

He cut his hand through the air. "It's not."

This was getting her nowhere. She drew in a frustrated breath. "I'm not Fae, Cael."

"We're all aware of that."

"I don't know where I came from or even what I am!"

His silver eyes regarded her patiently as he smiled. "You are Death. You keep the Fae in check, and we're your Reapers."

She glanced at the sword. "I swore never to pick up that weapon again."

"Will it help you win against Bran?"

"Yes."

"Then use it," Cael urged.

Shock went through her. "You say that because you don't know who I was when I wielded it. If I take up that sword again, if I become who I once was, I may win against Bran, but the person you see before you now may be gone, eaten up by the bloodthirsty being who lived for wrath and hate, for battle and the waste that followed."

"Bran will be gone. That's our first step. We can deal with whatever you become later. And that's a big *if*. You're strong enough to stop it."

"Am I?" she asked, brows raised. "I wasn't the first time."

A cocky smile flashed over his handsome face. "You didn't have us with you."

Was it any wonder she had fallen so hard for him? "You might be right. But that means you and the others will see who I once was. The Mistress of War."

Erith watched Cael closely, but he didn't flinch in shock or turn away in alarm. He held her gaze as if she had just told him it was going to rain tomorrow. Maybe she needed to get the point across better.

"I destroyed worlds, Cael. My power feeds on the physical act of war itself. I swung my sword, uncaring who was at the end of the blade. All I wanted was blood and death and destruction. I didn't stop until a realm was annihilated."

He dropped his arms to his sides. "To be frank, it's the Mistress of War that we need right now. If Bran succeeds in killing you, he'll be the one destroying Earth."

"I came to the same conclusion. That's why I decided to get the sword." That and to protect the Reapers, despite the repercussions that brandishing the blade might bring. "Though, I'm not anxious to use it."

"You'll be fighting for yourself and all you've created here. Not to mention the Fae, Halflings, and even the humans."

She nodded. If only Bran would forget about the Reapers. If she could know for sure that he would be satisfied with her death, she would accept her fate. But before she gave up her life, she would go to Constantine, the King of Dragon Kings. Because there was no way the Dragon Kings would stand by and let anything destroy their realm.

But Bran wouldn't stop with her. His hatred extended to the Reapers because he knew how much she cared for them. And to hurt them would be like tearing out her heart.

"You were right," she said.

Cael quirked his head. "About?"

"You said I should've killed Bran instead of putting him in the Netherworld. I believed the prison would hold him."

"That was a long time ago, and I was angry," Cael said. "I wanted vengeance for what Bran had done to us and you. The Netherworld would've held him had Seamus not released him."

Her gaze followed a hummingbird as it flew past her to drink from a flower.

"Did you get all the information from Seamus? Should we question him again?"

Erith inwardly cringed. "Seamus isn't here."

A muscle ticked in Cael's jaw. "Did he escape?"

"No one leaves here if I don't wish it."

Cael looked away, seeming to fight to control his anger. "Why did you let him go?"

"So he could get close to Bran. Seamus was supposed to find you and tell you his plan."

"He didn't. Which means, whatever he found out from you, he's going to tell Bran."

"Seamus won't betray me."

Cael's head slowly swung back to her. "I don't have your faith in him. The vision I saw of the coming battle? Seamus was with Bran."

"Where he's supposed to be."

"If I see him, I'm going to kill him."

She closed the distance between them so much, she had to lean her head back to look up into his eyes. "No, you won't."

"Was this plan your idea, or Seamus's?"

"Seamus."

Cael shook his head and gazed into the distance. "That's what I thought. He deceived you."

"What if he didn't? What if he will help us?"

"Then why didn't he tell me what he was doing as you bade him?" Cael demanded, his silver gaze boring into her.

She shrugged. "I don't know. If he's going to betray me, then let him."

"Is there anything he could've found out here that would help Bran?"

Erith thought of the book Seamus had brought to her—the volume about her, the Mistress of War.

"You're taking too long to answer," Cael stated, his gaze narrowed.

"There might be something."

Anger simmered in Cael's eyes, but he never let it into his voice. "What was it?"

"There is a book."

"About?" Cael pressed.

She gave him a pointed look.

He let out a loud snort. "About you. Dammit, Erith. If there were any secrets in there, Bran now knows them."

"That book was written by a Fae who knew very little

about me, other than that I loved war. It details all the realms I ended, and all the lives I took."

Cael took a deep breath, his chest expanding as the air filled his lungs. "So there could be a chance Bran doesn't know you're the Mistress of War?"

"I can't answer that for sure. I don't know how he's draining my power."

"And your life," Cael added.

Erith nodded. "And my life. Once I begin fighting, my power will build back up."

"But he can take it away again, unless we figure out how he's doing it and stop him."

"Exactly."

Cael looked at the sword again. "I'll get Kyran and Talin on it."

"You don't like being around the sword, do you?"

His head snapped back to her. "I feel something from it, but it doesn't make me want to move away. Why?"

"It has always repelled Fae. Why do you think there were none in Killarney? It should affect you, as well."

He lifted one shoulder in a shrug. "Perhaps before, but I'm a Reaper, which means, I'm part of you." Cael suddenly frowned as he thought of something. "You didn't take away Bran's Reaper abilities."

"You know I didn't."

"Aye, but if you had, he wouldn't want to be around the

sword."

Erith had made many mistakes in her long life. Not taking away Bran's Reaper powers before she threw him into the Netherworld was one of them. She'd wanted him to suffer, so she allowed the magic she'd given him to remain in order to draw out his torture instead of his life ending too soon.

She walked past Cael to the sword. Right before she wrapped her fingers around the pommel, she hesitated for just a heartbeat. The moment her fingers closed around the cool metal, she felt the power of the blade.

"I made this," she said and lifted the weapon. She turned to face Cael. "This is part of me. With each life this blade took, it grew stronger with me. Just holding it replenishes some of what Bran took from me."

Cael grinned. "Good."

"It will be enough to restore me before we go into battle, but that's not why I told you all of that."

"Then why?"

"Because I want you to know that Bran will never be able to hold this weapon. I allowed Ettie to use it when Bran came for her. If Bran tries to do anything with this weapon, he's in for a big surprise."

Cael nodded solemnly. "I'll let the other Reapers know not to touch it."

She lowered her arm so the point of the sword was directed at the ground. "I don't want to draw this war between Bran and me out any longer."

"Give me a little time to talk to Xaneth. And perhaps find the Dark who could also help us."

"I won't force either of those Fae to fight for me. Everyone who joins us must do it of their own free will. Otherwise, Bran will be able to turn them."

Cael's lips twisted into a rueful smile. "I suppose that means you won't *convince* Xaneth to join us?"

Erith shook her head. "You also need to make sure the women are secure. Especially River. I won't have Bran taking the baby."

"My men are already working on that."

"And what of you?" she asked. "What do you intend to do?"

He gave her a flat look. "Remain with you."

"Bran can't get into this realm."

"I don't care. I'm not leaving."

Cael would never know how his words gave her courage. "You're a leader, Cael. Go to your men. With them is where you're supposed to be.

"I don't like leaving you."

"You're not. You're doing your duty."

Several tense minutes went by as Cael seemed to try and find an argument to remain. Finally, he bowed his head and turned on his heel.

As he walked away, Erith kept her eyes on him as she brought the pommel of the sword to her mouth and whispered to the metal. "You will answer to Cael."

Chapter Five

The tattered paper was smooth beneath his fingers. Bran had unfolded and folded the ancient sheet so many times, he worried it might fall apart. Already, the seams were nearly transparent.

The page was burnt on one side, engulfing part of the lower righthand corner. But, somehow, this page had survived Death's attempt to get rid of it. Thankfully, it had fallen into his hands.

It had taken him quite a while to realize that his magic was getting stronger. And then, it had taken him even longer to comprehend that there was a correlation between his increased magic and each time he read the parchment.

Searlas strode into his office, pulling Bran's attention from the folded sheet. Their new location was a manor on the east coast of Ireland that Bran had forcibly taken from the former occupants—whose lifeless bodies had since been thrown into the Irish Sea.

Bran sat back with a smile as his lieutenant stood with his hands clasped before him. "Can I take that smug look you're wearing to mean that Seamus has finally been found?"

"Aye," Searlas replied. "It seems he was trying to find you."

"Is that so? Bring him to me then."

Searlas turned and motioned someone forward. Bran watched as a man with long, black and silver hair strode into the room. Bran smiled in greeting to Seamus. "I've been looking for you."

He wasn't at all certain where Seamus had been the last several months. He'd searched for the Dark, but not as thoroughly as he should have since his focus had been on other things. Perhaps if he'd tried harder, Seamus would've been with him the entire time.

Seamus crossed his arms over his chest. "I've always had enemies. You knew that, or you wouldn't have sent me that note so long ago. That's the reason I spent my life searching for the doorway to the Netherworld."

"Where have you been?"

Seamus's face contorted with rage. "You know exactly where I've been. Death took me."

Bran had been ready to kill the Fae if he tried to pass off some lie. The fact that Seamus answered honestly was a plus, but it was far from guaranteeing his life.

"And?" Bran pressed. "How did you get free?"

Seamus smirked, his red eyes brightening with glee. "She grew weak. So weak, that I was able to throw off her magic. I tried to kill her, but I wasn't able to. However, I did escape, and immediately came looking for you."

Bran leaned an elbow on the arm of his chair and propped his chin in his fist. "And the Reapers? They didn't come after you?"

"I've been staying out of sight and using all the magic I know to keep them away."

"You didn't keep the Reapers away," Searlas said, derision dripping from his words. "They're protecting Death instead of looking for your ugly arse."

Bran smiled as the two men glared at each other. "I have to agree with Searlas. The Reapers haven't come for you because they're not focused on you right now."

Seamus's red eyes swung back to Bran. "From what you're saying, they won't be bothering me ever again."

"That's right. Your concern, however, should be on whether or not I let you live."

The Dark's brows rose on his forehead. "This is the payment I get for freeing you from the Netherworld? Perhaps I should've left you there."

"Watch your tongue," Searlas stated angrily and formed an orb of magic, his arm rearing back, ready to release it.

"Searlas," Bran said calmly.

His lieutenant reluctantly collapsed the sphere as he pulled back his lips and snarled at Seamus. "I don't trust him."

"And I don't like you," Seamus said. He then turned back to Bran. "I'm Dark. I've spent my life doing evil. And I freed you. That should say all that needs to be said."

"You could be lying about how you left Death," Bran replied.

Seamus shrugged. "I've no way of proving it to you. If you don't believe me, then kill me. But do something, so I don't have to smell his nasty breath any longer," the Fae said as he threw his thumb in Searlas's direction.

"I'll gut you," the lieutenant threatened.

Seamus formed a ball of magic in each hand. "Bring it on, fekker."

Bran watched the exchange, his attention locked on Seamus. He'd known of the Fae while he'd been a Reaper. There hadn't been anything Seamus couldn't procure for any Dark who came to him. For the right price.

The moment Bran had told his lover who he was, he'd written the note Seamus had mentioned earlier and took it to a group of Dark Fae who delivered messages. The day he didn't check in with them, was the day they were to present the note to Seamus.

"Enough," Bran said. When neither Fae backed down,

he got to his feet and slammed his hands on the desk. "I said, enough!"

Searlas was the first to face Bran. Seamus took a little longer. Another few minutes were spent in silence as Bran walked around Seamus.

Finally, he turned to Searlas. "Leave."

The Dark wasn't pleased with the command, but Searlas did as he was told. Once Bran was alone with Seamus, the Fae relaxed, his anger evaporating.

"Sorry, Bran, but I really despise him."

Bran nodded and walked back to his desk, turning to face Seamus before leaning against the edge. "Searlas doesn't believe your story."

"I've no reason to lie to you. As I said, I'm a Dark."

"But she's Death."

Seamus shrugged as he frowned. "And, apparently, dying. Her power is waning significantly. Whatever fear I had of her left quickly."

"What did you tell her?"

"The truth. She asked how I freed you. There was no reason not to tell her."

"I suppose," Bran said as he gripped the desk on either side of him. "What else?"

Seamus's cheeks puffed out as he blew out a breath. "She wanted to know about you. I didn't spend much time with you after you were freed, so I had nothing to tell her."

"You forget, I was a Reaper."

"I've not forgotten anything," Seamus said.

Bran paused, his gaze steely. "I know full well Death's ability to get others to talk. There's no way that she gave up on you so willingly."

"She didn't have to try hard to get me to tell her what she wanted to know. I told her everything," Seamus said. "The fact that I left you and went back to my cottage was a good thing. I knew nothing of your plans, who you were with, or where you were going."

"So you couldn't tell her anything." Bran drew in a deep breath. Maybe Seamus was telling the truth.

The Dark grinned. "She realized pretty quickly that I had no information for her. She even sent Cael to talk to me."

"Oh?" The hatred Bran felt for Cael surpassed even what he had for Death.

"I'm not sure at all why he's the leader of the Reapers. He lacks what it takes to make others do what he wants."

The desk creaked as Bran's hold tightened. "I knew the moment Cael became a Reaper that he was Death's favorite."

"For the most part, they left me alone after they got what they wanted. Death would visit me every so often and see if I could tell her anything I might have forgotten.

That's how I saw her weakening."

Bran raised a brow. "Is that so?"

"She didn't have me in chains or even in a cell of any kind. I had free rein of the place."

"What place?"

Seamus twisted his lips. "The only thing I saw was the tower I was in. The only Reaper who came was Cael, and he rarely visited. So, when Death got weak enough, it was easy to bust through her magic and escape."

"You're lucky she didn't throw you into the Nether-world."

Seamus's smile was wide as he said, "Because I knew how to get out. I did worry that she might kill me."

"Death doesn't get blood on her hands." Bran pushed away from the desk and walked around it to sit in his chair again. "At least not anymore. She leaves that to the Reapers."

"You said if I freed you that I'd never have to fear my enemies again. I'm here for payment."

Bran raised a brow. "Cheeky."

"Straightforward. You set the terms, I accepted."

"So you did." Bran looked at the folded paper before him on the desk as he tried to find the lies in Seamus's story. Luckily, he couldn't find any. He lifted his gaze to the Dark. "Shall I decree to all Fae to leave you alone?"

Seamus shook his head as he grinned. "I want to help

you fight Death and the Reapers. I spent more years than I want to admit, fearing the stories of the Reapers. And then to learn they're true.... No one should have the right to judge us."

"I'll allow you to join us, but it'll be up to you and Searlas to work out something. I'm not going to be breaking up your fights at every turn."

"You won't need to."

"I'll hold you to that promise."

Seamus flashed a smile before he pivoted and left the room. A moment later, Searlas returned, looking even crankier than usual.

"Can I kill him now?" Searlas asked.

Bran shook his head. "He's joining us."

"You believe him?" his lieutenant asked in disbelief.

"I do. Is there a problem with that?"

Searlas wisely kept his mouth shut and shook his head.

"Good," Bran replied. "I expect you to keep a rein on that temper of yours when it comes to Seamus."

"You make it sound as though he'll be used instead of the other Dark."

Bran held back his grin since he knew the fury that was coming. "Because he will."

Searlas's red eyes blazed with rage as his nostrils flared. But despite the explosion of words he obviously wanted to say, he managed to keep silent.

"I'm well aware that he could be a spy, but I also know that Death is growing very weak. With no Reapers or chains to hold Seamus, there's a good chance that his story is all true."

Searlas remained quiet, a testament to how angry he was.

"I also want to know what he saw while with Erith. There are little things Death might have said or done in front of him that Seamus isn't thinking of now. I want to give him some time to settle in before I start grilling him about such things." Bran leaned forward to put his forearms on the desk. "Don't worry, Searlas, you'll be with me every time. And if Seamus is lying, you get to torture him."

Searlas's nostrils flared again. "Good."

Bran motioned for his second in command to leave. Once he was alone, Bran let his thoughts turn to Death. It was a shame to kill something so beautiful, but he alone knew that Erith was a monster that needed to be put down.

Her *rules* that he'd broken had earned him banishment for eons, but now those same edicts no longer applied to the Reapers. It wasn't fair that the Fae he'd fallen in love with should be killed, while the others got to not only keep their lovers but also have them near.

Bran suddenly smiled as an idea grew. It was time they

discovered where the Reapers' women were. Let the Reapers experience what it was to lose someone they loved. It was only fair since those were Death's rules.

"Searlas!" Bran shouted.

A second later, the door opened, and the Fae walked in. "Aye?"

"How do you feel about killing the Reapers' women?"

Searlas's smile was slow. "When do I leave?"

Chapter Six

Nothing ever went as he imagined it would with Erith. Then again, what else did Cael expect from Death?

She might be the most stunning creature in the universe with more power than any other, but she stood alone. Always alone.

Was it because she liked it that way? Or was it because she didn't trust anyone?

He ran a hand down his face as he arrived in his chamber at Inchmickery.

"That's not the face I hoped to see."

Cael closed his eyes at the sound of Eoghan's voice behind him. "I'm beginning to miss when you refused to speak."

"You just don't like me pointing out the obvious."

Turning to his oldest friend, Cael met Eoghan's gaze where he reclined in one of the two chairs. "What are you doing here?"

"You actually have to ask that after our conversation?" Eoghan replied with a black brow raised.

"You have your own Reapers to see to."

Eoghan crossed an ankle over his knee. "They're taking care of either collecting souls or trying to locate Xaneth."

"So you thought you'd come to bother me?"

"Actually, Thea wanted to see River. The prospect of a babe makes my woman smile. And I like making her happy."

Cael blew out a breath. "Perhaps you should get her with child."

"Who says I'm not trying?" The grin slipped as Eoghan dropped his leg and sat forward, resting his arms on his thighs. "I know I'm not the only one worried about the women here. Though Neve is a Reaper. She can take care of herself."

"But there's Jordyn, River, Cat, and Ettie. Not to mention Thea," Cael added. "Ettie has been training the others with weapons, and Cat has combined her magic with ours as protection around the isle."

"Cat and Ettie might be able to fight since they've already done so against Bran. But Jordyn's and Thea's skills lie elsewhere. And River's attention will be on her unborn child."

"If Bran attacks the women now." Because both of them knew that Bran would go after them. "If he comes at us, each Reaper should take his woman and go somewhere safe to protect them."

Eoghan's lips flattened. "Separating us. Giving Bran the advantage to go straight for you. I don't like that."

"Bran doesn't know you're back. He also doesn't know about Thea or her connection to Usaeil. And he doesn't know about the other Reapers."

"I don't want to even consider what he might do if he does find out about any of that."

Cael pinched the bridge of his nose. "The women need to be elsewhere. We need to move them quietly and quickly."

"I agree. But where?" Eoghan asked.

Cael shrugged and shook his head. "That's going to depend on each of you."

"And we don't tell each other."

"Precisely."

Eoghan pushed to his feet. "Before we go out there and inform the others, what happened with Erith?"

"She's fekking stubborn, that's what."

Eoghan had the gall to grin. "Of course, she is. She's Death. She's the strongest being I've ever encountered—physically, mentally, and magically. I wouldn't be concerned about Bran at all if he hadn't syphoned her magic."

Cael swallowed. His stomach knotted every time he considered that he might lose her. "Did you ever wonder why she created the Reapers?"

"To carry out her judgment against the Fae."

"You know as well as I do that she doesn't need us. She could do it all on her own."

Eoghan's gaze narrowed. "I'm guessing this has something to do with her past. And by your words, it has to do with that sword."

"What did you feel when you saw the weapon?"

"Like I wasn't too sure I wanted to be near it."

Cael twisted his lips. "Erith said the blade is why there were no Fae in Killarney. Apparently, it repels them."

"But not us?"

"We have some of her magic, so we don't feel it as strongly."

Eoghan's brows lifted as he sighed. "Fek."

"That's one way of putting it."

There was a brief silence, then Eoghan said, "She told you about her past, didn't she?"

Cael nodded. He didn't want to think about the idea that he might lose the woman that he'd fallen for so long ago, but if it took Erith becoming the Mistress of War to defeat Bran, then he would stand beside her.

Because a life without Erith in it—regardless of who she was or what she did—was better than one without her.

Eoghan ran a hand over his jaw. "Bloody hell. I suppose it all makes sense now."

"You didn't see her face. She's ashamed of who she was. And now I understand why she created us."

"Because she didn't want to kill anymore."

"I suspect it's also why she didn't take Bran's life," Cael said. "Though she did kill his Fae lover."

Eoghan shook his head. "I can't believe you didn't stay with her."

"She didn't want me there."

"So you left?"

Cael frowned. "What the hell does that mean?"

"Exactly what I asked."

"She's Death. She makes the rules."

Eoghan shrugged nonchalantly. "Now that Bran has taken so much of her magic, perhaps it's time someone else made such decisions. You want to be with her. Go be with her."

"I lead the Reapers. That's where I'm supposed to be."

"But there won't be any Reapers if Bran kills her."

Cael clenched his hands, fury rushing through him at the thought of the corner he'd been backed into. "You don't think I know that?"

"Cael!" someone shouted through the door.

He didn't wait for Eoghan to answer his question. Cael turned on his heel, threw open the door, and strode into the open area to find Xaneth standing between Aisling and Torin with Daire off to the side.

Cael looked from Daire, who had called for him, to Eoghan's only female Reaper and gave a nod before doing the same to Torin. Then he focused on Xaneth as Eoghan came to stand beside him.

Within the next heartbeat, the rest of Cael's Reapers filled the space. He kept his attention on Xaneth, who was none too pleased with being there.

"All you had to do was ask, and I would've come," Xaneth stated, shooting a scathing look at Talin. "I didn't need to be dragged here."

"Oh, please," Aisling said with a roll of her red eyes.

Xaneth glanced her way before he took a step forward and looked from Cael to Eoghan. "I gather the two of you want something."

Eoghan crossed his arms over his chest. "You could say that. Originally, you wanted to join Bran to be able to kill the Queen of the Light."

"Usaeil deserves to die," Xaneth said between clenched teeth.

Thea walked through one of the arched doorways. "No one knows that better than me."

Xaneth bowed his head toward her. His silver eyes swung back to Cael. "If either of you wants to know if I've joined Bran's army, I've not yet. I was in the Dark Palace, hoping to be approached."

"He and Balladyn have an agreement," Aisling added.

At the female's words, Cael saw Xaneth stiffen. Interesting that Xaneth was known for his ability to negotiate with both the Light and Dark Fae, but Aisling seemed to get under his skin.

Xaneth lifted his chin. "Aye, the King of the Dark and I came to terms. Balladyn wants Bran found so he'll stop taking Dark. I want to find Bran to fight Usaeil."

"I thought you gave up on that notion," Eoghan said.

Xaneth shrugged. "The only one looking out for me is myself. I always look at my options."

"And you still believe Bran is one of them?" Cael asked.

Silver eyes slid to him. Xaneth held Cael's gaze for a long moment before he said, "Aye."

"Death could've taken your life at the Light Castle after we confronted Usaeil. She chose not to. You should consider that, as well."

"I have."

Cael cocked his head to the side. "Obviously, you don't fully understand what's at stake here."

"Oh, I do," Xaneth said as he widened his stance and looked at the Reapers around him. "Bran is stealing Death's power. He plans to wipe her out before coming for all of you."

The room was quiet, all eyes on him. But Cael didn't care. He also wasn't concerned with how Xaneth might have discerned that bit of information. What mattered was getting Xaneth on their side any way he could.

"You fought alongside us once before," Eoghan said.

Xaneth snorted loudly. "So?"

"So. . . ." Cael said. "You know we keep our word. Bran is not only a traitor, he's a liar. As soon as he finds out you're Usaeil's family, he's likely to kill you or hand you over to her to make an alliance."

"I know," Xaneth replied.

Cael glanced at the floor. "Death has forbidden me from forcing you to side with us. I know you only do what benefits you, so let me give it to you straight. I've seen how things play out for us. There's Bran's massive army of Dark Fae that he's imbued with the same power he stole from Death. And us. Fourteen against hundreds—if not thousands."

"You don't stand a chance," Xaneth said.

Fintan gave a bark of laughter. "That response tells me that, despite fighting alongside us, you still don't know anything about Reapers."

"I second that," Aisling added, her red eyes narrowed dangerously on Xaneth.

Cael grinned. "Most of those in Bran's army are there by force. When it comes right down to it, they won't fight for him. Not when they realize just who they're fighting against."

"Fine," Xaneth said. "Maybe you're right, but that still doesn't explain how you believe you stand a chance against Bran when he's growing in power, and Death is losing hers."

Kyran's red eyes blazed as he said, "We're fighting for Death, for ourselves, and for those we love. We have something at stake. The Dark with Bran do not."

"Revenge drives Bran," Torin said. "There's nothing in it for anyone else. He cares for nothing but himself."

Neve fingered one of the many daggers on her person. "And that means he'll gladly sacrifice anyone to move his vengeance forward. I know from personal experience, as I watched him kill my parents and turn my brother Dark."

"I saw you in my vision," Cael told Xaneth. "I saw you standing between us and Bran's army. You've not chosen a side yet."

Xaneth frowned. "I have a better chance at continuing to live with Bran. As you said, the odds are stacked against you."

"Actually, you have a better chance of survival by disappearing, which I'm surprised you haven't done," Aisling stated, her voice dripping with derision.

A muscle ticked in Xaneth's jaw, but he didn't so much as look Aisling's way. His gaze held Cael's. "What if I can't decide now?"

"You mean you want to know if we're going to hold

you? We won't," Cael promised.

Eoghan said, "Nor will we do anything if you tell us you'll join Bran. But know that I'll come straight for you on the battlefield."

"So will I," Baylon said.

Talin nodded. "Me, too."

"I'll get to him before anyone else," Aisling promised.

Cael released a breath. "You see, Xaneth, we're a family. Each of us was betrayed and killed before Death came to us and offered us positions as Reapers. Blood doesn't bind us. Something much stronger does."

"Loyalty. Devotion. Honor," Eoghan said.

Xaneth's eyes lowered to the floor. "Thank you for giving me your side of things. You'll know my decision soon."

Cael watched as he disappeared. He held up a hand, stopping anyone from going after the Fae. "This decision is Xaneth's alone. As he said, we gave him our pitch. It's Bran's turn."

"While we have you all here," Eoghan said, glancing at Cael, "there's another matter."

Cael looked at each of his Reapers. Every one of them had found love, including Eoghan. He knew the joy love could bring, but he knew the heartache of it, as well. After everything his Reapers had endured, he didn't want any of them to suffer by losing their women.

"If I were Bran, I know exactly what I'd do next," Cael said.

It was Kyran who nodded in understanding. "Come after our women."

"He wants us to feel what he went through," Eoghan said.

Talin shook his head. "That's not going to happen."

"No, it's not," Cael replied. "Because we're going to make sure it doesn't. Each of you needs to find a safe place for your woman. Don't tell each other or me where you're going. And just to be safe, everyone should split up to make it harder for Bran to find you."

"He found them before," Baylon pointed out. "He'll do it again."

Eoghan held out a hand for Thea. "Bran won't be able to go after all of them at once. We need to make it as difficult for him as possible."

"The goal is for everyone to come out of this alive," Cael said. "But be prepared for anything."

"Shite," Fintan said as he ran a hand through his white hair. "Cat isn't going to like this."

None of them would. Hell, even Cael didn't like it. But he wanted them to live, so he'd do whatever he had to in order to ensure that happened.

"Let your plans be dark and impenetrable as night, and when you move, fall like a thunderbolt."

-**Sun Tzu,** *The Art of War*

Chapter Seven

It's only a sword. A weapon I wield. It does not control me. It does not control me.

"It doesn't control me," Erith said aloud as she held the sword. A memory of the life she once led with the sword tried to rise up within her, but she kept it back. Barely.

The rush of power that filled her was exhilarating, invigorating. The weakness that had plagued her vanished like an afterthought. She didn't know how long this would last, or how many more times the sword could revive her waning magic.

That's why she had to find Bran now and use her strength while she could. The sooner she discovered how he was taking her magic, the better.

She knew how long she'd used the sword, letting it build its power with each death. Countless fatalities, endless victims. Its might hadn't diminished over the millennia. Instead, it had grown stronger.

Erith stalked to the doorway, but she had only gone a couple of steps before she halted and looked down at the full skirts of her gown. Her current mission wasn't to fight Bran head-on, but if she did, this wasn't the attire for it.

For just an instant, she almost called up her old armor, but Erith decided it was best not to tempt her tenuous hold on the bloodlust that threatened to overtake her. Holding the sword was already taxing her control. The armor would remind her of the many battles she'd fought—and the lives she'd taken.

Just thinking of it made the pommel heat in her palm. Her eyes closed as she recalled the swiftness with which she'd descended upon a realm, the power that fed the blade with each kill.

The fear and reverence that had filled the eyes of those she selected to die.

When they saw her coming, they screamed one word—*Death*. It was the only name she knew until she had chosen Erith.

Cael.

It was because of him that she had wanted a name. Cael had made her . . . crave . . . so many things. It was because of him that she desired more than just a companion. With Cael, she wanted it all.

Erith was the first name she had used. The King of the Dragon Kings, Constantine, knew her by Heather, Iris, Blossom, and others that suited her purpose.

But she could never stop being Death or the Mistress

of War, no matter how many names she used.

She didn't know why she had been born, or for what purpose. Yet, she'd somehow found her way to the only thing she was good at.

And Bran wasn't going to take that from her.

Erith's eyes snapped open. The black gown disappeared, replaced by black pants and an armored corset that molded to her body and over her shoulders. Matching armored vambraces graced her forearms. Tall boots came up to her knees, as her long hair formed into a thick braid. Next was a coat that came up high in the back but hung down to her knees on either side. The best part was the hood. The humans had a vision of what Death looked like to them. Perhaps it was time she incorporated some of that into her outfit.

She loved the color black. Not because it signified death. It was the Fae who made that connection since she was always seen in the color. No, she wore black because it was her color. The queen of colors, she'd always called it.

It was strong but serene. It was a color that trumped all others. A color that was bold and commanding.

And it was hers.

Erith looked down at her hand that gripped the sword. It had been so long since she'd held the weapon, but she still knew the weight of it, still recalled how it felt to swing the blade and end a life. Still recognized the absolute authority she commanded with it.

Erith had lied to Cael. She knew exactly how to defeat Bran. All she had to do was become the Mistress of War again. First, she would need to destroy a few realms to build back the last of her power that the sword couldn't provide, and then she could return and take on Bran.

But in the process, she might very well destroy Earth—and Cael.

Which was only one of many reasons she wouldn't go that route. Besides, she knew she would never come back from that if she did.

She didn't want to think about how Cael and the others might look on her if they saw who she'd once been. No matter how much she tried to deny it, Cael's opinion of her mattered more than anything else.

If she saw his gaze change from respect and admiration to revulsion and horror, she would never recover.

She continued toward the Fae doorway. The animals came toward her as always, but they didn't get close. Not that she blamed them. She was a different person with the sword. Anger and loneliness and resentment had helped forge the weapon. And it radiated from the metal so all could feel it.

Erith approached the doorway. Just before she stepped through it, she wondered if Cael would be on the

other side, protecting it as he once had. She didn't want
to see him.

Liar.

Yes, it was a lie. She yearned to see him, to talk to him.
To . . . lay her hand on him and feel the heat of his skin,
the strength of his muscles.

It might have been ages since she had first touched
him, but the memory was still as fresh as if it had just happened. She would never forget the way he'd looked at her
with a mixture of awe and desire.

No one had ever gazed at her in such a way before—or
since. She had lost Reapers in the past, but she couldn't
lose Cael. It would destroy her more quickly and savagely
than anything Bran thought to do to her.

Erith tightened her hold on the sword and walked
through the doorway. The disappointment that filled her
at not finding Cael was so great that her knees nearly
buckled.

If she didn't push aside such feelings, Bran would suss
them out and use them against her. Before Bran syphoned her essence and magic, it had been easy to keep
her feelings not only in check but also hidden.

Now, it felt like an open wound rubbed raw, one that
could only be healed by Cael. The fact that she ached so
desperately for him just made her stay away from him
even more. Because she didn't trust herself not to do

something stupid like blurt out how she'd been in love with him for hundreds of years, even before she came to him to be a Reaper.

To have love so close yet so far away that it could never be hers was a crushing blow. She'd done it to herself, and while it was hard to bear at times, she wouldn't change any of it. Simply because the Reapers needed Cael.

She needed him.

There was one person who could truly understand her dilemma like no other—Rhi. The Light Fae had fallen hard and fast for a Dragon King, but he'd foolishly ended the affair. It had nearly killed Rhi. While Erith understood his motives, she didn't agree with them. Now, Rhi was helping the Dragon Kings with their many enemies.

Though none of that was why Erith had had Daire follow Rhi all those months. That was for something else entirely. Something that was quickly approaching. Erith just prayed Rhi was ready for it, because if she wasn't, then everything could go sideways in a blink.

Erith hated that she wasn't able to locate Bran as she could with others, but then he couldn't find her either. It worked both in her favor and against her. But there was someone she could track—Seamus.

Erith veiled herself and smiled when she located the Dark Fae. In the next breath, she stood outside a grand mansion on a lavish estate with an immaculate garden as well as hundreds of acres of land. Of course, Bran would be in Ireland. It was close to the Fae, where he felt secure.

Unlike the Fae, her Reapers could not only see each other but also anyone else who was veiled. Since Bran was giving those in his army the same power she gave the Reapers, they could do the same.

But she was different. No one would be able to detect her, no matter what kind of magic they used.

No one but Bran.

She looked at the mansion, her eyes moving from window to window. On the bottom floor toward the left corner, she spotted a shape through the sheer drapes. She moved closer, making her way around the Dark, who were veiled and standing guard.

Ten feet from the window, she jerked to a stop when she saw that it was none other than Bran. She could end it all right now. The overwhelming need to fight him almost consumed her.

Just as she was about to take another step, she felt the magic before her. A thick barrier ran around the house. Anyone who touched it would alert Bran that they were there. And she had nearly done exactly that.

Erith couldn't believe how blind she'd become from her anger, enough that she'd almost done something incredibly idiotic. She couldn't afford to screw this up. Thankfully, she had felt the magic in time.

Frustrated, she began to turn away, when she heard a voice she recognized. Seamus. She walked around the side of the mansion, careful to keep clear of the magical barrier. She found Seamus with two other Dark, discussing how to get more Fae from the Dark Palace.

No one realized what type of king Balladyn was, but they were about to learn. And, frankly, she was looking forward to the showdown.

The conversation went on much longer than she liked. It was twenty minutes later before Seamus finally walked away. She fell into step beside him, wondering if the Dark had betrayed her as Cael suggested.

Erith considered herself a good judge of character, even though she'd made a few mistakes—Bran being one of them. She really didn't want to include Seamus in that, as well.

Suddenly, the Fae stopped and, without moving his head, swung his eyes from right to left. "Is someone there?" he whispered.

She wanted to ask him what he'd found, but she wasn't sure she could trust him. She didn't wish for Bran to know that she'd discovered him. Right now, whether Seamus knew it or not, he was her key to Bran.

"Erith?" he whispered.

She moved to stand before him while remaining veiled. "Have you betrayed me?"

"No," he replied immediately, his eyes jerking to where her voice had come from. "I can't stay still. We need to walk."

She moved out of the way and fell into step with him again. She said nothing else, waiting for him to answer her question.

"This is about me not telling Cael," Seamus said, trying not to move his mouth. "I didn't go to him because I knew as soon as I left your realm that Bran would have others looking for me. I was right. Within an hour, his men found me. If I'd called to Cael, Bran would've known."

It was a plausible explanation. Then again, Seamus was used to talking himself out of difficult situations. He could, in fact, be lying straight to her face right now and she'd never know.

"I'm not lying," he said as if reading her mind. "Bran already suspects me. I swore I'd help you. I'm not going back on that, but I've not been here long enough to get you anything. I have to do everything right, or Bran will kill me. Please, Erith. You can trust me."

She leaned close to him so that her mouth was near his ear. "Don't make me regret this."

He flinched away, causing her to grin. She liked Seamus. It would be a shame to kill him, but she would in a heartbeat if he betrayed her.

She teleported away from the mansion before she gave in and went after Bran. It would feel good to get it over with. This had been going on for too long. If only she'd known he was syphoning her essence. She could have put a stop to it much sooner.

But Bran wanted her weak. What had she ever seen in him that made her think he'd be a good Reaper? Perhaps because he'd been reckless. She'd once thought Cael was reckless, too. But in actuality, he was anything but. He was calculated, deliberate, and unhurried.

Because he saw everything so clearly.

Bran was nothing like Cael. And, now, she was paying the price.

Chapter Eight

His patience was running out. Normally, Cael didn't have a problem, but then again, he hadn't been fighting someone like Bran.

He stopped walking and turned to lean against an old, brick building in Limerick. He'd come to look for the Dark he'd seen in his mind—an impossible task, considering he had no idea who the Fae was. But he was the missing link to winning against Bran.

Yet it was thoughts of Erith that brought Cael up short.

No matter how he looked at it, he wasn't upset about the upcoming battle with Bran. He was actually looking forward to it. What troubled him to the point that his mind was in such turmoil was Erith.

She didn't need him. If anyone could face Bran and have the odds be in her favor—even in such a weakened state—it was Death. But it felt wrong that he wasn't by her side.

Cael was all too aware that it was his feelings for her that ruled him. Those few minutes when he lay dying, watching her, he'd fallen head over heels for her.

Even if he'd known who she was, he wouldn't have steeled his heart from loving her.

It was a beautiful kind of torture to be associated with her but never allowed to have her. Never able to hold her. Never able to kiss her.

Never able to love her.

She was the reason he was so wound up. Because he knew just how easy Bran could win.

After all the centuries with Erith, Cael had never imagined there could be anyone who could defeat her. There were some, like Bran, who would abuse power such as hers. But she didn't.

She might have at one time, but that wasn't who she was now. If Bran gained her power, every realm in the universe would be destroyed, one by one. Cael didn't need to meditate to see that outcome.

Out of nowhere, rain began to fall. Others on the street ducked their heads, pulled up the hoods of their coats, or rushed indoors. Not Cael. He stood beneath the downpour and closed his eyes.

The feel of the drops on his face acted as the tears he wouldn't—and couldn't—shed. All the love, frustration, and despair within him filled each water droplet that tumbled from his face to the ground.

He could stand beneath the rain for a thousand years, and it still wouldn't touch a thimbleful of his emotions for Erith. Nor could he allow himself to fall into such desolation. Whether he found the faceless Dark Fae he searched for or not, he wouldn't let Erith or the Reapers down. They counted on him. So he would do what he did best.

Cael focused on the Reapers and Death because if he allowed himself to think about all the Fae, humans, and the various other beings in the vast universe, he would be crushed under the weight of it.

The rain soaked his clothes. He didn't care about the cool temperatures or how the drops felt like needle-pricks on his skin. These few minutes were his to wallow in doubt and self-pity before he squared his shoulders and continued doing what he had to do.

When he opened his eyes, he found a woman across from him. But not just any woman. It was Rhi. The Light Fae held an umbrella over her as she stared at him as if he'd lost his mind.

"I'd ask if you were all right, but clearly, you're not," she stated.

Cael still didn't know why Death was so interested in Rhi, but he'd seen firsthand the Fae's incredible power. "I like the rain."

"So do I, but that doesn't mean I want to be soaked by it." She flicked her long, black hair over her shoulder and propped a hand on her hip. "What's up, studly?"

He took in her black outfit of stilettos, leather pants, and a sweater with a wide neck that fell off one shoulder. Rhi was always impeccably dressed. Most Fae were, but she took it to the next level. The one thing the Fae was known for was her constantly changing nail designs.

She frowned when he didn't answer. Then, she looked at her hands and grinned before bending her wrist to let him see the bright pink, yellow, and white colors.

"The newest in my collection," she stated. "No Turning Back from Pink Street, Sun, Sea, And Sand In My Pants, and Suzi Chases Portu-geese. Now, as flattered as I am that you noticed my nails, tell me what's wrong."

"I'm walking in the rain."

"Yeah. I'm not buying that load of shite. Try again," Rhi demanded, giving him a look that said she was prepared to stand there all day.

Cael ran a hand down his face, flicking off the water. "I'm looking for someone."

"Oooh." Rhi's silver eyes brightened. "That sounds like fun. And I need something to do. I bought six pairs of shoes this morning, and I'm eyeing another three. So I'd like something else to do. Who are we after?"

He shrugged and shook his head, not bothering to hide his tight grin that was borne of anxiety and desperation. "I've no idea."

"That just makes it harder, handsome. And that means

things get fun." Rhi moved closer so that her large umbrella covered him, as well. Her smile faded as she stared solemnly up at him. "Care to share why you need this Fae?"

Cael swallowed, wondering how much to tell her. Death had allowed Rhi to live despite her knowing who the Reapers were. Perhaps it was because Rhi tracked them with her own magic while they were veiled. Or, it could be because Rhi had fought against Bran.

Whatever the reason, Rhi was alive, and Cael didn't want to change that. He might not know everything Death knew, but even he was aware of Rhi's importance, not just to the Light Fae but to the Dragon Kings, as well.

Rhi adjusted her earring—a rhinestone skull dangling from her lobe—and flashed a bright grin. "You're a Reaper. That means you can find anyone, anywhere. Right? I mean, at least I thought it did. Yet you're wandering the streets. I know because I've been following you for the past half hour."

For fek's sake. Cael was really off his game if he hadn't noticed that. He sighed and shrugged. "There's a lot going on. And we're only able to locate those that have been judged. Not just anyone."

"I'm gathering that. I can also guess that you can't tell me?"

"I'm not sure. You fought with us once. Maybe Death

would let you again."

Rhi rolled her eyes. "If you're going to war, then you need all the allies you can muster. Just ask the Dragon Kings. I take it that wanker Bran is still causing havoc?"

"More than you know."

"I really don't like him. Why don't you fill me in?"

Cael shook his head. "I'd love your help, but I'm not sure it's wise. You're going to be needed elsewhere."

The beautiful Fae stared daggers at him. "I get to decide who I help and when. I still haven't discovered why Death had Daire following me, and I want to know. If I help the Reapers, maybe she'll impart something."

Cael dropped his chin to his chest.

Rhi continued. "What I want to know is why Death doesn't just snap her fingers and end this Bran dude? She is that powerful, after all. For all I know, she could be some goddess." The Fae gasped in amazement. "She is, isn't she?"

"I've no idea," Cael answered honestly.

Rhi bent slightly and turned her head to look at him. "You've got me worried, studly. I don't know you all that well, and the few times I've been around you, you've been really quiet, but even I can tell something is eating at you."

"If something happened to this realm, the Dragon Kings would fight it, wouldn't they?"

The Fae frowned as she straightened. "What *something* are we talking about?"

Cael lifted his head before he twisted his lips. "Something like Bran."

Rhi searched his face before she gave a nod. "The Kings will fight anything and anyone who tries to harm their world."

"They've never fought against someone like Bran."

"He's just a Reaper."

Cael gave a shake of his head. "He's been syphoning Death's magic and life essence."

"Damn." Rhi stood there as the rain pelted the umbrella. "And the Dark you're looking for? Does he work for Bran?"

"He could either side with us or Bran. I believe he could be one who turns the tide of the war."

Rhi put her hand on his arm. "Now I understand why you've been walking around in a daze."

"Bran won't just kill Death and the Reapers, he'll come after this world, as well."

"Good luck with that," Rhi said with a snort. "The Dragon Kings are fierce, Cael. Not even they know the extent of their power. If Bran faced off against them, my bet would be on the Kings."

"You have that much faith in them?"

She gave him a dose of side-eye. "Honey cakes, I've

seen them fight."

"Bran has an army of Dark."

"The Kings are one unit. It doesn't matter how many men Bran has. He won't be able to compete with that. But we're getting ahead of ourselves. You're already thinking Death has lost."

Cael shot her a hard look. "I have not. I like to look at the options and attempt to find my way through each of them."

"Maybe you don't need the Dark Fae you're searching for. Maybe all you need is me."

"No," he said emphatically.

She smiled and batted her thick-lashed eyes at him. "You don't think I'm capable?"

"I think you're more than capable. But you fought against Bran before. He'll recognize you."

"I'm counting on that."

"The hell you are," Cael said as he pushed away from the wall and brought himself nose-to-nose with her.

Rhi shoved him back. "Do you know how he's stealing Death's power?"

"No, but th—"

"I'm going to find out." She turned and started walking away.

Cael glanced at the sky in annoyance as he was once more drenched before he hurried to follow her.

"Dammit, Rhi. Stop being so stubborn. This is madness."

"Actually, it's smart. It's a new concept you might try sometime."

"You're maddening!" he shouted as he came to a halt.

She stopped and slowly turned to face him, leaning the umbrella on her shoulder. "Let me put it to you this way, handsome. Bran knows I'm strong. When he finds me, he's going to attempt to have me fight for his side. I'll tell him he's lost his mind, and we'll have some more words. Then, after some careful thought, I'll agree. When I get close to him, I'll be able to find out what he's doing to Death, and we can stop it. That way, she becomes her powerful self again and can crush this insignificant cockroach once and for all."

"I like the crushing part," came a seductive voice behind Rhi that Cael knew all too well.

Erith.

He wanted to go to her and wrap his arms around her, pull her against him and feel every inch of her. But he didn't.

Rhi jerked around, slamming the umbrella into Cael since he was so stunned at seeing Erith that he didn't duck in time. He winced and shoved the umbrella away as he stepped to the side.

"You're looking pretty spiffy to me," Rhi said and looked Death up and down where she stood beneath the overhang of a building. "I'm totally loving the outfit, by the way. I've got some boots that would complete it to perfection."

In the next second, Rhi was holding a pair of black boots with tall stiletto heels that had small silver spikes lining them. There were six buckles from the top of the boot down to the top of the shoe—each a silver skull.

"Perfect for Death," Rhi said with a wink.

Erith didn't so much as glance at Cael before she smiled. He blinked, and the boots were suddenly on her feet. Even he had to admit, they were indeed perfect.

"Thank you for wanting to help," Erith told Rhi. "It means more than you will ever know. But your path lies elsewhere."

"But—" Rhi began.

"We'll speak soon. I promise," Death said before she touched Rhi. In the next instant, the Fae was gone.

Then, Erith's gaze slid to Cael. Their eyes clashed. His balls tightened at the sight of her standing so defiantly before him in an ensemble that showed she was becoming more than just the Death he knew. She was letting in more of the Mistress of War.

Her pants were sculpted to her lean legs, and the corset accentuated her small waist and full breasts. Even the asymmetrical coat she wore was hot.

Desire swelled within him. He'd seen her many different ways, but this was a new Erith.

And this one might very well be his undoing.

Chapter Nine

It hadn't been her plan to search for Cael. Once Erith left Seamus, she found her thoughts going again and again to Cael. Before she knew it, she was in a city, watching him and Rhi talk.

The moment Erith saw Rhi touch him, jealousy, sharp and true, cut through her. She wanted to lash out, to hurt Rhi. And it was only by sheer will alone that Erith didn't. Oh, but how she craved it.

In her mind, she ripped the Light Fae to pieces again and again. It was only the sound of Rhi's boots on the sidewalk that made her realize the duo was walking right toward her. That's when she heard their conversation.

Relief swept through her when she realized the Fae wasn't flirting with Cael. Which made Erith relieved that she hadn't attacked Rhi. Erith should've known better. The Fae's heart belonged to another—and would until the end of time.

But when it came to Cael, Erith didn't always think clearly.

She was mortified by the feelings that had nearly gotten the best of her. But she managed to stay in control. This time. Would she the next time? It was just another reason to stay away from Cael.

Erith knew the Reapers found comfort in the arms of women all the time. But she'd never seen or heard Cael talk about anyone like the others did—before the Reapers found love. Erith was grateful that she didn't know about Cael's lovers because she wasn't sure how she would react.

Her emotions were all over the place, and that didn't bode well for anyone. Especially when she faced Bran.

Erith decided to make herself known to Cael and Rhi. She dropped her veil, yet neither saw her because of the umbrella Rhi held. It wasn't until she spoke that both looked her way. Erith fought against looking at Cael.

Soaked from the rain with his shirt sculpted to every hard muscle, he'd never looked so damned gorgeous.

Or untouchable.

Erith kept her attention on Rhi. It would've been so easy to take the Fae up on her offer to help, but Erith couldn't. She knew what was coming, and Rhi needed her attention focused elsewhere.

Once Rhi was gone, Erith had no choice but to look at Cael. She knew it was a mistake the moment she did. Because, for the briefest of seconds, desire flashed in his eyes, making her blood pound in her ears, and her heart race.

"The boots suit you," Cael said.

She pulled her gaze from him to the shoes Rhi had given her and smiled. "I quite like them."

"I also like the new look."

Warmth filled her as she slowly raised her eyes to him. This time, she heard the need in his voice, and it made shivers race over her skin. "I couldn't very well fight in a dress."

Cael's black brows snapped together as his gaze hardened. "Are you going after Bran now?"

The sound of authority and anger in his voice did something strange and unexpected to her, something exciting and . . . *exhilarating*. It took her three tries before she found her voice. "No."

"Damn right, you aren't," he replied testily.

Cael turned away, only to spin back to her. "What the hell is wrong with you wanting to go after Bran? We have to stop him from taking your magic first. I thought you understood that."

He'd never spoken to her that way before, and damn if she didn't like it. A lot.

Too damn much.

"Believe me," he continued his rant. "I know you don't need me or anyone, but that doesn't mean you should go alone."

"I know."

"That's reckless, and that's not something you've ever been. At least not while I've known you. And wh—" His words halted. "What did you say?"

"You're right," she said.

Cael ran his hand through his long, wet locks, pushing them away from his gorgeous face. Seconds later, the downpour shoved them back down again. She watched the rain fall into his thick lashes before he blinked the drops away.

She moved out into the rain, coming near him. It was a mistake to tempt herself so, but she couldn't seem to help it. She would never have done such a thing before her magic was taken—or before she'd gotten the sword.

But now was different.

Now, it felt *good*.

"You're getting wet."

She shrugged. "It's only water."

His gaze dropped to her chest before he cleared his throat and hastily looked away. "Shouldn't you be scolding me for talking to you like that? I apologize."

"Don't," she told him. "You spoke your mind, which is what I want right now."

Silver eyes met hers. "You don't really want to know what I think."

"Try me."

He put his hands on his hips as he stared at her. Cael blew out a breath, sending water droplets flying as he did. "It's better if I don't."

"Whatever," she said and teleported to the tiny isle that held the doorway to her realm.

Once there, she quickly stepped through and strode toward her tower. She was angry. No, she was livid. She'd liked Cael's tone. And she'd given him permission to keep doing it. Why had he stopped?

Why hadn't he continued? Didn't he realize that she needed exactly that right now? That she needed *him*?

She threw open the door to the tower and started up the winding stairs that led to her chamber.

"What the hell is wrong with you?"

Her foot missed the step, and she had to quickly right herself before she fell. Erith turned, her gaze snapping to the doorway to find Cael standing there, fury sparking in his eyes as he still dripped with water.

"I don't know what you mean."

She hated how happy she was that he was there, and even more pleased that he was furious. In fact, her heart beat double-time that he had followed and then confronted her.

She faced forward and continued her ascent, intending to ignore him—just to see what he would do. Then she heard him taking the stairs three at a time, and her stomach quivered in anticipation.

Within moments, he was beside her as she reached the landing to her chamber. Except she didn't go to her room. It had a bed, and with the way her emotions were darting here and there, she didn't want to give herself any kind of reason to put her lips on Cael's. She diverted to another room.

"You know exactly what I mean," Cael said as he followed her into the library.

Erith turned around, her long braid swinging out before slapping against her arm with a thud. "Why? Because I told you to speak your mind?"

"You've never wanted that before."

"When did I say that?" she demanded, anger slowly churning within her.

He opened his mouth, then closed it. A muscle ticked in his jaw. "I don't know."

"Because I didn't. You assumed that."

"No," he said as he took a step closer. "We always knew we worked for you. You make the rules. We follow them."

"And each of you was chosen because you're warriors. Did that ever cross your mind? Because I never wanted sheep to just follow me blindly."

Cael jerked his head back as if slapped. "Sheep? You think I'm a fekking sheep?"

"Far from it. But when I tell you to speak your mind, I

expect it."

"Because you're still calling the shots. You ignored me for weeks, and now I'm supposed to act as if that didn't happen? As if my concerns didn't matter."

All her fury vanished in a second. "It wasn't because I didn't care. I did it because I didn't want you to see what was happening to me."

Instead of appeasing him as she'd hoped they would, her words only incensed him. His eyes narrowed as he stalked toward her. "Because you didn't want any of us to see you weakening and try to join Bran? Is that what you think of us? Or was it because you feared we wouldn't follow you anymore."

"What?" She gaped, unsure where he was getting the ideas.

"You went to Eoghan."

She shrugged. "Of course. He'd just returned to this realm. I needed to see that he was himself and give him control of the other group of Reapers."

"That you didn't tell me about. You didn't trust me enough with any of that. All these years, I thought there was trust and maybe even a little friendship between us, but I was so bloody wrong."

He pivoted on his heel to leave, and Erith couldn't handle that. It had killed her to keep him away. But if he left on his own this time, it would devastate her.

"Cael. Stop," she ordered before he reached the door.

He halted, his fists clenched by his sides. "What more do you want from me? I've given you everything I have. I'm here to serve you, not because I want revenge or because I am afraid of dying." He looked at her over his shoulder. "I'm here because of you. Because of what you created with the Reapers. I wanted to be a part of something so amazing."

"You're a natural leader. I knew it the first time I saw you." She bit back a smile when he turned to her. Erith fought not to go to him and ease the anger that marred his features. "You were an inspiration for the Reapers."

She'd never intended to tell him that, but it seemed right that he knew now.

"I don't understand."

This time, she did grin. "I walked the Fae realm for thousands of years after I gave up my sword. I watched the civil war between the Light and Dark rip the planet apart. And I saw one warrior who was more courageous, more heroic, and more noble than any I had seen before. You."

Confusion flashed across his face for a moment. Then, he took a step toward her, making her heart leap.

Erith glanced at the floor and decided to tell him everything. She knew if her emotions weren't so out of control, she'd never even contemplate such a thing. But perhaps it was good that this was happening. Maybe it was time.

"I watched you for days, and as I did, I came up with the idea for the Reapers. It wasn't long after when I found Theo and saw his betrayal and subsequent death. He was the first I asked to be a Reaper. The betrayal he suffered was something that resonated with me, so I used that as the basis for the Reapers. I never imagined I would offer you a position."

"Everyone can be a fool."

"You weren't a fool, Cael. You were tricked. There's a difference."

Silence filled the room as he silently watched her. Erith grew uncomfortable under his silver gaze, wondering what he was thinking. She wasn't all-knowing, and there were times—like now—that she wished she were.

"Cael, I—"

Her words locked in her throat as her knees grew weak, and it became difficult to breathe. She could feel her magic draining from her as if someone had turned on a faucet. Worse was the lethargy she experienced from her life being drained away, as well. She pitched forward, and suddenly, she found herself in Cael's arms.

"I've got you," he whispered and lifted her.

He brought her to the window seat and sat, still holding her. His warmth helped ease the coldness that had enveloped her.

"What just happened?" he asked.

She rested her head against his chest, uncaring that his shirt was wet because he felt that good. "It hasn't been this bad before."

"Bran," he stated angrily.

Erith closed her eyes as the weakness consumed her. Her body wouldn't respond properly, making it nearly impossible to even hold up her head. She liked the way Cael's hand stroked her hair. In fact, she could stay just like this forever.

"I thought I could take him," she murmured.

"You can."

She shivered against the weakness and their wet clothes. "My sword revived me, but he took that little bit away again."

Before her words finished, she was wrapped in a thick blanket while still in Cael's arms. He dried their clothes with magic, but he never let go of her.

"I wouldn't use the sword again until we stop whatever Bran is doing to take your power."

"You'll never get close enough."

He rested his chin on the top of her head. "Maybe. Or Seamus could come through and give us the information as you believe."

"I tracked him and found Bran. I think you might be

right about Seamus. He said he didn't go find you to tell you the plan because he knew Bran would have men looking for him."

Cael blew out a breath. "Since he's already with Bran, that's probably exactly what happened. Had he called to me, Bran's men would've seen that, and Seamus would've never gotten close to him."

"Or, he could be lying."

"We'll know soon enough." Cael tightened his hold. "Let me worry about that. You need to find a spell that will slow down what Bran is doing."

"I've tried."

Cael smoothed a lock of hair away from her face. "Try harder."

She wanted to look up at him, but the lethargy pulled her toward sleep, and she couldn't find the strength to fight it.

Chapter Ten

A hunger he wasn't sure he could control, ran through him. Cael refused to release his hold on Erith. She felt so good against him, better than anything he'd ever dreamed or imagined. She fit perfectly as if she had been made just for him.

Partly because he'd seen her face go pale right before she crumbled and he caught her. But now that she was finally in his arms, he never wanted to let go.

If only she weren't fighting against her very essence being taken from her. It was a cruel, painful way to die. And not something Erith deserved.

"I'm not leaving you," Cael vowed as he inhaled the scent of her hair that was a mixture of all the flowers of her realm.

Now that she slept, it was the prime opportunity for him to look around the tower for a possible way to battle Bran. It gutted him to see Erith so weak and vulnerable. She was anything but. Bran putting her in such a position made Cael's blood boil.

He looked down at her. In all the years he'd served her,

not once had he ever seen her thus. Still, yes. But lifeless, never.

The idea that this might be a preview of what was to come infuriated Cael. It didn't help that he felt powerless. He had no idea how to aid her. The one thing he could do was go after Bran, but nothing he did would destroy his nemesis. Just as none of Bran's army could hurt Erith.

Frustrated, angry, and feeling more exposed than he ever had before, Cael realized it was a dangerous combination.

He slowly rose to his feet with Erith in his arms and gingerly walked out of the library in search of her bedroom. He was a bit surprised to find it was the first room he came to. He gently lowered Erith to the bed and made sure she was covered with the fur blanket. She had stopped shivering, but her skin was still extremely pale.

Unable to help himself, he ran the backs of his knuckles down her cheek. Her flawless skin was cool to the touch. He longed to curl up beside her, but that would be pushing things a bit far.

Besides, he needed to help her win against Bran, the bastard.

Cael's eyes lifted from Erith, determination swarming him. He straightened and turned on his heel before returning to the library. There, he searched each book, hoping he might find some kind of magic that would put an end to whatever Bran was doing to hurt Erith.

He found nothing, which didn't help his mood. In all the various books, there wasn't even one that could aid him. Cael left the library and made his way to the stairs. He ascended them to the next level and looked in each chamber on that floor.

It was the first time he'd ever had free rein within the tower, and he knew it would anger Erith if she knew he was roaming. He didn't care. He'd rather her be pissed than dead.

Level after level, he searched until he reached the top. It was just one massive room. He halted at the doorway, shocked that there was something from each of the Reapers inside. From a weapon to the helmet Cael had worn in the Fae army. Every item had once belonged to a Reaper before they were betrayed and became Death's warriors.

Cael was curious about the room, but he didn't enter it. This was Erith's domain, a private sanctuary that he didn't want to invade. He took a step backwards and pivoted before leaving to return to her bedchamber.

The entire realm was nothing but an oasis of beauty for wildlife and plants. The only structure was Erith's tower, so there was no point in searching anywhere else.

Cael checked on Erith. With every rise of her chest, he sighed in happiness, knowing she was still alive. He lifted the edge of her braid, feeling the soft locks before he made his way to the window. The picture below was stunning with the forest and lake and the mountains on the horizon. There were birds everywhere, their songs mixing together to create a beautiful melody that lulled him.

He leaned against the edge of the window, his gaze moving to the water beyond. Cael stilled when he saw a pack of wolves loping from the woods to drink. He'd had no idea there were such creatures there, but it didn't surprise him.

Erith loved all animals. The ferocious to the timid. He wasn't sure if she preferred the beasts or the plants more. In truth, each time he saw a blossom of some kind, he thought of her.

But even he was aware that there were many aspects of her life that he knew nothing about.

He pushed away from the window and turned when he spotted a book on the chair, half hidden beneath a pillow. Curious, he moved the throw cushion aside and lifted the hefty tome. The title, *Tales of Death*, left him cold.

His gaze jerked to Erith, but she remained asleep. Cael sank into the chair and opened the book to discover that it was a Light Fae's account of what he'd witnessed from the Mistress of War.

Cael devoured each word, page after page. Before he knew it, he was halfway through the book. He'd sensed the power within the black sword, but reading about the things that Erith had done brought home just how formidable she was.

When he finally finished, he softly closed the book and set it on the floor, dazed and astounded by what Erith had accomplished. Whether she wanted to return to being Mistress of War or not, that was how she would win against Bran.

Erith's reluctance to become that being of death and destruction now made sense. She *was* death in all its terrifying, daunting glory.

Not just powerful, but alarmingly so. If Cael had to guess, he'd say that Erith was a goddess of some kind. He'd always assumed that she was Fae, but only because she judged them, keeping them in line. But even she admitted that she wasn't a Fae.

Cael turned his head to the bed to find Erith on her side, her eyes open, watching him. He couldn't tell what she was thinking, and that set him on edge. But she didn't look nearly as pale. "How long have you been awake?"

"Long enough to know what you were reading."

He scooted to the edge of the chair and leaned his arms on his knees. "Was any of it true?"

"I'm afraid so."

"Good."

She frowned and sat up slowly. "Good?"

"Just as I told you yesterday, you're the key to winning this war." He watched her carefully, looking for any hint of fatigue, but it seemed the sleep had helped her body repair some of what had been taken.

"You don't understand—"

"I do," he cut her off. "I read the book, remember?"

She shook her head and sat forward, pulling her legs toward her chest while holding tightly to the blanket. "It took a lot for me to let go of the sword the first time."

"Did you ever think you weren't meant to let it go?"

She snapped her head to him. Her expression was a mix of shock and outrage. "If you had seen me, you wouldn't be so cavalier about it."

"I did see you," he stated, thinking back to when she'd come to him when he was dying.

She hesitated before looking away. "That wasn't really a fight, and it wasn't my sword."

"I beg to differ. I know what I saw."

"You never mentioned it before."

He shrugged. "There wasn't a need before. There is now."

She moved to the edge of the bed and swung her legs over so that her back was to him. "I don't fear dying. What tears me up inside is knowing what Bran will do to all of you."

Cael got to his feet and walked around the bed until he faced her. "Stop this idiocy. You're too fekking strong to be acting as if everything is decided. Take the damn sword in hand. Return to being Mistress of War. You get to control things, Erith. Not the other way around."

Lavender eyes churned with anger.

But he didn't care. "You wreaked havoc last time because you had nothing to anchor you. That's what's different. You have us now. The Reapers will remind you not to let the wrath take over."

"You seem to have a lot of faith in what I can do."

"That's right. So, get up off your beautiful arse and get it done."

A black brow quirked at his words. "Telling me what to do now?"

"You urged me to give you my thoughts. That's what I'm doing."

She got to her feet and tossed the blanket aside. Erith ran her hands over her head, and as her palms passed, her hair changed from one braid to small ones running from one side of her head to the other and ending at her crown where the midnight locks fell freely down her back.

He smiled when he saw the resolve in her eyes. This new Erith was a combination of Death and the Mistress of War. And he couldn't wait to see what she did.

"I take it you approve?" Erith asked.

"Absolutely."

Her lips softened slightly at the corners. "I never wanted to wait around and die. You need to understand that."

"I do," he said with a nod. "You feared becoming what you were before."

She licked her lips and blew out a breath. "There's a difference between the Fae's fear of me now as Death and the one they knew when I was Mistress of War. I judge the Fae now. Back then, anyone was fair game."

"You already told me."

She shook her head, her black locks shifting with her. "I need you to understand just how risky this is. If I return to being the Mistress of War, I'll be no better than Bran. If that happens, you have to stop me."

"And how do you propose I do that?"

Her chest rose as she inhaled deeply. "You need to get Con."

"The King of Dragon Kings?" Cael asked in confusion. "What does Constantine have to do with this?"

"I've been his friend for a long time. There is something I've given him that will help him defeat me or Bran."

Cael crossed his arms over his chest. "When were you going to tell me about this?"

"When the time came. And it's now."

"Why Con? Why not someone else?"

She glanced away. "Because you wouldn't use it on me."

Damn right, he wouldn't. Cael didn't know what *it* was, but he could guess it was something that would kill her. No way would he allow that to happen, but he'd keep that part to himself.

"Why not just have Con destroy Bran now?"

Erith's gaze met his. "This is our war. Let's keep it that way. The Kings have enough to deal with at the moment."

"It's the same reason you wouldn't let Rhi help us."

She gave a nod.

Cael dropped his arms and ran a hand down his face. "We need allies, and you're making sure that none can help us."

"Is that so?" she asked testily. She gave him a steely glare. "In the vision you saw of the war, did you, at any time, see Rhi or the Dragon Kings?"

Damn, he hated when she was right. "No."

"You saw the Reapers and two Fae—Xaneth and a Dark—who could decide to join us or Bran. Right?"

"You know you are," he bit out.

"That's who will be on the battlefield, Cael. And if I had my way, none of the Reapers would be there."

Fury that he barely held in check ripped through him.

"You would keep us away?"

"It's too late for that now."

"You're so used to standing alone that it really bothers you having to take help, doesn't it?"

She closed the distance between them, her lavender eyes blazing with more emotion than he'd ever seen. "You don't know what you're talking about. I don't want any of you there because the moment one of you gets hurt or killed, it's going to wound me more than anything Bran could ever do to me." She paused but didn't look away. "I can't lose any of the Reapers. Especially you."

He wished her feelings ran to something other than his leadership skills because her words went straight to his cock that was now hard and aching for her.

Only her.

Always her.

Chapter Eleven

DARK PALACE

The cries of pleasure from the many humans captured by the Dark didn't register with Xaneth. He'd returned to the palace as soon as he left the Reapers. But if he thought he could get back to his life, he was sorely mistaken.

The warriors' words kept ringing through his mind. The fact that Cael had seen him standing between the two armies was significant. Xaneth might not know any of the Reapers well, but he knew *of* them.

Also weighing heavily on his mind was the fact that Death hadn't killed him. He hadn't thought much about it after helping Eoghan and Thea, but since then, Xaneth had done some asking around. It took quite a bit of prodding to learn anything about the Reapers.

The Fae—both Dark and Light—were a superstitious lot. They feared even talking about the Reapers, but Xaneth was used to prying information out of others. So it wasn't long before he saw a pattern in the stories—anyone who claimed to know about the Reapers was soon dead.

As in, hours later.

Now, he understood why Eoghan and Cael had sworn to talk to Death on his behalf. He had thought it was just a ploy to get him to do what they wanted. Apparently, he'd been wrong.

Xaneth felt someone come to stand beside him, but he ignored them. He wasn't in the mood to talk. He wasn't even sure why he was at the palace. After fighting so hard to stay alive and avoid his insane aunt—who just happened to be the Queen of the Light—he wasn't keen on losing his life because he chose the wrong side in a war.

But that might very well be what happened.

"It's not polite to leave the king waiting."

Xaneth blinked as the words registered. He turned his head and found himself looking into the face of Balladyn, the King of the Dark. "Mingling with us now, huh?"

"I really should gut you for such insolence," the king said, though there was no heat in his words. "Something is troubling you. I've been watching you for thirty minutes. Ten of which, I've been beside you. I expected you to be more aware of your surroundings."

Xaneth blew out a breath and faced Balladyn. "I have a problem I need to sort out. And quickly."

"Then sort it."

"I can't make up my mind."

Balladyn chuckled and pushed away from the huge column. "Take a walk with me."

Xaneth had already had a few run-ins with the king. Balladyn had known that Xaneth was using glamour to appear as a Dark Fae, which didn't please the king at all. Yet Balladyn didn't throw Xaneth out or kill him—which would have been the king's right.

Instead, he'd listened to Xaneth about Bran and struck a deal with him. Xaneth could remain at the palace for as long as it took for him to find Bran. Xaneth wanted someone to help him kill Usaeil, and Balladyn wanted Bran's kidnapping of the Dark for his army to stop.

So far, neither had gotten their wish.

Xaneth fell in step with Balladyn. They walked in silence as the king nodded to others as they passed through the many wide corridors of the palace.

It was quite a shock to Xaneth when he found himself on the top floor and in Balladyn's private chambers. He eyed the soaring ceilings and large windows, but it was the seemingly endless shelves stacked with books on the far side of the room that caught Xaneth's eye.

"Have a seat," Balladyn said as he made his way to the book area. He turned and smiled at Xaneth. "I have the largest Fae library outside of the Light Castle. And I know for a fact that I hold books that can't be found anywhere else."

Xaneth raised a brow, impressed. He walked to the large table where several books lay open. Before the table were two chairs. He took one and stretched out his legs before him, crossing his ankles.

Balladyn propped a hip on the edge of the table. "If you need a place to think, I've found quiet normally works. Less distractions. Or time for anyone to sneak up on you and kill you."

"True." Xaneth expected to be told to share his problem, but Balladyn always seemed to do the opposite of what people imagined. "I watched you fight in the Fae Wars once. I was only a small lad, but I knew even then that you were a badass."

The king grinned, a faraway look crossing his face. "That seems like a lifetime ago."

Neither mentioned that it was when Balladyn had been a Light Fae and Commander of the Queen's Guard. Xaneth had no idea how Balladyn had become Dark, but he did know that somehow Usaeil had had a hand in it.

"I've done some digging on you, Seeker."

Xaneth sat up straight in the chair. For all the casualty Balladyn showed, he hadn't gotten to be king for nothing, and Xaneth would be wise not to forget that. "You wouldn't be where you are if you didn't know who was in your palace."

"You've worked both Light and Dark without siding with either. In fact, you've done what no other has. Well done. I'm impressed," Balladyn said.

Xaneth wasn't fooled. The King of the Dark was cunning. He'd been Taraeth's right hand for thousands of years before killing him and taking the throne. Balladyn had forged his way in the Light and then did the same with the Dark. He wasn't a Fae to be trifled with.

"Why do you want Usaeil dead?" Balladyn asked.

Xaneth held Balladyn's red gaze. The king's long, straight, black hair hung down his back. "Isn't it enough that I hate her?"

"It should be. But rumors have a way of changing things. And one has reached me. There are those who say you became the Seeker to keep hidden from Usaeil. The only ones needing to hide from the queen are those she wants dead."

"Should I clap that you figured it out?"

Balladyn stood and walked to the other chair. He sank into it and smiled, his gaze shrewd. "Skip the clap. If you don't want to tell me why Usaeil is after you, don't. I'm merely curious as to why you wish her dead."

Xaneth looked down at the ornate red and gold rug at his feet. Then he had an idea. "I'll tell you what you want to know about Usaeil, if you tell me what you've discovered about the Reapers."

"You assume I know of them."

"You do," Xaneth stated.

Balladyn stared at him for a long minute. Then he gave a nod. "Deal. You first."

"Usaeil is my aunt. She killed our family and took the throne. She's been searching for me since I fled."

"Interesting," Balladyn said. "And you want to kill her to take the throne?"

Xaneth snorted as he jerked back his head. "I don't want to rule. I just want to be able to return to the Light and live as I should have all along—freely."

"I think I might be able to help you out with that. But first, Reapers." Balladyn jerked his chin at the table. "There are all the books I've found that have any sort of mention of Reapers. But, I believe I've met one. Fintan."

"The infamous Dark assassin?" Xaneth asked with surprise.

Balladyn nodded. "White hair and red-rimmed, white eyes. There is no other who looks like him."

"Did this Fae confirm who he was?"

"Nay, but he didn't deny it either. Why are you curious about the Reapers?"

Xaneth shrugged, unwilling to share what he knew. "There's been a lot of whispers about them lately."

"It's more than that. You know something."

"I'll neither confirm nor deny that," Xaneth said, repeating something he'd heard a human utter.

Balladyn gave a bark of laughter. "Damn, if I don't like you." His smile dropped. "There's another rumor that has reached me. Some say this Bran we're both after was once a Reaper."

"From all the things I've heard about Bran, combined with him kidnapping the Dark, I'm guessing he's not going to go down without a fight."

"My people don't scare easily, but it's to the point that they're asking me to spell the palace so no outsiders can get in. It means I'd have to mark each Dark personally. While it's a decent plan, there are ways Bran can go around it."

Xaneth nodded in agreement. "By using a Dark already in his army that's stationed in the palace."

"Precisely. That's how I'm guessing Bran's finding those he wishes to take. Are you still trying to get noticed by him?"

"That's the problem I'm sorting out. Someone has given me incentive not to."

Balladyn gave Xaneth a droll look. "What you really mean to say is that there is someone else wanting to go up against Bran, and they want you on their side."

Xaneth didn't reply, unsure how to act.

"I know the signs of oncoming war, lad," Balladyn said. "I've fought in too many of them. Bran isn't taking Dark for shites and giggles. He's building an army. And a man only does that when he plans on something big. Like going for my throne."

"What if it's something else entirely?" Xaneth asked.

Balladyn frowned as he sat forward, bracing his elbows on the arms of the chair. "If this has anything to do with the Reapers, then perhaps you should side with them. From what I read, they're a fearsome lot—no matter who Bran might be."

Xaneth ran a hand down his face, more confused than ever.

"Then again," Balladyn said as he began to smile, "you could kill two birds with one stone."

"Meaning?"

Balladyn sat back in the chair. "Infiltrate Bran's ranks as a spy."

"Two birds. One stone." Xaneth liked the idea. Because it would allow him to go with whichever side won. "I can't believe I didn't think of that."

"Your mind was focused on choosing one or the other. Remember, go somewhere quiet next time," Balladyn advised.

Xaneth got to his feet. "You will get your revenge on Usaeil for whatever she did to you."

"This is what she did to me," Balladyn said. "She left me for dead on the battlefield. Taraeth was supposed to kill me, but he brought me here and turned me Dark."

"Shite," Xaneth murmured. He'd suspected that something devious had made a warrior of Balladyn's character Dark. It was no surprise that Xaneth's aunt had been responsible.

Balladyn looked away. "Watch your back, lad. Always."

"I'm going to spy for you, as well. The Dark will feel safe again."

The king's head swung back to him. "You would've made a great king for the Light, Xaneth. I'm sorry your family was taken from you in such a heinous way."

He shrugged. "Life goes on, right?"

"That it does. If you need anything, call for me. I'll help."

Xaneth held out his hand to the king. They clasped forearms, staring into each other's eyes. With a nod, Xaneth released his hold and made his way back downstairs to the main rooms.

With his focus renewed, he observed others with a sharper, more intent concentration. And that's when he spotted a Dark watching the others intently. Xaneth watched him for a long while before he was certain this Dark worked for Bran. Then Xaneth made his way over to the Fae.

The Dark glanced at him in annoyance. "Go away," he replied gruffly.

Xaneth smiled. "I thought you'd want to talk to any-one wishing to join the army you're building. That is why you're taking Dark, right?"

The Fae narrowed his gaze, instantly wary.

"I want to escape my meddling family and get some fighting experience," Xaneth finished.

"I don't know what you're talking about."

Xaneth shrugged, his lips twisting. "My mistake. I heard a rumor that someone was helping Dark get out of bad situations with the payment being joining an army."

The Dark said nothing as he stared.

"Too bad," Xaneth said. "I guess I'll go try someone else."

He got two steps before he felt a hand on his shoulder. Xaneth hid his smile before he whirled around.

"Hold on," the Dark said.

Xaneth widened his eyes. "So, the rumors are true? Tell me where I need to sign up."

The Dark looked him up and down before he smiled. He held out a piece of paper. "Go to that address. And if you have any more friends wanting to get away from their meddling families, send them my way."

"Will do," Xaneth said and walked away.

As he made his way to the back of the palace, he saw Balladyn watching. Xaneth gave a nod to the king and kept walking.

A lot hinged on Xaneth being able to act as a spy. He'd done it before, but only for himself. This time, it was for the Fae in general—and the Reapers.

This time, there was no room for any kind of screw-ups.

Xaneth glanced at the address on the paper and teleported to it.

Chapter Twelve

She'd said too much. Erith knew it, but once the words were out of her mouth, they couldn't be taken back. After she'd let it slip to Cael that she couldn't lose him, she'd left her chamber—because being so close to the bed with him was too much to handle.

Especially after he'd held her so tenderly not that long ago.

"Where are you going?" Cael demanded as he followed her out.

Erith stopped on the landing. She knew without having to ask that he had been to every nook and cranny in the tower. Even the top, which was her special place.

She turned to face him. "I'm no longer going to sit around, waiting for something to happen. I've done that for too long, and look where it's gotten me."

"What if Bran takes more of your magic again?"

"He will," she told Cael. "That's inevitable unless I find out how he's doing it."

"We."

She frowned. "What?"

"You said until *you* find out what Bran is doing. I corrected it to *we*."

Erith became lost in Cael's silver eyes. He was the strongest Fae she knew. He was the type who always bent beneath the weight of something but never broke.

He'd been born for great things, but a betrayal had delivered him into her hands. She didn't want to be happy about that, but the simple fact was that she was. Very much so. Cael was everything that was honorable and admirable. He held the qualities she wished she had herself, the traits that Erith strived for every day to make up for the lives she had so ruthlessly taken.

"I'm the only one who will be able to get close enough to Bran to find out how he's taking my magic."

Cael shook his head. "There's still a chance Seamus will come through."

"A slim one, yes. But I refuse to hinge everything on him. That's something an inexperienced and naïve person would do. I'm neither."

"You saw the good in him," Cael stated as he moved closer. "When I would've killed him, you showed him compassion. You gave him free rein on your realm. You trusted him."

She shrugged and glanced away. "And, as you pointed out, he probably betrayed me." She laughed as she turned and strode into the library, the place where she did most of her work. "You think I would know a betrayal before it happened. I've seen so many."

"As you've often said, you aren't all-seeing."

Erith halted in the middle of the room and looked toward the open windows that let in the songs of the birds, the scents of the flowers, and the breeze. "Maybe this is my punishment for all the death I delivered across the universe."

"Stop," Cael stated as he came up behind her. "Since when do you wallow in self-pity?"

She spun around. "Self-pity? Is that what you think this is? I'm being practical."

"You're being dramatic. We've all done things we regret."

"Have you killed millions simply because it felt good?" she demanded.

His lips flattened before he said. "Nay."

"Have you eagerly descended upon a realm, happy to hear the screams of terror?"

Cael glared at her and shook his head.

"Then don't tell me I'm being dramatic. I'm being realistic. Everything comes back around on us. *Everything.*"

"And you believe this is your penance?" he asked, crossing his arms over his chest.

Erith swallowed and looked away, unable to hold his gaze any longer. "I do. I just hate that the Reapers will be taken down with me."

"I thought you had stopped thinking like that. I told you, we need Death *and* the Mistress of War."

Oh! He infuriated her. Hadn't he listened to anything she'd said? Didn't he understand?

Erith strode to him until their bodies were nearly touching. She lifted her head and glared up at him, though some of her anger dissipated at his nearness, a reminder of his effect on her body. "It might be too late for that."

"Might," he replied succinctly.

She hated the emotions that rolled through her like the waves upon the shore. Regardless of what she did, she couldn't seem to control her reactions or her feelings, no matter how hard she tried.

How easy it would be to lift her hands and lay them on his chest, to run her palms over his hard muscles. To . . . no. She had to stop. Otherwise, she might take herself down a path she couldn't come back from.

Normally, she would've dismissed Cael and sent him back to the Reapers. Instead, she found that she had an overwhelming desire to roll her eyes.

"I've laid out the facts," she stated, proud of herself for not giving in to the eye-roll. "As you pointed out earlier, before we can begin to think about fighting Bran, *we* have to stop him from taking any more of my magic."

Cael smiled at her emphasis of *we*. "Precisely."

"But . . ." she pressed when he hesitated.

He sighed as he dropped his arms. "You need to get a handle on yourself."

Erith didn't need him to explain exactly what he meant. Her emotions.

"If Bran sees that he's rattled you, he'll mercilessly go in for the kill," Cael continued.

She nodded absently. "Ever since I picked my sword back up, along with my weakening state, I can't seem to control anything."

"I've noticed."

The fact that there was a note of amusement in his voice had her struggling not to smile. "I expected you to say something sooner."

"There was no need. I could see you were fighting it. Though I probably shouldn't, I'll admit that it's nice to see that you can feel out of control like the rest of us."

Was he joking? She gaped at him. "I can't remember a time when I've ever felt *in* control."

"That's not how you appear." He twisted his lips. "It's not how you sound or even how you approach things."

"A façade. I've gotten good at masking my feelings." So good, in fact, that she could almost pretend sometimes that she didn't love Cael.

Almost.

Cael turned his head as he looked away, his black hair slipping over one shoulder as he did. She recalled just how silky the strands felt sliding through her fingers. She had allowed herself a quick touch while he lay dying so long ago.

"Why are you alone?"

She was taken aback by his question. The fact that he wouldn't look at her when he asked was even worse. Erith pivoted and walked to a bookcase to give herself something to do. She looked at the spines but didn't read the titles.

Behind her, Cael's voice reached her once more. "I understood and agreed with your rules for the Reapers, but that didn't mean you had to follow them, as well. You shouldn't spend eternity alone."

"I'm not alone." She had the Reapers. She had Cael.

From a distance.

And that was enough. It had to be.

"Was there someone you loved and lost?" he pressed.

Erith didn't want to go down this road. She wanted to keep their conversation on something safer, like the upcoming battle. But Cael had flung open the gates and was barreling through with his prying inquiries. Questions she couldn't answer.

"You mean as you did?" she asked, squeezing her eyes closed each time she thought of Cael holding the pretty

Fae in his arms.

"Nay."

The word came from close behind her. He'd moved as stealthily as a feline. "I know you did," she said.

"I thought I loved Corla, aye," Cael replied. "I realized I didn't. So, no, I didn't leave anyone I loved behind."

His words, husky and soft, were so near that she wondered if he would be there to mold his body against hers if she leaned back. Erith closed her eyes against the desire to find out.

Her will to stand fast against her need for Cael was crumbling fast. It had been dealt a crushing blow when he held her. And his sexy voice was like the straw that broke the camel's back.

"You have loved, haven't you?" Cael pressed.

She wanted to deny it, but the words wouldn't get past her lips. When she tried to shake her head, it also wouldn't obey her. The lie—because it *was* a lie—wouldn't manifest in any form.

"Go to him—or her. If they don't know how you feel, tell them," Cael urged.

Erith slowly turned to face him, his words slamming into her like a punch to the gut. Just as she thought, he was close. So very close.

She saw the white flecks in his silver eyes and the laugh lines around his mouth. Finally, she said, "I can't."

"They're gone, then? I'm sorry."

Her eyes pricked with tears. "No."

The word came out of nowhere, of its own volition. Erith was shocked by the sound and terrified that Cael would push to know more.

"No?" Cael asked, a brow arched. "They aren't gone?"

"No." That damn word again. Not only couldn't she control her emotions or say a little lie to save her heart, apparently, her mouth was also working on its own and giving away secrets.

A frown furrowed Cael's brow as his gaze searched her face. "Then why can't you tell them?"

She clenched her teeth together, refusing to give any sort of answer. She'd already said too much. Somehow, someway, Cael had no idea about the confession she'd made earlier when she said she couldn't lose him. And that's how she wanted to keep it.

Didn't she?

Or . . . maybe. . . .

No. Things had to stay as they were. It didn't matter that he claimed not to love Corla.

Aye, it most certainly does.

For fek's sake. It did. It really, really did. That was one of the reasons Erith had kept her distance from Cael, never letting him know of her feelings. One of a hundred different reasons.

Because she didn't want to be second best. She wanted a man who loved her—and only her—fiercely, ferociously, and without any barriers.

Because that's how Cael loved.

"Erith?"

Her name, spoken in that sensual voice that made her knees weak was all it took to break through the last of her willpower. She pressed back against the bookshelf in a last-ditch effort to keep her feelings hidden instead of leaning into Cael as she longed to do.

"I'm Death," she said in a hoarse whisper. "I can't have the one I want."

"If it were me, I'd take what I wanted. I'd move Heaven and Earth itself to get to her," he declared vehemently. "Nothing and no one would stop me."

She blinked back tears as her stomach fluttered at his words. If only he were saying those things about her. "Take it?"

"Aye," he murmured, leaning closer.

Her gaze carelessly dropped to his lips. Cael had the sexiest mouth she'd ever seen. Wide, full lips that should look out of place were the final, perfect piece to his gorgeous face.

For the first time in . . . eons . . . she forgot that she was Death. Forgot what she was supposed to do and what she shouldn't do. She allowed herself, for one instant, to just be a woman who craved the touch of the man she loved.

Erith rose up on her tiptoes and pressed her lips to Cael's. She held there for a heartbeat before moving away, but his arms snaked out and yanked her against him again.

She gasped at the feel of his warm body, but he swallowed the sound as his mouth returned to hers. But he did more than just touch his lips to hers. He nibbled and licked, each kiss growing longer and deeper until, with a contented sigh, she leaned her head to the side as his tongue swept into her mouth.

Chapter Thirteen

The taste of her was sublime.

Transcendent.

Better than anything Cael could've dreamed of. And he was going to take his fill of her. Nothing could make him stop now.

He groaned when her hands rested on his chest and seductively moved up and around his neck. Her fingers slid into his hair, her nails softly scraping his scalp. Desire had exploded the moment she put her lips on his.

Now, it pounded through him, turning his blood to fire.

He didn't want to overwhelm her, but his efforts to keep their kisses reserved were failing. Not that she seemed to notice.

Cael pressed her against the bookshelf, his hand against the back of her head to keep her from slamming it against anything. The way her tongue dueled with his made his knees weak.

But it was the feel of her breasts that had him achingly hard and yearning to thrust inside her, to claim her as his.

It was all he dreamed about each time he closed his eyes, all he wanted.

And, somehow, she was now in his arms.

The kiss deepened, her soft moan filling his ears. He'd never craved, never yearned for anyone as he did Erith. The moment he'd seen her so very long ago while he was in the middle of battle and she'd stood on the sidelines, she had stolen his heart.

It wasn't until she came for him as he lay dying that he recognized the feeling within him—love.

Her hand pushed against his shoulder as she tore her lips from his. With her head turned away and her breathing harsh and ragged, she whispered brokenly, "We can't."

"Says who?" he demanded.

His gaze was on her mouth, her lips wet and swollen from their kisses. Gradually, she looked at him, doubt filling her face. But it was the desire darkening her lavender eyes that he focused on.

"Tell me you don't want me," Cael demanded. "Tell me you're repulsed by my touch, and I'll leave."

She gave a small shake of her head. "I can't."

"Then kiss me again, Erith, or I might go up in flames right here, right now. I've wanted to do this for far too long. You've given me a taste. I need more."

She touched his lips with a shaky hand before meeting

his gaze again. "This is folly," she murmured huskily.

"Nothing that feels this good can be bad." He lowered his head, rubbing his cheek against hers. "Admit it. You want this. You *need* this."

He felt the brush of her lashes on his cheek as she closed her eyes. A warm rush of breath skimmed his ear when she sighed and sagged against him, her silent acquiescence that he was right.

"I do want this," she whispered.

Elation swept through him. Cael lifted her into his arms and strode to her bedroom before she could change her mind. He set her down and cupped her face to kiss her deeply, thoroughly. If this were a dream, he hoped he never woke. Because the woman who held his heart was finally in his arms.

He ended the kiss and took a step back. Then he gave her a nod. "Undress." She raised a brow, and before she could use magic, he held up a hand. "Yourself."

A slight smile curved her swollen lips. His cock jumped, impatient to be inside her, to feel the slick heat of her body surrounding him.

Erith pushed the long, leather coat off her shoulders before straightening her arms and letting it fall with a *whoosh* at her feet. Without taking her eyes off him, she bent forward and unfastened the boots, stepping out of first one, then the other.

He swallowed a moan. His gaze dropped to her cleavage, his mouth going dry as he imagined cupping the globes in his hands.

She reached behind her and, a second later, a soft zipping sound filled the air. Erith held the front of the corset with her other hand as it sagged open. She lifted her chin, her lavender eyes seductive.

Then she tossed the corset aside.

Cael's breath left him in a rush as his balls tightened. Stunning. Gorgeous. Striking. All words that described her, yet they lacked the depth to properly portray her exquisiteness.

He swallowed hard as he gazed longingly at her pink-tipped breasts. They would fill his palms perfectly. He fisted his hands, fighting not to reach for her.

Yet it was his turn to smile when her nipples hardened beneath his gaze. For several seconds, he watched the way her chest rose and fell rapidly, imagining all the ways he was going to tease, lick, and suckle at her amazing breasts.

Finally, he lifted his eyes to her face. Only then did she unbuckle the pants and peel them down her legs to remove them. Then she straightened and tossed back her hair.

The wildness he saw in her eyes made his blood rush in his ears. Before him stood a goddess, a warrior woman as violent and furious as a storm, and as tender and affectionate as a summer breeze.

Her gowns—and even her current outfit—had left little to the imagination. But seeing her now in all her glory left him speechless.

Her hourglass figure was stunning. His gaze traveled from her breasts to over the indent of her waist to the flare of her hips and then lower to the triangle of black curls nestled between her legs.

He wanted her. Now. Right that instant.

No foreplay, no touching. Just thrusting inside her so he could finally end the ache that had been burning in him since before he was a Reaper.

"Take my clothes off," he demanded.

Without any hesitation, she made her way to him and put her hands on his abdomen. Her touch made him sway toward her, but he held himself steady.

She gazed up at him with eyes shining with need. Erith unfastened one button at a time. Then she ran her hands up his chest, pushing the shirt over his shoulders. A shiver went through him at the feel of her hands on him. She leaned to the side, her breast brushing his arm as she tugged off one sleeve.

He had to close his eyes when she leaned the other way, and her nipple scraped against his flesh. He sucked in a breath at the temptation before him. He was so lost in his own desire that he didn't realize that his shirt was gone until she tugged at his leg.

Cael glanced down to see her kneeling before him. The sight of her on her knees, her wealth of black hair cascading around her made it difficult to breathe.

Shifting from one foot to the other, he watched her remove his boots. She lifted her face to him as she rose up on her knees. With her lips inches from his straining cock, she put her hands on the waist of his pants.

He swallowed the moan and the desire for her to put her hand on his arousal. Ever so slowly, she unbuckled his pants before sliding the zipper down. Her fingers hooked in the waistband of his jeans and tugged them down his hips. He couldn't look away as her eyes focused on him.

When his cock sprang free, she smiled, causing his rod to jump. Erith took her time removing his trousers, her gaze locked on his arousal.

Once freed, she raised her gaze to his face, waiting for him to tell her what to do. He'd always been the dominant lover in a relationship, and he hadn't once thought about how Erith might react to that.

"Touch me," he commanded.

The corners of her eyes crinkled briefly before she cupped his sac with one hand and wrapped the fingers of the other around his cock. His body jerked, the pleasure was so intense. Warmth spread through him with every soft stroke of her hand up and down his shaft.

~

Erith was utterly enthralled. She hadn't realized that she wanted or needed someone to take charge until Cael did it. The moment he demanded that she remove her clothes, she shook from the desire pooling within her.

As soon as he ordered her to take off his clothes, she hastily complied, eager to get a look at the body she knew was hidden beneath the garments.

Her mouth was devoid of moisture as she took in his sculpted chest and the washboard stomach. The sight of his muscular arms and legs left her panting.

When his cock sprang free of his pants, she forgot to breathe. She was far from a virgin, but the sight of him was spellbinding.

Though she shouldn't have been surprised. Cael was superb in every way. In any other life, he would've been a god. His confidence, quiet leadership, and cool head only added to his handsomeness, causing both men and women to lust after him.

Erith didn't want to know if she was simply fulfilling a need he had, or if he really wanted her. She wasn't sure she could handle the former, and if it was the latter, she didn't know what to say to that. It was better for them both if she didn't think about it.

Which was easy to do when he told her to touch him. She'd wanted to do nothing else since they began kissing. Now, she had her chance.

The feel of his hard length in her hand made her sex clench, hungry to feel him pushing inside her. She glanced up to find that his head had dropped back, and his hands were clenched at his sides.

How many times had she dreamed of bringing him pleasure? How many times had she wished she could have him in exactly this position, that same pleasure-filled expression on his face?

Erith worked her hand in a steady rhythm, slowly increasing her tempo. His hips were rocking in time with her movements, and each time she squeezed his sac, he moaned. The moment a bead of pre-cum appeared, she brought his arousal to her mouth and wrapped her lips around him.

"Erith," Cael ground out as his fingers tangled in her hair.

Her stomach quivered at the sound of her name spoken with such raw desire. She took him deep into her mouth, using both her lips and hand to work him into a frenzied state.

But if she thought she would get him to climax, she was sorely mistaken.

One moment, she was on her knees. The next, she was flat on her back on the bed with Cael leaning over her. His long, black hair fell to one side as he stared at her for a long minute, his breathing ragged.

He ducked his head to look down her body. She knew he could see her desire. His knees were between her legs, and she wanted him to take her, craved it.

She knew he wanted it, too. It was there in his eyes, the look that said he was nearly past the point of no return. The expression that said he wanted inside her right then.

Erith waited for him to make up his mind while her body throbbed for relief. She closed her eyes when he lowered his hips to hers and rocked against her. There was that one instant of friction, and then it was immediately taken away—replaced by his mouth.

There was no slow build, no tender caresses. His tongue found her clit and began teasing it ruthlessly. She arched her back, a moan falling from her lips as pleasure engulfed her.

Cael's hands held her firmly, preventing her hips from moving as he licked and laved until she was on the verge of orgasm. And as if he had some link to her body, letting him know how close she was, he pulled away.

Her eyes flew open, but before she could even form a thought, she issued a startled—and bliss-filled—cry when his lips wrapped around a nipple and began to suck while he rolled the other turgid peak between two fingers.

She tried, again and again, to rock her hips against him, but he had situated himself in such a way that she couldn't. Desire built inside her. She was ready to explode, and he kept pushing her higher, giving her more and more pleasure.

Erith was a shivering mess, need strumming through her, when she felt something at her sex. She stilled, waiting, hoping it was Cael.

Then her mind stopped working when he slowly pushed a finger inside her and began to move it back and forth.

Chapter Fourteen

This might be the only opportunity Cael had to make love to Erith, and he was going to take full advantage of the time he had.

Every second listening to her cries of pleasure, watching the seductive movements of her body, and feeling her desire only cemented his love.

Cael knew full well that there were better men than him for Erith, but he didn't care. She was the center of his world, of his universe, and, like a dying man, he was grasping at any chance he could to be with her.

To hold her.

To show her how much he loved her.

How much he couldn't live without her.

Cael watched ecstasy pass over Erith's beautiful face as he brought her to the brink with his fingers. Her body was exquisite and made to be loved. She was passionate, just as he'd always suspected. She kept that and so many other things tightly locked away.

He wanted to know that secret and all her others. If only they had the time for him to prove his worth to her.

If only he'd had the balls to tell her of his feelings before now.

If only. . . .

He closed his mind to those kinds of thoughts and returned his attention to her amazing body. Her legs were growing stiff, and her breathing ragged. She was close to orgasm once again.

"You were made for loving," he said as he pulled his hand from her.

Her fingers were tangled in the sheets. She rolled her head to the side and opened her eyes a crack to look at him.

Only then did he say, "By me."

"Yes," she whispered.

He crawled up her body, inwardly smiling when she reached for him. Cael kissed her then. It was a languid caress filled with dreams and hope.

And love.

Her palm tenderly slid along the side of his face. Whatever willpower he had shattered a thousand times over. In his arms was the woman he'd love for millennia, a being so powerful and lovely that he couldn't fathom what she saw in him.

He ended the kiss and lifted his face to look into her lavender depths. Her eyes were heavy-lidded, making his balls tighten in response.

Shifting slightly, he reached between them and guided his arousal to her entrance. Her lips parted as she sucked in a breath. He moved his hips forward, pushing a fraction into her tight sheath.

"I've craved this for so long," he said. All the centuries of keeping his feelings to himself were gone. She would know everything. "I've hungered for you in ways you can't even imagine."

A shudder went through her as she brought her knees up. Her arms wrapped around his middle, her chest rising and falling rapidly. "Don't," she whispered.

He pushed farther inside her, causing her eyes to roll back in her head. She tried to move her hips, but he held perfectly still.

"I'm tired of being silent," he said into her ear. "I need you to hear me."

Her voice was broken as she said, "I am."

"I need you to feel me." He slid another inch inside her. She was panting now. "I do."

Cael thought he could hold out, that he could rule her body, but he was wrong. So very wrong.

He was the one who had his fingers twisted in the sheets while doing everything he could not to simply thrust hard and bury himself deep into her wet heat.

It didn't help that her hands were moving over his back. But the final thread snapped when she locked her ankles behind him.

Cael clenched his teeth, and with a groan, drove himself in to the hilt. For a moment, he couldn't move. The feel of her was overwhelming, blinding.

"Please," she begged, her nails digging into his skin.

His need matched hers. There was no more holding back for him. Not now that he was inside her.

He began to move his hips in a slow rhythm, in and out of her, his thrusts sliding deep. He couldn't take his eyes from her face, watching as she gave herself fully to him, to the pleasure between them.

Cael moved a hand beneath her and shifted them so he was sitting. Her eyes opened, meeting his. He wrapped his arms around her, holding her tightly as their bodies began moving against each other once more.

Sweat soon glistened over their skin, their breaths mingling, their hearts beating in time with each other. He felt her body stiffening, a signal that she was close to peaking. And that made him smile.

~

Erith had expected Cael to pull back when she drew near to her orgasm. But, to her surprise, he didn't. She moved her hips faster, the friction of their bodies gliding along her clit, as well.

In the next breath, she went over the edge. The pleasure was so forceful that she forgot to breathe. While her body shuddered with her climax, Cael kept moving, flinging her higher.

Just as one orgasm ended, another was right on its heels. Erith cried out, blinded by the bliss that swallowed her, that pulled her down into an abyss of decadence she never wanted to leave.

Ripples of pleasure continued even as Cael pushed her onto her back. Her limbs were lethargic, her blood still pumping furiously in ear ears.

But she'd never felt so good before.

She looked up at Cael to see him leaning over her. He gave her a wicked grin that promised more. Her stomach quivered in anticipation of the carnal pleasures that awaited.

He began moving then, plunging in and out of her, hard and fast with short, quick thrusts that felt just as good as his long, slow glides.

Cael was relentless as he pounded her, hurtling her toward another climax that took her completely unawares. Erith forced open her eyes and looked at Cael to find him watching her with so much emotion blazing in his silver depths that it made her heart catch.

His feelings were there for her to see—and accept.

Cael gave a final thrust and buried himself deep. His

neck muscles corded when his orgasm took him, and his cry of pleasure made her sigh in contentment. She reached for him, pulling him down atop her. They held each other, limbs and hearts tangled together as each became lost in their thoughts.

Erith couldn't help but wonder why she hadn't given in years before and admitted that she wanted Cael. Oh, she knew why, but looking back, it seemed so . . . silly. Especially when there was a very real chance she could die.

She'd never thought about her death before. Sadly, she'd just expected to always live. But now, with Bran taking her essence, she looked at life with new eyes. She saw all her regrets in blazing Technicolor.

"I can feel your brain," Cael said, a smile in his voice.

Erith couldn't help but grin. "Is that so?"

"Do you ever stop thinking?" he asked as he rose up on his forearm to look at her.

She moved a lock of black hair out of his face. "Probably no more than you do."

"Point taken." He ran his thumb over her bottom lip. "Tell me you don't regret this."

"Nay," she replied immediately. "I don't."

"Good. Because if you said you did, then I was going to have to show you why you shouldn't."

She laughed at his certainty. "You don't lack for self-confidence, that's for sure."

"That's a good thing."

"I think it might be."

This—whatever *this* was—was amazing. It felt normal and perfect, a setting she had only had in her dreams. Something she never believed could be hers. Could it be now? Did she dare try to hold onto it?

"Why the frown?" Cael asked.

She didn't want to talk about what she was feeling. Instead, she put the conversation on what was to come. "We can't stay like this."

Cael fell onto his back and sighed. "I know. But we also don't have to leave for some time yet."

She turned her head to look at him and found him staring at her. He was asking her—with a silent plea in his eyes—to let them continue as they were for a little longer. How could she refuse when it was what she longed for herself?

Erith rolled toward him, resting her head on his chest as his arm came around her. She couldn't believe that she had actually worried about taking up the sword again. After this brief respite with Cael, she knew she'd fight however she needed to.

Because she wouldn't lose him or any of the other Reapers. And for them to survive, she had to, as well.

Whatever might come of taking up her sword again, she was prepared for it. She'd worked too hard to get to where she was, and Bran wasn't going to take it from her.

Cael kissed her forehead and rested his cheek against her head. Her gaze was locked on the window and the white puffy clouds that drifted lazily by.

This was her private realm, a place she came to in order to be alone and get away from everyone and everything. A place where she often wallowed in her solitude and cried tears of loneliness.

But it was also a place where the Reapers' women would be safe. She couldn't believe she hadn't thought of it sooner. It should've been the first thing she offered.

Just as she couldn't lose Cael, her Reapers couldn't have the ones they loved taken away. She realized that she had come full circle from when she first put the Reapers together and made her rules. She was all too aware of how the Reapers' love of their women divided their loyalties.

Because they would help their women before they did their duties. Erith knew this because she would do the same for Cael in a heartbeat.

If she survived this war with Bran and managed to keep from turning into the Mistress of War again, she would have to reconsider the Reapers. She should free them and allow them to live the lives they had been denied.

She closed her eyes as she thought of Cael. There was a

good chance that she wouldn't be able to let him go, that she would hold onto him with everything she had.

But was that wise?

She refused to even go down that road right now. Her body was satiated from their lovemaking. Somehow, that had cleared her mind of all the static that had been there since she'd discovered that Bran had broken free of the Netherworld.

Now, she could think straight again, and she knew that she and Cael both needed to be focused on the battle. They couldn't talk about their feelings or what their lovemaking might mean.

It went against everything she wanted to do while lying in his arms. But she had to think of the future—Cael's future.

She listened to his even breathing and realized that he'd fallen asleep. In all her eons of life, she'd never slept in another's arms. The fact that her first time was with Cael made the moment all the sweeter.

Suddenly, she was rolled onto her back, Cael's silver eyes locked on her. "No more thoughts," he ordered.

"But—" she began.

His eyes narrowed. "No."

A little thrill went through her once more. For a being who had always been in charge and in control, she'd longed to find a man who didn't let who she was intimidate him in any way.

And Cael gave her exactly what she needed without her even having to tell him.

Their lips met in a frenzied kiss as desire exploded again.

Chapter Fifteen

Not even in the comfort of Erith's arms could Cael shut off his mind. He'd joked with her about her thoughts, but only because he hadn't been able to stop his own.

He'd lost count of the many times they had made love. Sometimes, it was slow. Sometimes, fast and hurried as if they knew they were running out of time.

The sun had set long ago. Through the open window, he heard an owl in the distance. He should be relishing every second with Erith, but his mind was locked on one thing—Bran.

Cael cursed the very thought of the bastard, but he had to grudgingly admit that if Bran hadn't come back into their lives, Cael would never be in Erith's bed. He knew that as surely as he knew that his love for her would never end.

He lay curled around her, his front to her back. One of his hands was entwined with hers. For such a small woman, she tended to take up more than her share of the covers, but it didn't irritate, it only endeared her to him. He never used the blankets anyway.

"I can hear your thoughts."

The way she threw his words back at him made him grin. She tucked her head in such a way that half her face was in the sheets at all times. He discovered that there wasn't anything about Death that wasn't fascinating, if a little peculiar.

He kissed her bare shoulder. "Did I wake you?"

She shifted the covers and drew in a deep breath as she turned her head toward him. "I go to sleep, then I feel so guilty about having this time that I wake up."

"Guilty?" That's not how he wanted her to think of their time together.

Erith turned in his arms. They lay facing each other, her usually perfectly coifed hair in complete disarray. With her mussed hair, sleepy eyes, and soft smile, she was stunning. Disarmingly so.

"Here we are, having quite a lot of enjoyable sex, while the others are preparing for Bran."

Cael smoothed back a lock of her hair, tucking it behind her ear. "Trust me, every single one of them is going to have sex as soon as they can."

She smiled, but it was fleeting. "You know what I mean."

"I do. I told my men to find places to hide their women, just as we spoke about."

"That's just it." Erith licked her lips. "It never dawned

on me that I know the perfect place for them."

Cael frowned, wondering where that could be. "Where?"

"Here."

He studied her closely. The one thing Erith didn't do was make an offer without thinking it through, yet he had to play Devil's advocate. "This is your sanctuary."

"A place where Bran can't come. A place only you, me, and Eoghan know about."

"If you bring the others here, they'll know, as well."

She grinned, the smile so bright that it blinded him. "We bring them here as they sleep. The women will never know. I can still have my sanctuary, the females will be safe from Bran, and the Reapers can fight without worrying about those they love."

No matter how Cael looked at it, it was a solid plan. "Are you sure?"

"I want to do this."

"Then I suppose we should do it now." The sooner the women were safe, the better, but Cael was irrationally angry that his time with Erith was coming to an end.

She put her hand on his jaw and gently rubbed her thumb across his cheek. He thought she might remind him that what happened between them needed to stay private. As if he needed to be told that. He had no intention of letting anyone know what had transpired.

Instead, Erith leaned forward and briefly placed her lips against his. "I don't want this amazing time we've had to end, but I'm needed."

Gone was the pliant, passionate woman who had waited for his command. Death had returned, and that meant Cael was back in his role as leader. He would always stand beside her, ready to do as she ordered.

But he would get her in his bed again. Because he wouldn't be able to survive without her. That much he knew.

He stopped her before she rolled away and dragged her against him for a long, blazing kiss that had them both breathing hard.

It took everything he had to end it and pull away. Cael rolled over and stood before he forgot about Bran, the Reapers, or the war and made love to her again.

With just a thought, his clothes were back in place. By the time he turned, Erith was also dressed, every one of her impossibly long strands of hair in place as if they hadn't spent hours rolling around on the bed, his fists clenching her hair, or her head thrashing from side to side.

"You do know that Neve won't remain with the women," he said, needing something to think about other than how his body still yearned for Erith.

She gave a nod. "Neve is a full-fledged Reaper, just as

Aisling is. She'll remain with the others."

"Is that wise? Bran will go straight for her, if for no other reason than to get at Talin."

"Then you need to talk with Talin. You and Eoghan both know how Bran fights. You stood alongside him for many centuries. You know how he thinks, how he acts. We need to use that against him."

Cael grew hard just listening to her. He'd loved seeing her at his mercy while they made love, but there was something about her authoritative, imposing attitude that always turned him on.

Erith glanced down. As soon as she saw his erection tenting his pants, she raised a brow and slid her gaze back to his face. She smiled, her lavender eyes full of desire and a primal hunger that made him groan with need.

"We're not done here," he told her.

She shook her head. "No, we certainly aren't."

With that settled, they walked from the bedroom, down the stairs, and out of the tower. Neither said anything while making their way through the flowers to the realm's doorway. It wasn't until they reached it that Erith stopped and faced him.

"I'm going to Eoghan and Thea," she told him. "I want you to get River here first."

"Good idea."

Erith hesitated. "As far as I know, no human has gone

through a Fae doorway while pregnant."

"You're worried something might happen to the baby?"

She shrugged. "It's magic. Not only that, but River will be traveling through realms."

"I'll talk to Kyran. And the rest?" he asked.

"We each take one until they're all here."

"Be careful," Cael told her, hating that he wouldn't be with her. Not because she couldn't handle herself, but because he didn't like being apart from her.

Erith held out her hand, and the black sword appeared. She slid it into the scabbard at her waist. "I won't be without this again. It may not always show, but it'll be with me. I know what I have to do."

Already, he could see the Death he knew transforming into someone even stronger and more extraordinary. "Then I'll meet you back here."

With a smile, she stepped through the doorway. Cael paused. He looked over his shoulder at the tower shining a pale blue in the moonlight. Then he squared his shoulders and walked through the portal.

As soon as he was on the other side, he teleported to Inchmickery. He appeared in the concrete compound and hurried to the room Kyran shared with River.

"Cael?"

He halted and turned around at the sound of Kyran's

voice. Cael frowned and walked to his friend. The Fae had lines of strain on his face, and his hair was sticking out in every direction as if he'd run his hands through it multiple times. "What is it?"

"I don't know where to take River," Kyran said helplessly. "And she doesn't want to go. Honestly, I don't want to leave her, but I know I have a duty to the Reapers."

Cael put a hand on his friend's arm. "I know exactly where to bring her."

"I didn't think we were supposed to tell each other."

"Different plan. Where is River?"

Kyran ran a hand through his shoulder-length black and silver hair. "Asleep, finally. I used a spell to get her to rest."

"I need her to stay asleep."

Kyran stepped in front of Cael when he made to move. "You're my leader, and I will follow you anywhere, but you're not touching my woman until you tell me what the bloody hell is going on."

Cael wasn't offended by the statement. He knew exactly how Kyran felt because he'd dealt with something similar every day he'd been a Reaper. "Death has offered River and the others protection on her realm."

The obvious relief that swept through Kyran had the Reaper physically doubled over, his hands on his knees as he tucked his chin to his chest. After a few moments, he straightened. "I didn't expect this."

"Neither did I. But," he said, "this isn't without risks. Death isn't sure what could happen to the babe going through the doorway."

Kyran glanced at the closed door to his room. "If River remains here, she's certain to die, along with our baby. If she goes to Death's realm, then she and the child have a fighting chance."

"That's true. Do you want to talk it over with her? She should get a say."

"I should, but I've got this nagging feeling there isn't time. My goal is to get my wife and child as far away from danger as I can. Whatever happens, I'll take responsibility for it," Kyran said.

"You'll feel differently if River loses the baby."

Kyran licked his lips and shrugged. "If I don't let you take them, then I lose them both. She's going."

"Let's get River moved then so I can get the others."

Kyran ran down the corridor to his room. He opened the door and rushed to the bed where he gathered his wife in his arms. He kissed her forehead before handing her to Cael.

"Take her," Kyran said. "I'll tell Baylon, Fintan, and Daire."

Cael gave a nod and teleported to the isle. He paused before the doorway, Erith's words coming back to him.

He glanced down at River and set his jaw before making his way through the portal. Thea was waiting for him on the other side. The fact that River remained asleep was good.

"Death already told me her concerns about River," Thea said to Cael. "I'll keep an eye on her."

Cael smiled at her. "Thanks."

They quickly got River settled in the tower, and then Cael returned to his Reapers. Death had already been there and had taken Ettie, while Eoghan grabbed Jordyn. Cael saw the happy looks on his Reapers' faces—everyone but Fintan.

Now Cael knew why Erith and Eoghan hadn't taken Catriona. She was awake and standing with her arms crossed in her and Fintan's bedroom, glaring daggers at her man.

"Sweetheart, please," Fintan pleaded.

Cael stared at the infamous Dark assassin who was still feared by every Fae. Who would have thought Fintan, who'd once buried his emotions so deep that Cael didn't think he'd ever feel again, would fall so hard for Cat?

"Not happening," Cat stated with an angry shake of her red head, her Irish brogue deepening with her fury. "I'm going to fight with you. That's what we agreed. Remember?"

Fintan squeezed the bridge of his nose with his thumb

and forefinger. With a loud sigh, he dropped his arm to his side. "We don't have time for this. I can't fight if I'm worried about you, and it's time we dealt with Bran once and for all."

"That's right," Cat said. She took a step toward Fintan, her arms dropping. "I've already fought him. I know what to do."

"He'll come at you differently," Cael said. He glanced at Fintan, waiting for his friend to give him the nod to proceed. When he did, Cael focused on Cat. "Bran is crafty, and as much as I hate to admit it, it's his sneaky attitude that lets him win more times than not."

Cat's green eyes filled with worry. "I'm the strongest Halfling there is. Let me help."

"He'll go straight for you. It's what I'd do. It's what I know Bran is going to do," Cael told her. "That's why we're getting all of you to safety. We need to go. Now."

No sooner had the words left his mouth, than there was an explosion behind him. The force sent Cael flying forward—straight into a concrete wall. His ears rang, and debris and dust swirled in the air as he caught sight of a wave of Dark Fae coming for them.

Neve and Talin stepped out, throwing magic. Baylon and Daire joined in while Kyran snuck around the back of the Dark.

Cael's head jerked to where he'd last seen Cat. He

found her lying on the floor with Fintan covering her with his body, shielding her from any further damage. Fintan then helped her to her feet, gave her a quick, hard kiss, whispered something, and shoved her at Cael.

Cael wanted to join his Reapers, but he had to get Cat to safety first. The Dark had spotted her and were coming straight for her.

As calmly as he could, Cael turned toward Cat and held out his hand. Once she took it, he teleported them to Death's realm and into the arms of the other women. He didn't look for Erith or Eoghan as he returned to his Reapers, he just jumped into battle with a bellow and a swing of his sword.

"In the midst of chaos there is opportunity."

-**Sun Tzu,** *The Art of War*

Chapter Sixteen

Something was wrong. Erith knew it without having to be told. She rushed from the tower, running toward the doorway where she found Cat staring wide-eyed at the portal.

Erith exchanged a look with Eoghan as he walked up. "What happened?" she demanded.

Cat swung her green eyes to Erith. "Bran attacked the base."

Without so much as a word to anyone, Erith stepped through the doorway. Before she could teleport, Eoghan grabbed her arm. She whipped her head around to look at him. "Let go."

"You can't fight him."

She raised a brow at her commander. "Excuse me?"

Releasing her arm, he flattened his lips for a second. "If you go into that battle now, you've lost the element of surprise with Bran. He thinks you're weakening. To show up and begin ripping through his men . . . one of them will go back to him and tell him all of it."

Erith looked away, hating that Eoghan was right, but

she wanted to be by Cael's side, to fight with him against their enemies. He shouldn't have to stand alone.

"It's just as difficult for me," Eoghan added, his jaw tight from his frustration. "I want nothing more than to call my Reapers and join the others."

"But we can't," Erith said with a nod.

Eoghan looked out over the calm water surrounding the isle. "Bran was after the women. They can't hurt Cael and the others. Not even Neve."

"Neither can the Reapers hurt Bran's men." And that's what angered her most of all. It was needless fighting. The only good thing was that she didn't have to worry about Cael being killed.

She faced Eoghan. "I won't fight or even show Bran's army that I'm there, but I'm going to be with my Reapers."

"How do you know his army can't see you? He shares his power with them like you do with us."

"Because I tested it," she told Eoghan before teleporting away.

Erith veiled herself the moment she arrived on Inchmickery. She gasped at the never-ending number of Dark that flooded the fort. Cael and his Reapers were spread out, each battling dozens of Fae.

She searched for all seven of the Reapers. Talin and Kyran stood near Neve, making sure none of the Dark got close to her. They couldn't kill her, but they could take her.

Erith's gaze returned to Cael. Every time she saw him in battle, he took her breath away. Every movement was fluid and timed perfectly. His transitions were sinuous, effortless. Natural.

Turning, Cael sliced his sword through two Dark before blocking a bubble of magic. In the next instant, he used not just his weapon but also magic to pummel the Dark around him with merciless abandon.

Every kill made Death ecstatic, but that didn't last long as the Dark rose and returned to fighting. She still wasn't sure why the Reapers couldn't kill Bran's army or vice versa, but it did allow the Reapers to blow off some steam.

One by one, the Dark realized that the women weren't there and that they couldn't get close to Neve. It wasn't long before the Fae retreated. The sounds of battle diminished until the only noise was the Reapers' harsh breathing.

Erith's gaze was riveted on Cael, who was soaked in sweat and blood, violence in his silver eyes. Suddenly, he turned, his gaze locking with hers. Shocked, she dropped her veil. No one should be able to see her, not even Cael. But, somehow, he had.

His torn shirt strained over his wide chest. All Erith

wanted to do was rip his clothes off and have him inside her. She saw the raw hunger, the visceral need that had both of them in its grip flash in his eyes.

Cael took a step toward her, then stopped as if remembering that they weren't alone. She hated that she was both relieved that he hadn't come to her and so disappointed that she wanted to cry out.

"Is she safe?" Fintan demanded.

Cael dragged in a breath and turned his head to Fintan. "Aye. Cat is with the others."

Fintan closed his eyes as his head dropped back, relief filling his face. Erith looked at the Reapers, each comforted that their woman was far away from harm.

Talin and Neve embraced, talking low, their words private. Erith looked away, her gut twisting with jealousy that she didn't have such a relationship.

You could.

No, she really couldn't. How could Cael command the Reapers if he was with her? And how could she continue on as Death if she were constantly making love to Cael? It just couldn't work.

"Thank you," Kyran said as he approached her. "Thank you for giving River and the others shelter."

She looked into his red eyes and inclined her head. "I should've done it earlier."

"How is she?" Kyran asked. "Is everything... all

right?"

Erith glanced at Cael. "As far as I know. I'm just glad that we got everyone out in time."

"It was close," Baylon said.

"Too damn close," Cael added.

Despite trying to keep from looking at him, Erith's eyes slid back to Cael of their own volition. Their gazes met, and she saw anger and irritation in his gaze. She understood it because she felt it, as well.

There was a war inside her, with one part wanting to go to Cael, letting everyone know that they were together. But the other part, the one that had spent countless millennia masking her feelings, went through all the things that could go wrong if the others discovered the truth.

So she stayed where she was, wishing she was touching Cael.

"They got through our spells easily," Daire said. "I don't like that."

Talin gave a shake of his head. "None of us do."

"When are we going after Bran?" Fintan demanded to know.

It was Cael who said, "I want Bran more than any of you, and while I wish nothing more than to descend upon him and his army, patience is what will win us the day."

"Death does look better. Did you stop Bran from taking your power?" Daire asked her.

Erith shook her head. She'd known this was coming, but she hadn't thought about what she'd say. She took a deep breath and slowly released it. Then she let her sheathed sword appear at her side. Everyone's gaze immediately went to it. The sword was the source of everything. She'd known it the moment she crafted it.

For so long, she'd tried to forget her years as Mistress of War, but that was no longer possible. The Reapers had given her their loyalty all these centuries. It was time that she did the same. They'd each earned it a hundred times over.

Slowly, she withdrew the weapon for everyone to see.

Their gazes locked on her blade before returning to her, waiting for her to speak.

She sheathed the weapon and lifted her chin. "I should've told you about the sword when you asked, Daire. I thought I could leave that part of my past behind, but Bran has made sure I can't.

"The blade is mine. I forged it long ago in the Fires of Erwar, and I used it to wage war on . . . everyone. Some knew me as the Mistress of War, but everyone feared me. I was Death even then, but I took innocent souls simply because I wanted to."

Fintan asked, "What changed?"

Erith glanced at the white-haired Fae and saw Cael watching her out of the corner of her eye. "One day, I just didn't want to do it anymore. I thought it was the sword that ruled me, so I took it someplace that I didn't believe anyone would ever find it."

"Earth," Kyran said.

She nodded. "I buried it so deep in the realm's core that no one could ever reach it. It is part of me, so it would only answer my call."

"Then why was Ettie able to use it?" Daire asked.

"I wanted some good to come out of the weapon. When I knew that Bran was after Ettie and her family, I bade the sword go to the sister strong enough to fight Bran."

Daire smiled and bowed his head in thanks.

Erith swallowed, wishing she were finished with the story. "When I set aside my sword, I told myself that I would no longer take life. That's when I decided to create the Reapers."

"With Theo," Baylon replied.

"Theo was the first, yes." Her gaze went to Cael. "But he wasn't the one who gave me the idea. That was another." She quickly jerked her gaze away from Cael. "I put the burden of taking souls I judged on each of you, but I realized two things. One, I'm still taking life, just not with my own hands. And, two, I can't do that anymore."

Talin frowned. "Why the hell not? We're doing a bang-up job."

"Damn right, we are," Kyran stated.

Erith found herself grinning. "What I meant to say, is that I'm not going to stand on the sidelines anymore. I'm Death. I've hesitated in taking up my sword again because I didn't want to become Mistress of War, but if I don't do something, Bran will kill me. And then he'll come for each of you."

"I'm guessing this new thinking goes with the new look?" Neve asked, jerking her chin toward Death's outfit.

Erith looked at Cael. Damn, but she couldn't stop it. "I was told that I needed to be Death *and* the Mistress of War."

She forgot everyone as she stared into Cael's silver eyes, remembering what it felt like to be in his arms, to have him kiss her senseless. To be *loved*. She would do anything to return to the tower with him and spend days making love to him.

His slight grin that told her he knew exactly what she was thinking was the thing that reminded her they weren't alone. But when she looked at the others, none of them gave the impression that she and Cael had let anything slip.

"Every kill my blade has taken is stored in the metal. It has returned enough power to restore me so that I can fight," Erith told them.

"But Bran can still take her life force from her," Cael added. "He did yesterday after she let go of the weapon."

Erith frowned at the reminder. The thought of becoming so weak again, where she couldn't even lift her arm, terrified her. She'd never felt so . . . helpless. And she hated it.

"Unfortunately, Bran is going to keep taking my essence until I stop him."

"How do we help with that?" Baylon asked.

"I know where he is. His men can't see me when I'm veiled, but he has a barrier around the mansion, preventing me from getting close."

Kyran crossed his arms over his chest. "The fekker is scared of you."

"Damn right he is," Talin added.

Cael used his magic to hide his sword before he said, "We suspect that whatever Bran is using to take Death's power is with him."

"So we call him out," Daire suggested.

Fintan shook his head. "He'll suspect something. We'll never get close enough."

"That's right," Cael agreed. "It's why I'm hoping to find the Dark I saw in my meditation vision. Perhaps he can destroy whatever it is Bran has."

"That could take weeks. Months," Neve stated in out-

Donna Grant

rage. "We don't have that long."

No, they didn't, but Erith kept that bit to herself. She didn't want to worry any of them more than they already were. Besides, it was her damn fault for taking so long to make the decision to fight.

She was disgusted with herself for even considering not taking a stand. No one knew better than she that warfare was her expertise.

All those wasted months that she could've been preparing for battle, implementing a plan to infiltrate Bran's army, and any number of other scenarios.

But she wasn't going to think about that now. She'd made a decision, and had a path before her. It was time she focused solely on that instead of the past.

"What other plan do we have?" Baylon asked.

Erith looked at each of them, ending with Cael. "You attack him in retaliation."

"Not that I don't enjoy fighting his army," Kyran said, "but why? We can't kill them."

Cael was smiling as he realized her plan. "Because we're going to keep Bran busy while Death finds whatever it is Bran is using to drain her."

"Tell me we're going now," Neve said with a smile.

Fintan cracked his knuckles. "I'm in."

"As if you need to ask," Kyran replied.

Talin gave a bow of his head.

"Hell, yes," Daire said with a smile.

Baylon nodded, grinning widely. "Oh, yeah."

Erith smiled at each of them. Then she found herself looking at Cael again. He held her gaze for a long time in silence. He closed the distance between them, making her lean her head back to peer up at him.

He had that same commanding look in his gaze, the one he'd had when they made love. Her blood heated at the sight of it. He was close enough to touch, but somehow, she managed to keep her hands to herself, though it was likely the hardest thing she'd ever done.

"Do you really need to ask?" Cael questioned. "I gave you my vow to follow you anywhere. That still holds. It always will. You point the way. We'll be beside you."

She shifted, her fingers brushing his and sending a shock rushing through her. That brief touch was better than nothing, but she would've preferred to grab his face and pull it down so she could show him with a kiss just how much his words meant to her.

"I need as long as you can give me," she told them. "Be prepared for anything."

Chapter Seventeen

A calmness swept over Cael as he stared at the mansion where Bran had taken up residence. Cael didn't even want to think about what had happened to the humans who owned it. No doubt they were dead.

Cael and his Reapers were veiled and hidden behind some trees, staying just out of sight of the veiled Dark patrolling the perimeter of the home. Any human driving up would have no clue that anything was amiss until it was too late.

After following Death to the location, Cael kept his group at a distance until they could scope out the property. He sent Fintan and Daire to one side, and Talin and Kyran on the other.

While Cael waited for them to report back, he found his gaze locked on Erith, who stood near the mansion, looking into a window on the left side. There wasn't an ounce of fear in her. She could face anything and come out the victor.

Just as she would with Bran. Cael was sure of it.

He didn't know how he could see her and the others

couldn't. He didn't question it, but he was immensely grateful that he could. At least now, he would know where she was at all times.

Cael knew the window she was at must be where Erith had last seen Bran. It killed Cael not to be with her, to watch her back. None of them should be going into the residence alone. If Cael were Bran, he would've set traps for just such a scenario.

But Erith was smart. She would be prepared for such things. Still. He should be with her. He *wanted* to be with her.

Fingers snapped in front of his face. Cael jerked his head to the side and shot Baylon a scowl. "What?" he barked.

"I was about to ask you the same question."

Cael bit back a terse reply. Everyone was on edge, and it wouldn't do him any good to snap at Baylon.

With a sigh, Baylon said, "I know you have good reason to hate Bran, but so do the rest of us."

"I realize that. I also know each of you wants a piece of him for what he's done to you and the women you love."

Neve came up on Cael's other side. "What Baylon is trying to say is that you, Eoghan, and Death, don't have to take Bran on by yourself. We're here. We would like a piece of him. But," she said, her gaze darting to Baylon when he tried to interrupt her, "he betrayed your group first. He killed your friends and divided the Reapers. We'll wait for our slice of him once you're all finished."

Cael held Neve's silver eyes for a moment before he swiveled his head to Baylon, who grudgingly nodded.

"Right," Baylon said tightly.

Cael nodded to both of them. "I doubt there will be anything left of Bran for me or Eoghan by the time Erith is done with him."

Neve smiled widely. "As long as I get to see him being crushed beneath her gorgeous boots, I'll be fine."

The talk ceased as Talin, Kyran, Fintan, and Daire made their way back to him. With a last lingering glance at Death, Cael listened to their report.

"We should do a coordinated attack surrounding the mansion," Talin suggested.

Daire shook his head. "We should focus on one section. The weakest point is a side door into the kitchen."

Cael wasn't listening as the others voiced their opinions. In his head, he looked down on the area as if from above, mentally placing the Reapers and then letting his mind sort through how the attack might happen, including where and when Bran would appear.

All of it was to see how Erith would get into the house and if she would have enough time to find what she sought. When that scenario didn't work, Cael tried another, and another. And another.

Finally, he blinked and realized that it was quiet. He looked around to find the others staring, waiting for him to speak. It had been a long time since Cael had been in this sort of situation.

The skirmishes he and the other Reapers had been involved in with Bran in the past hadn't involved such huge numbers—or weighed as heavily as this one did. Everything had to be perfect. There could be no mistakes. And since Cael was in charge, planning that fell on him.

"We've each faced Bran one way or another these past months," he said. "Some have confronted him alone, while we've all been together in other situations. We're not here to kill him. We're here as support for Death."

Kyran gave a nod, his brow furrowed. "We'll be taking our anger out on the Dark. You don't need to worry about us forgetting our mission."

"I'm telling myself this, as well." Cael drew in a deep breath. "I've looked at this from all the angles. We're going to surround the mansion."

Talin grinned. "Like I said."

Cael cut him a glance to silence him. "Neve, Bran is going to come straight for you as soon as he learns you're here."

"Let him," the newest Reaper stated.

A muscle ticked in Talin's jaw. "Yes. Please let him."

"Bran thinks he's smarter than we are, and we're going

to let him believe that," Cael announced.

Fintan's brow furrowed deeply, a sound rumbling in his throat to let Cael know he didn't like the idea.

"Shite. This is going to be harder than I thought," Kyran mumbled.

Cael gave a nod. "For me, as well. Talin, I want you to stay close to Neve, and then let yourself be separated from her. We want Bran to think that he's isolated Neve and that none of us can get to her."

"So his attention will be on me," Neve said with a grin. "I like it."

Talin's lips compressed tightly. "I don't."

"Your woman is a Reaper. She can handle it," Baylon said to Talin.

Neve gave him a nod. "Damn right, I can."

"She won't be alone," Cael said. "We're setting this in motion. We're going to make sure that we can get to her in time."

"He can't kill me," she said.

Cael caught her gaze. "We're not going to test that theory. Look what he did to Eoghan. He came for the females, but they got away. You're the only one he can get to in order to hurt us."

Neve swallowed and glanced away before taking Talin's hand in her own. "You're right."

"You want all of us to come running to Neve's side

when Bran attacks?" Daire asked.

Cael smiled as he shook his head. "Talin and I will do that. Two of you will go for the kitchen door to get in."

"Daire and I'll do that," Baylon said.

Fintan grinned. "That leaves more Dark for me and Kyran to go through."

The two bumped fists as Kyran said, "Hell yeah, it does."

"We fight the Dark. Taunt Bran all you want, but stay out of his reach," Cael cautioned them. "Once Death gets what she needs, we leave."

Fintan cracked his knuckles. "They came for our women. Bran intended to kill them. I'm prepared to slice my way through as many Dark as needed."

"We all are," Daire agreed.

Cael turned his head to look at Erith. She hadn't moved from her spot at the window. And just as he suspected, it was where Bran was. Cael caught a glimpse of his nemesis and felt a wave of rage rise up within him.

"Erith," he whispered.

It felt like the softest caress when her lavender eyes landed on him. She shot him a smile and nodded.

He watched her for another heartbeat and then returned his attention to the Reapers. "I don't need to tell you to keep your anger in check. Bran will say and do anything to get us riled. We know the others are safe.

No matter what, he can't use them. But he'll find another way."

"Like my brother," Neve said softly.

Cael nodded. "We each have a reason to hate, but we cannot let that emotion rule us."

"We won't," Baylon promised.

Fintan rubbed his hands together. "Can we fight now?"

Cael told each of them what positions to take around the mansion. They stood in silence for a moment. Fintan was the first to teleport away, with Neve and Talin quickly following. One by one, each of them appeared around the residence. Cael was the last to get into position.

Seconds later, the alarm was raised, and the guards dropped their veils to attack the Reapers. It was only a moment later that Dark Fae flooded the area.

Cael wanted to be where he could see Erith, but he knew that would be a mistake. He put himself on the other side so he'd remain focused on his warriors and not the woman he loved.

Just as he'd known, the Dark quickly focused on Neve. Cael lost sight of her for a second as he widened the tightening circle of Dark fighting him.

He ignored the pain of their magic that repeatedly landed on him as he turned, swinging and slicing his sword. He didn't go after specific Dark. Instead, he kept the area around him as clear as possible so he could keep an eye on Neve and the others.

During one of his spins, he caught sight of Bran standing in a doorway of the house, his gaze locked on Neve, who appeared—even to Cael—to be in distress and overwhelmed by Dark.

It wasn't until Bran was making his way to her that Cael saw her take down four Dark with one swing. Talin let out a shout as he plowed through the throng of Fae to get to his woman.

Cael grunted as a Dark jumped on his back. He flipped his sword and swung it back, sliding it between the Fae's ribs. He threw the Dark off and blasted those nearest him with magic, knocking them down.

He took two steps and stepped on the back of a Fae trying to get to his feet. Cael then tucked himself into a ball and flipped over several Dark to land near Neve, right as Bran reached them.

"Show-off," Talin said to Cael with a grin.

Cael glanced at Talin and Neve as the fighting halted in their circle with Bran's arrival. He and Cael faced each other, their hatred there for all the world to see.

"I knew you'd do something stupid," Bran said with a laugh. "This little retaliation of yours will get you nowhere. And not only that, you're going to lose at least one Reaper." Bran's gaze shifted over Cael's shoulder as he pointed. "Her."

Cael smiled but didn't bother to reply. The things he wanted to say to Bran could wait until later when they were fighting each other. Bran had no intention of battling, but Cael would make sure he had no choice.

"Nothing to say?" Bran asked with a sneer. "Have you taken Eoghan's vow of silence? How . . . pathetic. You're all that's left of our merry little gang of Reapers, but that's going to end soon."

"You were part of that group, as well," Cael pointed out. "You plan on committing suicide?"

Bran's nostrils flared, his silver eyes narrowed. "I hated you from the moment you joined our ranks. What was it about you that Death liked so much? Hell, everyone liked you."

"Probably because I wasn't a wanker." Cael couldn't help the jab.

Bran snorted, a forced smile on his lips. "Death told me she regretted making me a Reaper. Right before she threw me into the Netherworld, she said I was her first mistake. Well, look at me now."

"Her real mistake was not letting me and Eoghan kill you." Cael took a step closer to him. "We had you. That's what really galls you, doesn't it? We had you beat, but Death stepped in and put you in that prison she designed just for you."

Bran eyed him with so much hatred that Cael thought he might get the fight he wanted right then. Out of the corner of his eye, he spotted Neve and Talin behind and on either side of him. Cael had no idea if Death was inside the house or not. By the sounds of battle, Daire and Baylon were trying to get through the kitchen door.

"You've failed here," Bran stated. "No matter how many Dark you kill, they rise again. What was your point in coming? What did you hope to gain?"

"Did you think you could come after the women and that we wouldn't do anything?" Cael asked in disbelief.

Bran gave a little shrug as his lips twisted. "I'll give you that one. You got them out in time. Barely. But I'll find them. There's nowhere you can hide them that I can't reach. And when I do, every one of your Reapers will know the crushing helplessness of losing someone they love."

"You're assuming a lot."

"Shall I show you the power I have? How about a little taste? To think, that bitch had this kind of power and didn't use it. It astounds me." Bran held out a hand, holding it palm up as a bubble of magic appeared.

It shifted from an iridescent color to a dark purple. Right before Bran threw it, Cael saw Xaneth in the crowd of Dark behind Bran.

"Move swift as the Wind and closely-formed as the Wood. Attack like Fire and be still as the Mountain."

   -**Sun Tzu,** *The Art of War.*

Chapter Eighteen

The moment Erith saw Xaneth, it was like a punch in the gut. She knew there was a good chance the Fae would go to Bran's side. But it hurt nonetheless.

She'd given Xaneth a chance, had allowed him to live. And this was how he repaid her.

A part of her—the Mistress of War side—wanted immediate retaliation. But she knew where to find him when this was over. Reprisal would come to the royal Fae who had chosen the wrong side. For now, she was there on another matter.

Erith paused and looked through the window of the mansion to the chaos of battle outside. Her gaze scanned the bodies until she found Cael. Her hand fisted, eager to feel her sword so she could join him.

With little effort, she could clear the Dark Fae, but it wouldn't end Bran. That couldn't happen until she discovered how he continued to steal her magic—and her life.

She reluctantly turned away from watching Cael and remained veiled as she made her way through the rooms until she found the office Bran used.

Knowing Bran's past before he became a Reaper, she knew he liked to keep things that meant something to him close at all times. Whatever he used to drain her was either in the office, the bedroom he chose . . . or it was on his person.

Erith sincerely hoped that it wasn't on him. That would prove to be rather tricky to obtain. She could do it, but she wasn't looking forward to it. Perhaps luck would be on her side.

She quickly searched the office, looking in every drawer, every cabinet, and searching for anything that was shrouded with magic. When she found nothing that might be connected to her, she rushed up the stairs and quickly located the master bedroom.

But that ended up being another fruitless search.

Exasperation rushed through her. This couldn't be happening. She was sure she'd find something that would let her know how Bran was stealing her power and life force. Now, she had to concede that it might just be his magic.

"No," she denied vehemently.

Bran had been a good warrior, but his magic had never been anything special. His strength had been in his calculating, crafty ways of getting to his enemy. Now that was being visited on her Reapers. And she hated it.

Erith drew in a determined breath and strode from the room to the stairs. She passed a window and glimpsed Cael and Bran facing off. She came to a halt as a mixture of delight at seeing Cael preparing to attack and worry that Bran would use some underhanded trick to hurt him engulfed her.

Then she remembered just how savage a warrior Cael could be. Her concern evaporated.

Everyone but a small circle of Dark surrounding Talin and Neve were still fighting. She couldn't see Bran's face, but Cael was as calm and collected as usual. But she knew that just beneath the surface was a wealth of rage, begging to be released.

"Soon," she whispered a promise.

Unfortunately, it wasn't going to be today. Erith wanted nothing more than to face off with Bran, but he'd taken so much of her essence already. She wasn't sure how much her sword could continue to give back, and until Bran stopped draining her, she was hesitant to test it.

Though, she might not have a choice soon.

"Cael," she called, letting him know that it was time for them to leave.

She waited to see if the Reapers would depart. Cael had heard her, and he should've already left. Why wasn't he?

"Cael. Now," she said.

His gaze lifted to the window, meeting her gaze so swiftly that she would've missed it had she not been looking at him. It was the only way he could let her know that Bran was somehow holding them. She should have suspected and planned for something like this, but she wasn't too worried. The Reapers were very good, better than Bran on his best day.

Better than the ex-Reaper no matter how much of her power he had.

In order to help her Reapers, she thought back to when she went through the barrier around the house. The Reapers had breached it first, so nothing should've alerted Bran and his men to one more passing through it. She had felt no other magic that indicated that Bran—

Erith's thoughts halted when she spotted something glowing between Bran and Cael. Her mouth went slack when she saw the purple bubble. No. That . . . it couldn't be.

A scream lodged in her throat when Bran threw it at Cael.

Her lungs locked when Cael dove out of the way. She put a hand on the window, waiting anxiously for some sign of Cael. She didn't release the breath until he slowly got to his feet and stood before Bran, murder in his silver eyes.

And much to her surprise, she found herself smiling.

Few had seen Cael in his true warrior form. There hadn't been a need as a Reaper. They simply collected the souls she judged. It wasn't until Bran returned that the Reapers had begun fighting again—though it came second nature to each of them.

Not even Bran knew the Cael that she had seen on the battlefield all those years ago. The intelligent, patient, clever Fae that Cael was. None of them knew how meditation allowed him to see a battlefield like a chessboard, moving pieces until he found the ones that would give him the win.

It's why he'd never lost a battle.

It's why he was so good at what he did.

It was also why he had been betrayed.

His ability caused others to fear him. But not Erith. Never her. His skill had only added to his power. And her desire for him.

Bran's laugh reached her through the walls, even over the sounds of battle. Erith was about to reveal herself to turn Bran's attention to her, but Cael shook his head. Cael wasn't looking at her, and she couldn't hear their conversation, but she knew the movement had been for her. It was confirmed a second later when Cael glanced her way again.

Cael's eyes spoke volumes, no matter how fleeting the

look.

Despite what Cael told her, she wouldn't leave the Reapers. He should realize that. Erith flattened her lips and quickly made her way down the stairs.

The house was empty with the Dark outside fighting, but she still went on her own power instead of teleporting. With the amount of magic Bran had now, she didn't want to trigger anything. It was fortunate that he hadn't detected her.

She stood at the door Bran had exited from atop the steps, but she still wasn't able to hear the conversation between Cael and the ex-Reaper. And that simply wouldn't do.

Just as she was about to throw caution to the wind and teleport to Cael, she felt a rush of magic near her. It was a barrier that surrounded the small group of Dark, Bran, Talin, Neve, and Cael.

A trap set for her or anyone who tried to help the Reapers. She would've sensed the invisible barricade if she hadn't been so worried about Cael. Thankfully, she had felt it in time. But how did she get them away?

As much as Erith wanted to hear the exchange between Cael and Bran, she knew she had to get the other Reapers away. She went to step down when she jerked to a halt as a Dark turned toward her.

He looked her way, frowning, his red eyes filled with

such malice and hatred that it made her shiver. Evil had never bothered her before, but this was different. This reminded her of what she had witnessed in Usaeil's eyes recently. The queen would have to be dealt with soon. Hopefully, Rhi would see to that, but if not, Erith would pass judgment on Usaeil.

Erith quickly slid out of the way as the Dark walked up the stairs and into the house. She knew that Bran had taken a lot of her magic, but she hadn't realized how much until now. She had been certain of her ability to remain invisible to Bran and his men, but now, she was having doubts.

She ducked and dodged her way through the battle until she found Kyran. He was surrounded by Dark, but she shoved her way to him. Luckily, the Fae fighting were more concerned about trying to get to Kyran than seeing who—or what—was jostling them.

"Kyran, leave. Now!" she yelled above the shouts.

He whirled around, searching for her.

She sighed. "Cael is trapped. Get away before it's too late."

His lips flattened as he kicked at a Dark, but he gave a nod. Erith made her way back through the mass of bodies, stepping over dead ones that had yet to revive and fighting the urge to join the fray. She looked back once to see Kyran following her command.

She made her way as fast as she could to Daire and Baylon, who had managed to get into the mansion and were battling the Dark there.

It took so long to get to them, that Erith worried she wouldn't have enough time to find Fintan. Erith hurried out of the barrier surrounding the mansion and yelled Fintan's name. Only then did she lower her veil enough for the Reapers to see her.

Seconds later, Fintan teleported beside her. "What happened?"

"Bran has Cael, Neve, and Talin confined."

Fintan's red-rimmed, white eyes lifted to where the Fae now gathered. "It's a trap for you."

"I know."

"You can't go," he stated.

She licked her lips as she gazed at the notorious Fae. Blood was splattered on his face, in his white hair, and all over his clothes. She'd once looked the same, but whereas she loved the bloodlust that consumed her, Fintan hated it. Always had.

Even now, he only took pleasure in ridding them of their enemies. He didn't enjoy killing. She alone knew how he'd nearly refused her offer to become a Reaper because he didn't want to take any more lives.

Erith sighed. "I can't leave them either."

"Where are the others?"

"I don't know. I told them to go."

Fintan wiped the back of his hand over his sweaty brow. "Tell me you found what you searched for. Please tell me that Cael and the others aren't trapped for nothing."

"I wish I could."

He spun around, his flowing, white hair swinging with him as he fisted his hands. Fintan stayed that way a long moment before he faced her again. "I'm not leaving Cael."

"Bran wants Neve. That's what this is about," Erith explained. "Since he couldn't get the others, he intends to take the only one he can. And if he can hurt Cael in the process, he will. This was exactly what Cael set up."

Fintan's chest heaved as he stared stonily at her. "But Cael didn't count on being confined. It might not bother you to lose a Reaper, but I can't lose another member of my family."

The calm Erith strived to keep vanished at Fintan's accusation. She let him see the fury his words had caused. "With just a thought, I can take away the magic and life that I granted you," she said, slowly advancing on him. "Don't *ever* claim to know how I feel, because you know nothing."

Instead of fear or even more anger, one side of Fintan's lips lifted in a grin. "About fekking time you showed how you really feel."

She blinked, taken aback. "What?"

"Trust me, I believe every word I spoke to you, but I also know that you care about us. And perhaps one more than the rest."

Erith opened her mouth to deny it, but Fintan continued talking.

"You trusted Cael to be our leader. We've followed him willingly because of who he is, not because you said to. And lest you forget, I know exactly who he is and what he did for the Light Fae."

She had indeed forgotten that Fintan had been sent by the King of the Dark to kill Cael and throw the Light Fae into disarray. Fintan had refused the order. The only time he'd ever rejected a mission. That had set the stage for his betrayal by the king.

Fintan glanced to where Cael and the others were. "I know how good Cael really is. If Bran knew, he wouldn't try to fight him. He'd run the other way."

Erith smiled.

"There is much more to Cael than we know." Fintan looked at her. "Except for you. You know, don't you?"

She nodded. "Yes."

"We serve you. If you go back for him, you defeat the purpose of staying out of Bran's hands. Cael will think of something."

"Before Bran hurts Neve, or after?"

Fintan blew out a breath, his face tight. "I hope before."

"Cael," Erith shouted, strong and clear. "They're all clear."

Her heart missed a beat as Cael whispered her name. It was like a caress on the wind, brushing against her cheek. She wanted to reach up and touch her face, but she didn't.

A moment later, Talin and Neve were beside her.

She frowned at them when she didn't find Cael. Her heart clenched painfully as she realized exactly what had happened. "Where is he? Where's Cael?"

Talin looked back at the mansion, tension tightening his body as fury rolled off him in thick waves. Neve held his hand, her eyes brimming with unshed tears.

"Where is he?" Erith demanded angrily.

Neve swallowed and said in a shaky voice, "Cael gave himself over to Bran in exchange for letting me and Talin go."

No. No! NOOOOOOOO!

The scream went on and on inside Erith's mind, but she didn't let it out. She couldn't. Because if she did, she'd never stop.

There was a way to get him back. All she had to do was face Bran. And that's exactly what she was going to do. Because she would do anything for Cael. Anything.

She started walking, but within steps, Fintan wrapped

an arm around her, yanking her back against him. He held her tightly as she fought him, kicking and hitting while trying to get to Cael.

"It's not time. It's not time."

She didn't know how long she struggled before she heard the words Fintan spoke calmly, over and over. She dropped her head back on his shoulder and looked at the sky of gray clouds.

Tears she didn't dare shed welled inside her. She couldn't lose Cael. Not now. Not after finally giving in to her feelings—and learning that he felt the same about her.

"I can't leave him."

"It's what he wants." Fintan set her down and turned her to face him. "But we won't leave him there."

She lifted her chin, resolve building within her. "No. We won't."

Chapter Nineteen

This was Hell. Xaneth was sure of it.

He walked among the Dark gathered behind the mansion. The beautiful garden had been destroyed. The grass trampled, the flowerbed ripped apart from the battle, and blood was everywhere.

Xaneth had thought he'd seen all there was to see of the Fae while living between both the Light and Dark. Now, he was getting a glimpse of another side—a side he didn't like.

He was one of five new recruits to Bran's army. Out of them, he was the only Fae who hadn't been taken against his will.

His gaze scanned the faces of the Dark. They were rabid with savagery, their bloodlust running higher than anything he'd ever witnessed before. If any of them had been abducted, they were content where they were now.

Xaneth had been in all kinds of situations before. Hell, he'd faced the Queen of the Light, but even he wasn't prepared for this. And that worried him. Because he might have stepped into a setting that he couldn't get out of.

His ego had put him here. He'd believed that he could sort through any situation, but he hadn't listened carefully enough to the Reapers. Otherwise, he would've realized that he was out of his depth. In order to survive, he would have to learn.

Fast.

He'd been trying to find Cael ever since the Reaper had given himself up to Bran. Even Xaneth had known that was a bad idea, but Cael had done it so the other two Reapers could get away.

The fact that Bran allowed Talin and Neve to go troubled Xaneth. Especially since Bran had made it clear to his army that his goal was to capture the women the Reapers had. Bran had something in store for Cael, and it couldn't be good if he'd willingly released a female.

When the group Bran had sent to the Reaper stronghold returned emptyhanded, Bran had lashed out at everyone in his fury. That's how badly Bran wanted the women.

The Fae around Xaneth suddenly let out a loud cheer. He saw them looking up and followed suit to find Bran standing on a terrace, looking down at them from the second floor of the manor.

The would-be leader of the Dark army wore a black suit with purple lining. His shoulder-length black hair was pulled back in a queue. But it was the delight in

Bran's silver eyes as he looked down at them all that sent a warning chill down Xaneth's back.

He'd spent a lot of time with the Dark Fae and had had dealings with some of the most dangerous of them. But none of them—not even Balladyn—came close to the evil Xaneth saw in Bran's eyes.

Bran might have lived and died a Light Fae, but something must have been done to him when he became a Reaper that prevented him from changing to Dark. Because the one thing Xaneth knew how to spot was a Dark Fae.

And Bran was most definitely Dark—even if his coloring didn't show it.

Bran didn't use glamour. And that's how Xaneth knew it must have something to do with the fact that Bran used to be a Reaper. Xaneth intended to ask Cael about it as soon as he could get close enough to him to do so.

Bran held out his hands, quieting the army. He rested his palms on the stone railing and smiled as he looked over the crowd. "I'd hoped we would be celebrating capturing the Reapers' women. Instead, the next one on my list has now fallen into my hands. Cael, leader of the Reapers."

More cheers went up as Cael was led out onto the terrace with a thick metal collar around his throat, connected to a chain that Searlas held.

Xaneth cringed when he saw the state of Cael's face. Reaper or not, he'd taken quite the beating from both fists and magic. The wounds were healing, but the blood was there for all to see, and it incited the Dark army.

"Cael is just the first step in our conquering of the Reapers!" Bran yelled over the noise. He raised his hand again for silence. "For too long, the Fae have stood in fear of Death and the Reapers. No more. We're going to take back that power."

Xaneth could well imagine that this was similar to what Usaeil had said before she slaughtered her family—*his* family. And while Xaneth didn't know much about the Reapers, he knew enough to know that Death was fair in her judgments. Bran wouldn't be the same.

A ball of magic formed in Bran's hand. It was a deep, dark purple. Xaneth had never seen anything like it before, and he wasn't sure he wanted to know what it did.

The thought ran through his mind an instant before Bran turned and slammed his hand—and the orb of magic—into Cael's chest.

Xaneth hid his grunt as Cael doubled over. His groan of pain brought a round of laughter from the Dark. With a motion of Bran's hand, two Fae straightened Cael to show the burnt patch of skin, the flesh eaten away to show Cael's ribcage.

"This is the start!" Bran said to the group, holding his

hand straight up into the air.

Xaneth clapped with the others, but all the while, one thought kept going through his mind—Bran had to be stopped. He knew it just as he knew that Usaeil's reign had to be ended. It was a good thing that Bran and Usaeil hadn't met because the two of them teaming up would be catastrophic.

Xaneth's thoughts came to a halt as the Dark released Cael. The Reaper leader's legs couldn't hold him, and he crumpled to the ground. Searlas sneered at the Reaper while everyone else laughed.

But all Xaneth felt was revulsion and anger. Both directed at himself for even considering joining Bran in his war against the Reapers.

"Where are the new recruits?" Bran inquired.

Xaneth stilled, dread going through him as he hoped that no one would point to him. One of the other four was hauled into the house by two Dark and led up to the terrace, all the while struggling against the others. Xaneth strained to hear what Bran told the Fae before he clasped the Dark's arm.

Almost instantly, the fearful Fae who'd just a moment ago had no desire to join Bran, changed into a rage-filled Dark who only wanted to kill. That's when Xaneth realized that Bran was giving everyone a little of his magic. Only Bran was sharing his malevolence, as well.

Xaneth hadn't counted on anything like this, and he wanted no part of it. In fact, the sheer idea of it terrified him. If he thought he could leave, he might try it. But he couldn't. Not just because Bran no doubt had something in place to prevent it, but because this was bigger than the trepidation Xaneth felt. This was about the way of life for not just the Fae, but every being on every realm—because that's how far Bran would take it if he won.

Xaneth had no desire to be turned, but he had a feeling there was no way to get out of it. He looked around and forced a smile. With the amount of Fae near him, it would be easy to get lost in such a mass. All he had to do was act like them. Maybe then, Bran would overlook him.

It was a big gamble, but what other choice did he have? If Bran gave him some of his magic, he would no longer be who he was. His desire to bring down his aunt would no longer drive him. And that just couldn't happen.

Xaneth took on the enraged expression of the others and began cheering just as loudly as them. One by one, the other three Fae who had been kidnapped were altered. Bran and his men searched the crowd for anyone not like the others.

Xaneth realized that the hunt wouldn't end until he showed himself. If he were going to spy, then he had to get close to Bran. In order to do that, he had to gain the maniac's trust. It was something he'd done countless other times. It was second nature.

With a deep breath, Xaneth shouldered his way through the others and came to stand at the front of the group. He looked up at Bran and simply stared. Bran's gaze held his for a long moment before he motioned Xaneth up.

Xaneth made his way to Bran on the terrace, hoping with every step that he maintained his thoughts and control after Bran shared his magic. Unfortunately, if the others were any indication, the chances of that were slim.

Finally, Xaneth stood before Bran. The ex-Reaper regarded him for a long minute. Xaneth was cognizant of how close Searlas and the other Dark were, but more than that, he was acutely aware of Cael just a few steps behind him.

"So," Bran said, "you're the one who asked to join my army."

Xaneth nodded. "You really think so many Dark can go missing without others becoming aware of what's going on? Perhaps for a little while, but eventually, someone takes notice."

"And that someone was you?" Bran asked, brows raised.

Xaneth grinned, not at all duped by Bran's deceptively calm words. "Actually, it was the king. I simply overheard some guards talking and realized that there was a way for me to actually do something other than hunting humans."

Silver eyes stared hard at Xaneth, trying to see through any lies. But Xaneth had learned to live off his lies—and use expert glamour to hide his Light coloring. No one had caught him yet.

"It's been some time since I've had a Dark willingly join me." Bran clasped his hands behind his back. "Is it what you expected?"

"More than I could've hoped," Xaneth replied. He felt the probing of Bran's magic in search of any glamour. But being a royal came with some perks, and that included powerful magic.

"I'm glad you've seen the possibilities of what I'm doing. It's always better to have someone wanting to join rather than forcing them."

Xaneth glanced down at the army. "They look more than ready to do your bidding."

"That they do. Come." Bran beckoned by holding out his hand. "Take your reward."

This could either get him closer to Bran, or it could all blow up in Xaneth's face. The endless centuries of hiding from Usaeil might have been for nothing. He'd wanted to join Bran so he could help Balladyn take down the queen. No wonder the Reapers had told Xaneth it was a bad idea.

For fek's sake. What had he gotten himself into?

There was no other choice for him. Xaneth grasped Bran's hand. A wash of ice ran from his palm, up his arm, and then through his body. He felt the swell of power almost instantly, and to his delight, he found that he was still very much himself.

Bran jerked him closer and grabbed Xaneth's shoulder with his free hand, squeezing tightly. "Welcome to our family. You'll forgive me if I don't trust you."

"I expected nothing less."

Bran grunted and tightened his fingers around Xaneth's hand. Then he released him and stepped back.

Xaneth turned and found his gaze clashing with Cael's. There was a split second where the Reaper let his disgust and fury show before it was masked.

Xaneth couldn't believe that had gone as well as it had. He walked away, not wanting to press his luck or get asked any more questions. He idly walked the manor while Cael was hauled away somewhere. While he wanted to see where they took Cael, he knew he was likely being watched.

Just as he expected, it wasn't long before Searlas caught up with him.

"Can I help you?" Xaneth asked the second in command, who stared at him.

"Don't think I didn't see you earlier when we surrounded the Reapers."

Xaneth shrugged. "What about it? I finally came face-to-face with one. I was curious."

"Do you want a closer look?"

All his instincts screamed that this was a test of sorts. Or a trap. Shite. "Sure."

"Follow me."

Xaneth trailed behind Searlas as the Dark took him out of the mansion to a building at the back of the house. It was meant to be a guesthouse but had now become Cael's prison.

Xaneth casually noted the number of Fae on guard and the amount of magic coming off the building. The moment Xaneth stepped over the threshold, he felt the wards that enclosed the structure. It was Dark magic, but even more malevolent, more wicked—and more controlling—than any he'd felt before.

The only other being who had such powerful magic was Death, and since Bran was syphoning from her, it was no wonder he was so strong.

They stopped before Cael, who was secured against a wall with his arms above his head and his legs spread wide. Even captured, there was defiance in Cael's eyes.

"He's mine to torture as much as I want," Searlas told Xaneth. "And after what was done to me by Fintan, I'm going to take pleasure in this. We can't kill him, but we can hurt Cael. And I plan on doing a lot of damage until Bran executes him. I know Bran has something special planned just for Death."

Xaneth forced a laugh, nodding in excitement when Searlas looked his way. He kept a smile on his lips as the Dark began throwing magic at Cael, aiming straight for the Reaper's chest that had yet to heal.

This wasn't the first—or the last—time Xaneth had seen such torment, but it was harder to watch this time. Maybe because he knew it was Cael. Or it could be because he knew the stakes were higher than they'd ever been.

"Want a turn?"

Xaneth shot his gaze to Searlas, his stomach tightening at the question. He had a part to play, and that meant doing everything in his power to ensure that he got close enough to Bran to extract the information Balladyn needed. But to hurt Cael? Xaneth wasn't sure he could.

He'd thought Bran was the winning team. In fact, Bran probably was, but the longer Xaneth was around him and the others, the more he knew that it was imperative he do everything he could to help the Reapers.

So he wouldn't just be spying for the King of the Dark. He was going to do it for Death, as well. Xaneth could only hope that he came out of all of it alive. But if he didn't, then he was doing something for someone other than himself. For once.

Then again, this was another test. And he didn't intend to fail.

He smiled at Searlas. "I'd love to."

The Dark stepped aside. Cael's fists were clenched tightly, his body straining against the pain, but not once had he cried out. The wound Bran had inflicted was ugly and gaping, and all the Reaper could do was stand there and bear every blow dealt him.

Until he got free.

When that happened, Xaneth knew Bran and the others would feel the full force of Cael's retribution. Not to mention when the other Reapers and Death joined in. It was going to be an epic battle.

Xaneth walked up to Cael, careful to keep his face blank of any emotion. Searlas had shifted to the side to watch him, but Xaneth wasn't that stupid. He might want to let Cael know that he was on his side, but that would have to come later after he'd earned some trust.

Hopefully, the Reaper would still be alive then.

Xaneth pulled back his hand and punched Cael in the jaw. The Reaper's head snapped to the side. Slowly, Cael turned his face forward and glared at Xaneth.

With everything inside him yelling *No!* Xaneth formed a ball of magic and reared his arm back, throwing it so that half of it hit Cael, while the other half slammed into the wall.

The sight of the Reaper leader's body jerking from the agony was heartbreaking. Knowing that he was adding to Cael's pain only made it worse. If Xaneth somehow lived through this, he would spend the rest of his life making it up to Cael somehow.

Searlas laughed and bade, "Again."

Chapter Twenty

He was going to kill Xaneth.

And it wouldn't be a quick death.

Cael had truly believed that the Fae would join them. How could he have been so wrong about Xaneth? Cael was usually a better judge of character, and after fighting alongside Xaneth and Eoghan against Usaeil, he'd discovered just how strong the royal Fae's magic was.

His thoughts halted for a moment when pain lashed through his body as the torture continued, adding to the agony from the orb Bran had hit him with. Cael let his mind wander while Searlas and Xaneth had their fun.

While their magic hurt, the real agony was in the wound delivered by the purple orb Bran had slammed into him earlier. Just thinking about it made Cael nauseous. He wasn't sure what was in the ball of power, but he needed to warn the other Reapers to prepare for it.

Cael didn't know how long they tortured him. The pain became so agonizing that he let his mind go to the one place that would soothe him—to memories of Erith.

He relived every second of their day together. Every

word, every sigh, every touch, every cry of pleasure. Nothing had ever felt so real, so perfect, as during those few precious hours. It had surpassed all of Cael's fantasies and dreams.

And in that time, he could believe that Erith was his.

He was so deep in his mind that it took him a while to realize that something was different. When he pulled himself back to the present, he saw that the torture had stopped for the moment. Searlas was gone, leaving Xaneth alone with him.

There were many things he wanted to say to Xaneth, but Cael didn't bother. The Fae had made his choice. Cael had survived too long on his own to know what it meant to belong to a group he could trust.

That's where Cael had gone wrong. He hadn't shown Xaneth everything the Reapers had to offer. Cael had believed after fighting together that Xaneth would see who they were and readily join them.

For Death to win, it meant that either Xaneth or the as yet unidentified Dark from his vision had to be on their side. They'd lost Xaneth, but there was still a chance for the unknown Fae. Except Cael had been captured. The others would look, but they had no idea what to look for.

But Cael didn't regret giving himself up so that Talin and Neve could get away. The way Bran had looked at Neve with such glee had made Cael's stomach twist with revulsion.

Bran wouldn't just kill the women the Reapers loved. He wouldn't just torture them either. He would inflict the most heinous kind of agony, prolonging their deaths to make the Reapers suffer as long as he could.

There was no way Cael would allow Bran to get his hands on Neve or any of the others. Not now, not ever. Even if it meant Cael died. It would be worth it to keep the women safe. It was his duty to his Reapers, and a promise that he'd made to them.

When he offered to hand himself over to Bran, he'd been surprised that the ex-Reaper had agreed so quickly. Then he'd realized that it was exactly what Bran had wanted. By the time Cael comprehended that, it was too late. The deed had already been done.

For once, Bran had outwitted him. And that infuriated Cael.

One mistake was all it took to topple everything. But there was still hope. Neve was out of Bran's hands—for now—and the Reapers were together. Not to mention, Bran didn't know about Eoghan.

Unless Xaneth had told him.

Shite. How had Cael forgotten everything the Fae knew?

Because you believed Xaneth would side with you.

Cael should have known better. He had accounted for

everything except Bran learning just how much power he'd taken from Erith. That was Cael's mistake. And it just might cost him his life.

Xaneth leaned against the doorway, flipping a knife end over end and catching it. He appeared bored, but Cael saw the way he noted the movements of everyone around the mansion.

Cael closed his eyes when he heard his name whispered in his head. The sound of Erith's voice was like a soothing touch against the pain that wracked him. He wanted so badly to answer her command. She understood that, but she let him know that she was still there, still fighting.

He hoped he would be alive to see her take on Bran. It would be spectacular. And Cael knew she would win. No matter what Bran had taken from Erith, she was stronger mentally. Bran would use brute force and his magic, but neither would be enough to end Death.

His woman.

Cael bit back a smile at the thought of her in his arms and how well they fit together. He should've told her that he loved her. The next time he had the chance, he was going to do just that.

He sighed as he thought of Seamus. Cael hated to admit that he hoped he was wrong about the Fae. The Dark could be the unknown he'd seen in his vision, and if so, he prayed that Seamus found a way to stop Bran from taking anything more from Death.

It was the sudden halting of the movement of the knife through the air that alerted Cael that he was about to have a visitor. He opened his eyes to see Bran and Searlas walking into his prison. His body had healed from the magic Xaneth and Searlas had inflicted, but his wound from Bran had yet to mend.

Bran smiled as he stopped before him. "You have no idea how long I've dreamed of having you just like this. For thousands of years as I suffered in the Netherworld, I imagined countless ways to kill you."

"Keep blaming me for everything that happened to you," Cael said, trying to hide his pain. "A real Fae would own up to his decisions and mistakes."

Bran's smile dropped as he looked at the ceiling with a sigh. "That sounds exactly like something Death would say."

"You hate it because it's the truth."

"You have your truth. I have mine."

"You broke the rules. That's all on you," Cael said.

Bran crossed his arms over his chest. "It seems like your Reapers have as well, but none of their women are dead. One is even now a Reaper to replace Eoghan. How does it feel to have lost your friend?"

"Do you want me to talk about my Reapers or

Eoghan?" Cael asked with a grin. This could be a trick to get him to say something about Eoghan's return. Or Bran might still be in the dark about Eoghan. "It seems you can't keep your thoughts straight."

Bran stared at him with narrowed eyes. "Both, of course."

"You want to know why Death changed the rules, then you need to talk to her."

"Oh, I plan on it," Bran stated.

Cael gave a shake of his head. "It doesn't matter what she tells you, it's not going to be what you want to hear. You want to know why your lover is dead? Then look in the mirror. You're responsible for that."

"No," Bran stated, spittle flying from his mouth as his arms dropped to his sides. He stalked to Cael until they were nose-to-nose. "Death could've spared her. I could've been happy."

"We both know that's a lie. You'll never find any sort of joy because your soul is twisted and black. You hid it well before you were a Reaper, but the power your position gave you as one of us changed you."

Bran snorted as he backed up a step. "You know nothing."

"Deny my words, but you know I'm right."

"It doesn't matter," Bran said. "I'm going to end Death and every one of the Reapers. I'm going to win. And then

I'm going to make the rules."

Cael released a breath, sharp pains shooting from what was left of his abdomen. Damn, but it hurt. What was in Bran's magic that kept him from healing? "You sound awfully sure of yourself."

"Even you know I'm going to defeat Death."

"Oh?"

"Why would you give yourself over to me?"

Cael frowned at Bran in confusion. "The answer is obvious. To save my Reapers."

"Are you sure it wasn't to separate yourself from Death?"

That was the last thing Cael wanted. "You really have lost your mind, haven't you?"

"Come now, old friend," Bran said with a slight curve of his lips. "You know you're going to die by my hand. I thought you'd wait until we met on the field of battle, and while I looked forward to that, I'll accept your death any way I can get it. At least now, your men—and woman—won't see what kind of coward you are."

Anger rushed through him, sharp and true. "Coward? Release me, and I'll show you what a true Reaper is."

"We both know you always liked to be the best at everything, but you were failing Death. To her and your Reapers, you look like the hero sacrificing yourself for them. But, like I said, that's a coward's way out."

"I should've let you have two of my Reapers to torture?" Cael asked in outrage.

Bran shrugged. "I'm going to eventually. You've just prolonged their deaths."

"You're the one who is going to die."

"Yeah, I don't think so."

"What makes you so sure?"

Bran's smile was slow and sinister. "I have a sure-fire way of defeating Death once and for all. I just need more time to take what little power she has left. And it is so very little, Cael. To think that you came here to prove yourself to her, to show your Reapers that you could retaliate, but it's been for naught. Death is all but finished. Where is she? If she were even half the being she used to be, then she would come to your defense. Shall we prove it? Call out for her."

Cael shook his head. "I won't."

A purple orb appeared in Bran's palm. "Call out to her."

Once more, Cael shook his head. He would die before he did anything that Bran wanted. But especially calling to Erith. He wouldn't bring her into a trap.

"Last chance."

"Just throw the damn thing and stop talking," Cael demanded.

"Oh, ho," Bran said with a laugh as he moved his hand in a slight circle. "Look at you, thinking you can tell me what to do. I'm not one of your Reapers."

Cael grinned. "And I'm thankful for that."

Bran walked to him and held the orb against the side of his face, just short of touching Cael. "Call for Erith," he ordered.

Cael held his gaze, unflinching. "Kiss my arse."

The moment the words passed his lips, Bran shoved the magic into the side of Cael's head. Cael ground his teeth together against the onslaught of pain that kept doubling with each second that passed. It became too much. Cael had no choice but to let out the scream of anguish that rose up within him.

His skin burned, yet at the same time, it felt as if it were freezing. His body jerked, trying to get free of the pain. The smell of burning flesh and hair surrounded him, making his stomach churn, knowing it was his own skin.

"Call for her!" Bran yelled in his ear.

Cael was locked in the roiling agony, but he still forced open his eyes to glare at Bran. It took everything he had to say, "Never."

Bran let out a bellow and shoved more magic into the wound. Cael gave himself up to the blessed darkness that swallowed him.

~

He was so close to winning. Why wasn't everyone bowing down before him? Bran pulled his hand away from Cael's head, smiling at the burnt mess he'd left behind.

"Is he dead?" Searlas asked hopefully.

Bran shook his head. "Not yet."

"What are you waiting for?"

"I want Death to be here. I want her to see what I've done to her favored Reaper."

"She won't come," Searlas said.

Bran faced his lieutenant. "She'll come if he calls for her. Cael and I both know it, which is why he refused. For now. By the time I'm done with him, he'll be begging me to let him call for her."

"He doesn't seem the type," Xaneth said.

Bran stilled before turning his head to the door where the Fae stood with one foot propped behind him on the wall. "Excuse me?"

"Cael," Xaneth replied. "He's not the type to beg for anything, no matter what kind of torture you put him through."

Bran still wasn't entirely sure about Xaneth. It was one reason he'd left him alone in the building with Cael to see if they spoke. The Dark had eagerly lobbed ball after ball of magic at Cael, but that could've been an act.

Leaving them alone with enough time to interact had been the deciding factor. Xaneth passed the test, but that didn't mean Bran would trust him so easily. It would be just like Death to send someone to spy for her.

Bran walked to Xaneth. "Do you know Cael?"

"No," the Fae said with a dismissive shake of his head. "I know his kind. He believes in something, and as long as he holds that belief, nothing and no one will be able to break him down."

As much as Bran hated to admit it, the Dark might be right. Bran looked at Cael. "I need Death to see him."

"You plan on fighting her," Xaneth said. "All you need to do is keep Cael until then. Bring him onto the battlefield. Kill him in front of Death and the Reapers. That should really kick them in the balls."

Bran laughed, nodding in approval. "I like you, Xaneth. You think just like I do."

Searlas mumbled something beneath his breath as he stalked from the building.

"Ignore him," Bran said with a shrug. "He gets his feelings hurt often."

"I should probably watch my back then."

"He won't hurt you. I'll make sure of that." Bran put his arm around Xaneth and led him from the structure. "I've already gotten one enemy out of the way. Soon, Cael will join Eoghan. Then, the final act in my plan will be put into motion, and I'll take down Death."

Xaneth smiled brightly. "I can't wait to see that."

Chapter Twenty-one

It had taken Erith far longer than she liked to gather Cael's Reapers and move them to another location. They couldn't return to Inchmickery, nor could they go to Eoghan because she didn't want to chance Bran tracking them.

Not once had she thought about what might happen if Cael were taken. In her mind, that had never been a possibility. What an utter fool she'd been. She knew Bran's hatred for Cael. She should've realized that he would do anything to separate Cael from the others.

Every time Erith thought about what Bran was doing to Cael, she reached for her sword, ready to attack and make sure Bran could never hurt anyone again.

Then she would feel the weakness within her, and she'd pause. If she were going to rescue Cael, she wanted to make sure she could actually do it and not fail in the middle—dooming them both.

She had ushered the Reapers through numerous doorways—many she hadn't used since her time as Mistress of War—to bring them to a realm where they could plan without Bran finding them. This world was deserted. She'd seen to that when she wiped everyone out so long ago.

The buildings were crumbling into ruin, the plants taking back the realm, but it was somewhere to rest and gather their thoughts. There were huge swathes of forest that hadn't been there before, and they were perfect places to hide.

"In all the time I've known you, I've never seen you move so much."

She halted at the deep voice, not even realizing she'd been pacing. Erith turned to Fintan to find the Dark watching her with his head tilted. "Is that so?"

He nodded. "You've taken us a long way from Cael."

"You think I'm abandoning him?" she demanded, stalking toward Fintan as fury churned like a storm-swept sea within her. "You believe I would do that to one of my Reapers?"

Fintan didn't so much as twitch. His red-rimmed, white eyes held hers. "I think it's tearing you up inside that you had to leave him behind."

All her anger evaporated, dispatched like mist through the universe. "Yes," she whispered.

"Cael did what he had to do to get Neve and Talin free."

"He gave Bran exactly what he wanted."

"Himself," Fintan replied.

Erith looked at the trees around her, hoping she would find solace in them as she usually did, but it wasn't working. "Bran will kill him. For all I know, Cael is already dead."

"He's not."

She shot a frown at Fintan. "How do you know?"

"Because Bran will want to kill him in front of you."

Her knees went weak as the truth of that statement hit. "Cael," she whispered, knowing he would hear her call no matter how far she was from him.

"What are you going to do?"

Erith swallowed past the lump of emotion in her throat and squared her shoulders. It was her decision. She'd put the Reapers together, she'd given them their extra power and abilities. They were her responsibility.

Just as Bran was. She should've killed him as Cael had urged her to do eons ago. Instead, she'd imprisoned Bran, which only fed his wrath.

The war she'd been preparing for was upon them. No longer would she hold off, waiting for an answer to fall into her lap. No longer would she hope to find an easy solution to ending Bran and getting back to her life.

By taking Cael, Bran set things in motion. It was now her move. While she didn't see the battlefield like Cael, she had other options. And she was going to use every one of them.

Because the minute she gave Bran the opportunity, he would kill Cael. And that was simply one death she refused to witness.

"Erith?"

She blinked and focused on Fintan. "We need to bring Eoghan and his Reapers here."

"War?"

"War," she replied with a nod.

Fintan grinned. "About bloody time."

"Tell the others. I'm going to get Eoghan and his group," she said before teleporting to the doorway.

Erith returned to Earth and chose New Orleans as her destination. The night was dark, the moon hidden behind the clouds as she walked the graveyard.

"Eoghan," she called, summoning him.

Within moments, he appeared before her. A small frown furrowed his brow as he looked around. "Interesting choice."

"Call your Reapers."

He hesitated, but he did as she commanded. Once the six stood around him, she looked at each of them.

"What's happened?" Eoghan asked.

She parted her lips to tell him, but the words stuck in her throat. Cael's face kept flashing in her mind as he looked at her with that sexy half-smile that made her melt. She knew exactly what it felt like to be held in his strong arms, an embrace she longed to have now.

Erith inwardly shook herself. She had to pull herself together. Cael's life depended on it. He was strong. He would think of something to remain alive, but she wouldn't fail him.

"After Bran's army attacked Inchmickery, we decided to return the favor. Cael knew that Bran wanted the women, so we dangled Neve as bait with the Reapers spread out around the mansion Bran now occupies. While they fought, I went inside to find whatever it is that Bran's using to take my power."

"Did you find it?" Eoghan asked hopefully.

"No." The word fell like acid from her lips. "Cael wanted Bran to come for Neve, where Cael and Talin would then join her against the Dark. It happened just as Cael planned."

Cathal asked, "What went wrong?"

"Bran's magic has changed. He trapped the trio, preventing them from leaving. I got to the others before the same fate could befall them. And . . . then Cael agreed to give himself over to Bran if Neve and Talin could go free."

Dubhan's face went slack with shock. "And Bran agreed? Why? He had all three."

"Because he knew what having Cael would do to Death," Eoghan said angrily.

Aisling shrugged. "But wouldn't having three of the Reapers be better? He had them. All three. And he just let Talin and Neve go?"

"She's right," Bradach said. "Bran could've killed all three right then."

Eoghan shook his head as he held Erith's gaze. "None of you understand Bran. Aye, he wants to kill us, but first and foremost, he wants to hurt Death."

"Bran also knows I'll come for Cael," Erith added.

Eoghan's forehead furrowed into a deep frown. "You can't. That's exactly what Bran wants."

"Wouldn't you go back for the others, as well?" Torin asked Eoghan.

Eoghan ran a hand down his face as he turned to his Reapers. "Of course, but you're missing the point."

"Nay," Rordan replied. "Bran believes he's already killed you. By capturing Cael and allowing Death to believe that Neve and Talin are safe, Bran is giving all of us a false sense of security while delivering the ultimate blow to Erith."

She nodded slowly. "Bran is waiting for me to show up. He'll kill Cael in front of me. Then, I suspect he'll take the last bit of my magic before he wipes out the rest of you."

"Fek me," Rordan mumbled angrily.

Eoghan looked at her. "We're ready for whatever you need."

Her gaze moved from him to the others. "I wish I could leave you out of it. Bran doesn't know about any of you, but if he defeats me, there's a good chance he will."

Aisling flicked her long, black and silver braid over her shoulder. "I'd rather meet him head-on in battle."

The other Reapers all nodded their heads in agreement.

"You know my thoughts," Eoghan said before Erith could look his way.

She shot him a quick smile. "I've taken Cael's group to another realm just in case Bran tries to track us."

Eoghan ran a hand over his jaw. "That's a good idea. I suppose you have a plan?"

"I know what Cael saw."

"Saw?" Cathal asked in disbelief. "How, exactly?"

Eoghan looked at his Reaper and shrugged. "I don't know how he does it, but somehow, when Cael meditates, he's able to see parts of a battle."

"Sometimes, the entire thing," Erith added. "It's why Cael was one of the greatest generals in the Light army."

Bradach asked, "Then why don't the Light know his name? Why isn't he revered as he should be?"

All eyes were on her. Erith had witnessed each Reaper's betrayal. She was the only one who knew everyone's secrets, their worst fears, and the things that they couldn't face in the darkest hours of the night.

Both Cael and Eoghan knew their Reapers' betrayal to better help them if the time ever came. It was a gift she gave every leader. Not once had she ever told of anyone's betrayal, and she wouldn't start now.

"His superiors feared him," Eoghan finally said. "Because Cael never lost a battle. Not one."

Aisling shrugged. "Too bad for the Light. He was the Reapers' gain, which I'm pleased about."

"What did Cael see?" Dubhan asked, getting back to the matter at hand.

Erith took a deep breath. "Xaneth and an unknown Dark that could go to either side."

"Let me have a chat with Xaneth," Torin said. "I'll get him to choose our side."

Erith glanced at the headstone near her. "He's already chosen. I saw him with Bran."

"Un-fekking-believable," Aisling muttered furiously.

Eoghan didn't seem fazed by the news. "Did Cael identify the other Dark?"

"No," Erith replied.

Eoghan put his hands on his hips and hung his head. "Unfortunately, I have news, as well. And you aren't going to like it."

"It's better to just spit it out."

Several tense moments went by before Eoghan lifted his head and met her gaze. "We happened upon some interesting information. Someone has sought out Bran in order to ally with him."

Erith thought of all the Dark Bran had been kidnapping, but couldn't imagine what Fae would willingly align with him. Balladyn certainly wouldn't. Or would he? No, there was something she was missing.

"Who?" she finally asked.

Eoghan's lips compressed briefly. "Usaeil."

Erith should've seen that coming. The Light Queen was power-hungry—and frightened that the Reapers were coming for her. Word would've reached Usaeil about the missing Dark, and she would've looked into the rumors and discovered Bran. Since Bran wasn't silent about what he wanted to do to the Reapers as well as Erith, it made perfect sense for Usaeil to ally with him.

If Erith had her full powers, she wouldn't hesitate to go up against the queen. Usaeil wouldn't come close to matching her. But the simple fact was that Usaeil's downfall was someone else's problem—namely Rhi's.

Erith inhaled deeply. "I have a plan that could succeed. A lot has to go perfectly, and there's a very good chance Bran will win. I'm telling you this so you have all the facts. There are three doorways here, leading to realms across the galaxy. Bran doesn't know that any of you are Reapers." She looked at Eoghan. "Or that you're alive and back. I'm giving you the option to get Thea and leave to live a life far from the chaos that could erupt on Earth."

"I'm offended you're even offering us that," Rordan said. "I'm a Reaper. I vowed to follow you. And that's what I'm going to do."

Bradach ran a hand through his short, black hair. "I'm tired of hiding from Bran. I want him to know my face."

"I don't run from anything," Torin stated.

Cathal reached behind him and began to braid his long, black hair. "I've been itching to kick some arse for a while now. Better Bran and his army than my fellow Reapers."

"If I'm going to die, it's going to be beside all of you, fighting our enemies," Dubhan said.

Aisling lifted her chin and shrugged. "My guys said it all perfectly."

Eoghan's head turned to Erith. "We're all that's standing in the way of Bran's reign of terror. I'm not going anywhere."

She smiled and motioned for them to follow her. "Come with me, then."

Chapter Twenty-two

The pain came in surges, washing over Cael like waves crashing onto the shore, drenching him in agony until he shook. And he knew it wouldn't end anytime soon.

His eyes were closed as he fought to escape the misery by taking his thoughts elsewhere. But he knew when someone was in the building with him. Most times, it was Xaneth, but Searlas was always waiting in the background.

Then there was Bran.

Cael was so wrapped up in the pain that he couldn't think straight. He tried to meditate, but he couldn't take his mind to that plane.

Instead, images of all the ways that Bran would trick the Reapers and kill Death kept rolling through his head. No matter how much Cael hoped otherwise, Erith and the Reapers would come for him. He would do the same in their place, but he wished they wouldn't.

The heavy thud of footsteps from the thick-soled shoes Bran favored warned Cael to prepare himself. Bran stopped before him and simply stood.

After a short time, Bran said, "I always get what I want, Cael. And I want you to call for Death. You *will* do it. You'll do it because I know how much pain you're in. And it's only going to get worse. Do us all a favor and call for her now."

"Why don't I do it?" Xaneth offered.

Searlas let out a hiss of anger. "As if she'd answer you."

"Well, I don't think the Reaper is going to do it."

There was a smile in Bran's words as he said, "Oh, Cael will do it. I've made sure of it."

Cael knew that Bran's words could merely be a threat. Or, they could be the truth. It was immaterial. No matter the pain, Cael wouldn't do what Bran wanted.

The stinging grew worse, and Cael retreated into his mind once more, seeking refuge anywhere he could. Unsurprisingly, he found himself in his most recent memories with Erith. He couldn't stop thinking about her, and no matter how hard he tried, he couldn't quit revisiting those memories. The pleasure, the contentment.

The happiness.

If Bran ever discovered Cael's love for Erith, the ex-Reaper would stop at nothing to use it to his advantage. Already, Bran was fixated on Death. But it would be worse. So much worse.

"You might as well give him what he wants."

Cael's thoughts came to a sudden halt at the sound of

Xaneth's voice. He listened for Bran, but Cael couldn't hear anyone else breathing other than Xaneth. Cael opened his eyes and pinned the Fae with a scathing look.

Xaneth smiled, faking a shudder. "If looks could kill. I don't know why everyone was so scared of you."

"Remove the magic holding me, and I'll show you," Cael stated.

Xaneth cocked a brow as he shook his head. "You think I'm that dumb?"

"Well, you did choose the wrong side."

"Is that right?" Xaneth wrinkled his nose as he briefly looked at the ceiling. "Yeah, I don't think so."

Cael didn't know why he was wasting his time with the Fae. Xaneth only cared about himself. If the Reapers began to win, he'd switch sides again. Why was he so important to the battle then? Why had Cael seen him in his vision?

Xaneth snapped his fingers and produced an oversized leather chair that he plopped into. "I'd probably be acting like a wanker as well if I was in your place. But everyone, even a Reaper, should know when they're beaten."

"Beaten?" Shite, but it hurt to talk, the muscles moving in his head caused the pain to double. "I'm far from defeated."

"Doesn't look that way to me." Xaneth yawned. "Why don't you show me how not beaten you are by healing that rather ugly wound on the side of your head? Or, better yet, break free."

Cael gave him a derisive snort. "Sod off."

"You're not my type, *amadán*."

"Moron, huh? Is that the best you can come up with?"

Xaneth covered his mouth as he yawned again. "Nay. I've got much better. I'm saving them."

Cael rolled his eyes when Xaneth began snoring a few minutes later. His vision had to have been wrong. Xaneth was the worst Fae Cael had ever met. Xaneth might be able to talk his way out of anything, but he was shite when it mattered.

~

Xaneth cracked open an eye as he gave a loud snore. Cael's eyes were closed again. He was cognizant of the fact that the Reaper was fighting the agony of his wound. It showed in Cael's eyes, and even in his voice when he spoke.

It was difficult for Xaneth to look at the side of Cael's head that was nothing but mangled, red flesh. Every once in a while, Cael's body would jerk, every muscle stiffening as pain obviously wracked the Reaper.

Xaneth could only imagine how torturous it was, but through it all, Cael stood strong and firm. Xaneth hoped the Reaper could continue on that path because Xaneth was no closer to getting near Bran than he had been.

It would likely take weeks, if not months, for him to gain Bran's trust, and Xaneth didn't have that kind of time. Listening to Bran and Searlas, Xaneth knew that the trap they were setting for Death and the other Reapers was one that would wipe them all out with a single blow.

The only good thing about all of it was that Bran didn't know about Eoghan or the second group of Reapers. That would come in handy when the battle began. But the others would need Cael.

It took Xaneth hours, but he worked his way closer to Cael to get a better look at the magic Bran used, not only to wound Cael but to hold him, as well. Xaneth intentionally spoke with the Reaper so that those spying on him for Bran could report that he wasn't attempting to help Cael.

If none of this worked, Xaneth would find himself strung up right beside Cael. And that simply wouldn't do.

A murmur of shock could be heard spreading through the Dark around the mansion. Xaneth jumped to his feet and walked to the door to determine what it was.

"Hey," he called to a Dark passing by. "What's going on?"

"Bran has a visitor."

Xaneth shrugged, not understanding what was so

shocking about that. "So?"

"So," another said as he stopped and gawked at him, "I'd say the Queen of the Light is enough to get all of us at the mansion to see if Bran kills her or kisses her."

Xaneth staggered backwards, astonishment and alarm roaring through him. Usaeil couldn't be there. If she saw him. . . .

"Fek," he murmured.

What the hell was she doing there? Surely, not looking for him. The last time Xaneth had seen the queen, she'd been running for her life, afraid that Death was going to kill her.

"Oh, shite."

Xaneth ran his hands through his hair. Usaeil was there to join forces with Bran. The queen didn't like fearing anyone, and like a fool, she believed that she could control Bran with his cock. She was in for a surprise, and Xaneth hoped he was there to see it, but he doubted he would be.

The one thing he was sure of was that Usaeil couldn't see him. She knew his face as both a Dark and a Light, and it was too late for Xaneth to use glamour to alter more of his appearance.

Yet Usaeil's arrival might be just the distraction Xaneth needed to get into Bran's office. Xaneth had enough information to take back to Balladyn, but he couldn't leave until he knew how Bran was stealing Death's magic.

Xaneth owed her at least that much. And maybe, if he were really lucky, he could get Cael free. Then again, that might be exactly what Bran was hoping for.

"Fek!" Xaneth yelled.

This is what happened when he stopped thinking about only himself and decided to help others. Everything got complicated. And he hated complications.

Xaneth glanced over his shoulder at Cael, who was so deep in his thoughts that he didn't know what was going on. Xaneth peered around the door. It was now or never. He stepped out of the building and began following the others.

Since there were too many Dark to be in the house, most shoved to get a glimpse from the outside windows. Xaneth squeezed and pushed his way through the mass of bodies into the house. He kept shouldering his way through the Dark toward Bran's office.

Unfortunately, that was also the direction everyone was facing. Xaneth paused for only a minute. He might not be able to get what he was looking for, but he could find out what was being said between Bran and the queen.

Once Xaneth was outside the office, he flattened himself against the wall near the door and listened. The other

Dark were all whispering so loudly that Xaneth couldn't make out what was being said inside.

With a frustrated sigh, he shifted and moved behind two rows of Dark. He was half-hidden if Usaeil should look his way, but now he had a view of both Bran and the queen. The fact that Bran had left the door open for everyone to see Usaeil spoke volumes.

They talked in low tones. Usaeil flirted outrageously, while Bran appeared almost disinterested. Xaneth watched them for over forty minutes before he realized there was a section of Bran's desk that he returned to again and again. It was done unconsciously as if something were there that he needed to touch.

Or protect.

An eternity later, Bran and Usaeil finally stood, sharing a drink of whisky that the Dark disbursed. Xaneth nearly veiled himself, but he remembered at the last minute that it wouldn't do any good. The others would see him, and that would just bring more attention to himself.

He melted into the shadows as the Dark slowly walked past, each wanting their own look at Usaeil. Then, to his surprise, Bran and the queen walked from the office. His aunt, the woman who had destroyed their family and taken the throne, came within inches of him.

But her attention was on Bran, so she never noticed it was Xaneth.

Long after they were gone, Xaneth stayed where he was. When the last of the Dark were gone, he casually walked into Bran's office—only to find another Fae already there.

The Dark stared at Xaneth. "What are you doing here?" he demanded.

"I could ask you the same."

With a loud snort, the Dark said, "You're new to the army. I doubt Bran trusts you enough to be in here."

"For all I know, you could be the one he mistrusts," Xaneth returned.

The Dark shrugged one shoulder. "I suppose our only recourse is to both remain to keep an eye on each other."

Xaneth saw how the Dark kept looking at the spot on the desk that Xaneth had seen Bran touching. He made his way toward the piece of furniture, his gaze on the rows of books behind it.

Once there, Xaneth leaned back against the desk and tried to discreetly feel what was hidden.

Suddenly, the Dark was before him, his red eyes narrowed. "Who are you?"

"No one of import. Who are you?"

"No one you need to worry about. What are you looking for?"

Xaneth was about to lie when he saw the Dark hastily step away as footsteps approached. Both men froze until the Dark passed by.

Xaneth straightened and raised a brow. "Are you looking for something?"

The Fae hesitated before giving a single nod.

Don't be wrong, Xaneth told himself. "In this area?" Xaneth asked, nodding his head toward the corner of the desk.

"Aye," the Dark replied.

"Why?"

The Dark rolled his eyes. "Lad, I don't have time for this. Either move or call for Bran, but I'm taking that."

That's when Xaneth knew. "You work for Death," he whispered.

The Fae froze, his red eyes searching Xaneth's face. His nod was barely discernable.

Bran's voice reached them, steadily growing closer.

The Fae suddenly grabbed his arm. "Get it and go. Tell Death Seamus is on her side, and I always will be."

Xaneth hesitated.

Seamus shoved him. "Go," he whispered urgently.

Xaneth turned and felt around on the desk. He found nothing at first, but then he felt the soft brush of an enchantment. He pushed his magic through his palms, lighting the spell. Xaneth worked his way through it, and when the magic was finally broken, he found a folded piece of paper.

"Take it to her," Seamus urged, his gaze pleading. "She might need it."

"What about Cael?"

"The only one who can help Cael is Death. And Bran knows it. Go, lad, before it's too late for both of us."

Xaneth clapped his hand on the Dark's arm and teleported out right before Bran walked into the office.

.

Chapter Twenty-three

The plan was good.

Actually, it was the best they had.

Still, Erith knew the odds weren't in their favor.

She stared down at the miniaturized mansion and grounds where Bran was as the others debated various ways to get the advantage. She should be focused, but her mind kept wandering to Cael.

She wasn't the only one who was having a difficult time, though. Kyran had told her the moment she returned that there was something wrong with River. He wanted to go to her, and Erith wished she could let him, but she couldn't.

And this was the main reason she had put the rule in place about her Reapers not having relationships. Because there would always be something that took their concentration away from their mission.

"Death. You're going to want to talk to me."

She jerked, not at the words but at the fact that they came from Xaneth.

"What is it?" Eoghan asked, concern clouding his

features.

Erith swallowed and looked down as she wondered what to do. It could be a trap. Was she willing to go and find out? If it meant learning anything about Cael, then the answer was a resounding yes.

"It's Xaneth."

"I'll take a piece of him," Aisling stated, her eyes flashing with ire. "After what he did to us, it's the least he deserves."

Bradach crossed his arms over his chest. "I agree with Aisling. Besides, I'd love to shove my fist in that wanker's face."

"What did he say?" Daire asked.

Erith looked around at the Reapers. "He said that I'm going to want to talk to him."

"It's a trap," Neve said.

Dubhan twisted his lips. "It could be, but it might not be."

"You're not going," Fintan stated.

Erith cut her eyes to him. While she liked when Cael became dominant, she didn't like it when the others did. "Since when do you tell me what to do?"

"Since Cael isn't here," the white-haired Reaper said. "That's exactly what he'd tell you. And, like the others have already stated, it could be a trap. We need you."

"And I need you," she argued.

Eoghan shook his head. "Fintan's right. I'm going instead."

"You?" Kyran repeated in astonishment before shaking his head. "I'll go."

Erith held Kyran's gaze, knowing that he would want to stop off and see River.

Rordan held up his hands at Kyran's words. "Whoa. Hold up there. Your group might have been first, but we've already dealt with Xaneth. We'll be doing it again."

"Enough," Erith stated, quieting them all. She blew out a breath. "Talin, you and Cathal accompany me to meet Xaneth. If, for even a minute, I think he's betraying us, he dies."

"Finally," Cathal said with a grin.

Talin gave a nod. "Understood."

"You shouldn't go," Eoghan said to her.

Fintan shook his head, his lips pinched. "Nay, you shouldn't."

Erith couldn't be angry about their concern. "I've stayed in the shadows for too long. I began this mess. I'm the one who decided to imprison Bran instead of taking his life. This is all on me. And I'm going to fix it."

She pivoted and walked through the forest to the Fae doorway, Cathal and Talin on her heels. When she reached the door, she turned her head to the side and said, "Be prepared for the worst. I'm going to be veiled, but know that if it is a trap, I won't let Bran take you."

"I say let him try," Cathal said with a smile as his sword appeared.

Talin held out his hand, a blade materializing in his palm. He exchanged a look with Death, then said, "I'm ready."

Erith took a deep breath and released it before she began the long trip from one doorway to the next back to Earth. She led Talin and Cathal to a Fae doorway inside Edinburgh Castle. Before they stepped through, she veiled herself.

Her eyes scanned the room, but she found no one—veiled or otherwise—with Xaneth. The Light Fae was lying on his side on a table, his head propped up on his hand. The fingers of his other hand stopped in the middle of drumming on the tabletop when he spotted them.

He sat up and swung his legs over the side with his hands braced beside him. Xaneth glanced at the rug and said, "She didn't come."

"What did you expect?" Cathal asked with a sneer.

Xaneth jumped from the table to his feet. "Take me to her."

"Not happening," Talin stated. "You tell us what you have, and we'll bring it to her."

Xaneth eyed him in puzzlement. "Do I look like an idiot?"

"Aye," Cathal replied.

"I'm not," Xaneth said over him. "What I have is for Death only."

Talin walked to stand in front of Xaneth. "You're lucky she even sent us. After you sided with Bran, I should kill you where you stand."

Xaneth held out his arms to his sides. "Do it then."

Erith watched everything unfold with interest. She wanted to believe Xaneth, but was it because she saw something in him, or because she didn't want to be wrong about anyone else?

"There's nothing I'd like better," Cathal said. "Trust me on that. The thing is, we have orders to get whatever you have."

Talin moved a foot behind Cathal and adjusted his grip on his sword. "We were also told that if, at any time, we think this is a trap, we should kill you."

A folded sheet of paper appeared in Xaneth's hand. He held it up by two fingers. "This isn't a trap. I have information about Cael, as well as Usaeil's visit with Bran. And, I have this."

No one ever got anywhere by being cautious. As Mistress of War, Erith would've appeared on her own, not veiled with two of her men. While the others had been talking, she'd extended her magic and searched for any

Fae.

Xaneth hadn't lied. He was alone.

Erith dropped her veil and moved between her Reapers. She put a hand on each of them, and, as one, they backed up several steps and lowered their swords.

Xaneth swallowed nervously as he dropped his arms. "I know what you offered me before. I didn't take it because I did what I always do, I thought of myself. But when I went to the Dark Palace, I had a chat with Balladyn. He reminded me that we made a deal. I promised him that I'd find out how Bran was taking the Dark."

Erith lowered her head, knowing full well why Xaneth had sought out Balladyn's help. She decided to remain silent and see what else the Fae had to say.

Xaneth shifted his feet as he caught her gaze with his silver eyes. "I got into Bran's army, but it was . . . nothing like what I thought. I got a glimpse of what he's going to do to this world, and the Fae in general if he takes over. Since I was already spying for Balladyn, I decided to spy for you, as well."

"I didn't ask that of you," she said.

"I know," he hurried to say. "But I also know that you need all the help you can get. Even if it is only me."

Erith cocked her head to the side. "Do you think so little of your worth?"

"I know what I am," Xaneth replied. "I know full well

what I've had to do to survive and remain in the shadows so Usaeil couldn't find me. I did it because I vowed to avenge my family."

Erith glanced at the paper in his hands, but she didn't ask what it was. Instead, she wanted to know something else. "What do you know of Cael?"

Xaneth visibly cringed at the sound of the Fae's name. "He needs to be freed. Soon."

"What did they do to him?" Talin demanded, anger in every syllable.

When Xaneth didn't immediately answer, Erith ordered, "Tell me now."

"Bran used the purple orb of magic on him, twice. Once on his midsection after Cael was taken. The second . . . on the side of his head and face when he refused to call for you," Xaneth said, unable to meet their gazes.

Erith's heart dropped to her feet. Fury and fear mixed within her to create an emotion she couldn't name and had never felt before. She didn't know whether to fight or cry. But she knew one thing—she was going to get Cael. "What did it do?"

"I don't know. Cael isn't healing. Bran said the pain would continue to get worse until he was begging to give Bran whatever he wanted."

Tears pricked her eyes, but she hastily blinked them

away. Now wasn't the time to show weakness. If Cael could endure all of that, then she could stomach listening to—and imagining—all he had been put through. "Cael won't break."

"He's fighting it," Xaneth said with a twist of his lips. "No doubt about that. I don't know anyone else who could have done it. But he's in agony. I'm not sure how much longer he can last."

Erith fisted her hands to keep herself from turning away. As Mistress of War, she wouldn't flinch and worry. She would act. And she was about to do just that. "Do you know where they're keeping him?"

"Behind the mansion. There is that same type of magic Bran used to trap Talin, Neve, and Cael earlier. It's not just around the building, it's holding Cael against the wall."

Erith could feel the rage building within the two Reapers with her. She understood their anger because she felt it, as well. "What else do you have for me?"

Xaneth's lips flattened. "I think Usaeil and Bran have aligned. I couldn't hear what was said, but both looked very pleased by the end of the meeting."

"You saw it?" Cathal asked.

"Bran purposefully left the door open. He wanted the Dark to see Usaeil come to him," Xaneth told them.

Talin squeezed the bridge of his nose with his thumb

and forefinger. "Bloody hell."

"That information is very useful," Erith said. She kept her gaze off the paper, wanting to let him bring it up. "Thank you for sharing it with me."

"That isn't all I have." Xaneth glanced down at his hand before holding out the paper. "I don't know if this will help. Bran had it shielded on his desk, but he touched it often while he was talking to Usaeil."

"Did you look at it?" Cathal demanded.

Xaneth shook his head.

Cathal gave a bark of laughter. "Like I believe that."

Erith reached for the weathered paper. It was old, very old, and there was something about it that looked familiar. She took it and started to unfold it, noting the burned edges. Before she opened it all the way, she knew exactly what it was.

A page from her journal. The same diary she had burned.

Her knees began to buckle. It was Xaneth who got her into a chair as she stared at the page and her own drawing of herself. Her vision blurred with tears as she read the words she had written so long ago.

It was the silence in the room that broke through her anguish. She sniffed and lifted her head to find the three men standing before her, looking anywhere but at her.

"You saved me," she told Xaneth.

The corners of the Fae's silver eyes crinkled in a grin that quickly faded. "Is that how Bran's been stealing your magic?"

"I believe so." She held the drawing out to Talin, who hesitated before taking it.

He read over the page before looking at her. "Your writing?"

Cathal leaned over Talin's shoulder and read. "It's long been said the pen is mightier than the sword."

"A person's own words about themselves hold a special kind of power, far greater than any magic I have," she explained. "I knew that, so when I cast off being the Mistress of War, I burned my journal. I knew when I reached the end of it and hated what I was that it was time to do something. I destroyed that. Partly to try and forget, and partly because I feared the book ever falling into the wrong hands."

"Then how did Bran get a page?" Talin asked.

Erith shrugged. "I wish I knew. I didn't watch it burn, but then again, I didn't think anyone was there with me. A mistake I keenly regret."

"What if Bran has more pages?" Xaneth said.

Cathal blew out a breath. "Shite. That could be a problem."

"We'll find out soon enough," Erith said and got to her feet. "It's time to go."

Talin and Cathal immediately turned to follow her. When she reached the Fae doorway, she looked back to find Xaneth staring out the castle window to the city below.

"Aren't you coming?" she asked.

Xaneth turned to look at her. "I'm not a Reaper."

"If you stay on this realm, Bran will find you, and he'll tear you to pieces."

"Maybe."

Cathal shot him an irritated look. "Don't be an arse."

Erith tried again. "You've helped me. That makes you one of my army. Unless you want out altogether."

"No," Xaneth said with a quick shake of his head. "I definitely want to fight Bran."

"Then you'd better come with us."

Xaneth strode to them but stopped and said, "I almost forgot. When I went for the paper, there was a Dark there trying to get to it."

Erith's heart sped up excitedly. "Who?"

"Seamus."

She smiled, happy knowing that she hadn't been wrong about him. "I knew he wouldn't betray me."

"He told me to bring it to you. He said he served you and always would. I barely got out before Bran returned to his office."

Erith's smile died as she realized that Xaneth was

telling her that Seamus might very well be dead. She put a hand on Xaneth's arm. "Thank you. When we go for Cael, we'll also go for Seamus."

It was Cathal who led them through the doorway this time. Erith was next, with Xaneth and then Talin bringing up the rear. It was nice to have Xaneth with them, and she wished she could tell Cael that they had another ally. And that his vision had been right.

Soon, she would be able to hold him again. To kiss and touch him.

To tell him of her love.

If you're not too late.

She ignored her thoughts and concentrated on knowing that Xaneth may very well have brought her the item that had allowed Bran to take her magic and her essence.

As soon as she was sure, she'd be able to face Bran on the battlefield and end this nonsense once and for all.

Chapter Twenty-four

His limbs were tangled with Erith's as they lay upon her bed, spent from hours of lovemaking. Cael smiled, utterly content.

The grin wavered as a twinge of pain developed. It grew, the stinging sensation expanding until it wracked his entire body. Cael opened his eyes to find Erith looking at him.

He wanted to ask for her help, but the words wouldn't form. Concern filled her lavender depths. She rested a hand against his cheek and whispered something that he couldn't make out. Then, her image began to fade.

Cael grabbed hold of her, trying with all his might to keep her with him. If she stayed, he could handle any amount of torture, any pain. If only he had her.

Erith evaporated into mist that leached through his fingers, floating upon the air to disappear entirely. He wanted to follow, to find her and hold her once more. It was pain that had turned into a storm of agony that kept him immobile—that kept him locked in unimaginable torment.

The wrongness of the entire situation made wrath swell inside him like a tsunami. He bellowed against the injustice, against the Fates or gods or whoever tried to keep him from Erith.

While he raged like a madman inside his head, still unable to move, he realized that none of it was real. It was just a dream.

His anger vanished, replaced by a soul-sucking sadness that made his fury turn to despondency. Cael had lost himself in his mind to get away from the pain, but the agony followed him even to his happiest memories, twisting and warping them so that he had nowhere left to go.

There was only the relentless, merciless throbbing.

Gradually, Cael became aware that he was no longer alone in his prison. He wanted to revert back to his memories, but he remembered that he was a Reaper. He served Death, and until his last breath left his body, he would continue to gather information for her. One way or another, he would get Erith what she needed to beat Bran.

Cael focused on the words, picking out two distinct voices. Male and female. Bran's laugh made Cael want to lash out at the ex-Reaper, but it was the woman's voice that made his blood turn to ice.

Usaeil.

His entire focus centered on the duo until their words became clear.

"I'm telling you," Usaeil said, "this isn't the Reaper who was in my chamber."

Bran blew out a breath. "There are seven Reapers in all. This is only one of them, but he is the leader."

"The one I spoke to had an authoritative air about him."

"They all have that," Bran said with a snort.

There was a brief pause before the queen demanded, "I want to see his eyes."

"His eyes?" Bran asked in confusion. "Why?"

"Because the one I spoke with didn't have regular Light eyes. There was no pupil. In fact, his eyes looked like liquid silver."

Cael bit back a yell when Bran's fingers clamped on his injured jaw and jerked his head up. "Open your eyes."

Cael grinned despite the pain and lifted his lids to stare at Bran. "You know my eyes."

"But the queen needs to see them."

Usaeil walked closer, her gaze narrowed as she looked him over. "No. That's not the one I talked to."

Bran's lips twisted in anger as he yanked his hand away. "It doesn't matter who it was. They're all going to die."

"No one breaks through the spells and wards in my castle, in *my* chambers," Usaeil stated petulantly, "and gets away with it. I'm going to gut this Reaper."

"If he was a Reaper," Cael said, taking in Usaeil's all-white ensemble. She tried to hide what she really was with clothes and glamour, but he knew the truth.

The silence that followed his statement made Cael inwardly do a little jig. If he couldn't fight Bran, he could at least make things difficult. And that's exactly what he was going to do.

In a blink, Bran was back before him. He yanked on what remained of Cael's hair and lifted his head, causing pain to cut through him. "Are you calling the queen a liar?" Bran asked.

Cael slid his gaze to Usaeil. "If the shoe fits."

He was prepared for the orb of magic that Usaeil slammed into his stomach, doubling him over. Seeing the anger that tightened her features was worth the pain. A punch in his jaw from Bran quickly followed the queen's magic.

"Who did you send to the Light Castle?" Bran questioned.

Cael looked his way and smiled through the blood that filled his mouth. "No one."

"He's lying," Usaeil replied.

Bran's nostrils flared, his gaze never leaving Cael. "He'll protect his Reapers to the very end."

Cael let them talk. Inside, he was smiling. Bran still

didn't know about Eoghan, and that meant that advantage was still in place. If only Cael could let the others know that. If they found out that Usaeil was with Bran, they might assume that she knew who Eoghan was and tell him.

Cael's thoughts halted when Usaeil spoke.

"I'm going to send my Hunters out for my nephew," she said. "It's long past time that the final member of my family is wiped away. You might want to be on the lookout for him. He uses glamour to appear as a Dark, but worse yet, he worked with the Reapers."

Bran's lips flattened. "Only Reapers work together."

"Not this time."

Bran shrugged. "I've my own betrayer I'm looking for. He took something from me that I need back."

"I can send my Hunters after him for you," Usaeil offered.

Cael frowned when he heard a third person in the room snort. He turned his head to find Seamus beside him, held with the same magic as Cael. Sweat dripped from what was left of the Dark's face. One eyeball moved and briefly met Cael's gaze.

Without a doubt, Cael knew that Bran had used his purple orbs of magic on Seamus, and if the Dark appeared that bad, Cael could only imagine how he looked.

Seamus coughed, blood dripping from his lips as he

returned his attention to Bran. "You can look all you want. Xaneth is long gone."

"That's not possible," Usaeil screeched as she glared at Bran. "You had him? You had Xaneth?"

Bran cut her an offended glare. "Xaneth joined my army before betraying me. You never said the name of the Fae you wanted. How the fek was I to know the Dark I now look for and your nephew are one and the same?"

Usaeil threw up her hands in disgust. "This is just great. What did he take from you?"

"Something he'll never get back," Seamus said with a laugh.

Cael looked at the Dark, hoping against hope that Seamus and Xaneth had somehow stolen whatever it was that Bran had been using to syphon Death's life.

Hope erupted into outright glee when Seamus shot him a smile before winking with his good eye.

Bran let out a bellow of anger and threw volley after volley of purple orbs at Seamus until there was nothing left of the Dark but a splatter on the wall.

"No one betrays me," Bran stated, his chest heaving from exertion. His gaze moved to Cael. "Don't think I haven't missed the optimism in your eyes. I want you to cling to that pitiful feeling so that I'll get even more gratification when I yank it away."

"I know you'll kill me," Cael said. "But you've lost your

treasure. The one thing you had over Death is gone. You had the opportunity to end her, but you prolonged her torment for too long, and now she has the upper hand again. You'll never win."

Usaeil put her hands on her hips as she came to stand beside Bran. "The hell he won't. He has me."

"You?" Cael said with a laugh. He instantly regretted the action because of the pain it caused, but it was worth it to see the queen's frown. "Death has already judged you. You think you've escaped the Reapers? You're wrong. So very wrong."

Usaeil crossed her arms and raised a brow, not quite hiding her worry. "Then why haven't you come for me?"

"Death has something special planned just for you." Cael had no idea what Erith intended to do with the queen, but he'd heard enough from her to know that it would be something big.

"Don't listen to him," Bran said to Usaeil. "He's trying to get under your skin. Besides, once I take over as Death, you'll be judged again."

Usaeil raised a black brow. "How do I know you aren't lying?"

"We made a pact," Bran answered.

"To fight the Reapers and Death together. My army is at the ready, waiting for my call."

Bran faced her, looking bored. "That pact also had the

part where I would back your play to merge the Light and Dark Fae together. Or did you forget that bit?"

"No," Usaeil said with a bright smile. "I just wanted you to say it again."

"We bound it through magic, Usaeil. Neither of us can break our word."

Cael looked between the two. He should've realized that Usaeil would join Bran, but he hadn't entertained that thought since he'd been so focused on stopping Bran from getting whatever it was he was after.

Now, Cael really wished he had Rhi there to help him. All he had to do was call her name, but he wouldn't do it. As Erith had told him, this wasn't Rhi's fight. It might very well get the Fae killed, and Death had plans for Rhi.

Usaeil motioned to Cael with her hand. "I'm tired of looking at his grotesque form. Kill him."

Bran raised a brow at her. "Are you giving me orders?"

"I am queen," she said.

"Not of me."

Usaeil rolled her eyes. "Of course, I am. You're Light Fae."

"Sweetheart, I've not been a Light since I became a Reaper. You seem to have a habit of not remembering things. I told you, a Fae stops being either Light or Dark when they become a Reaper."

Unfazed, Usaeil shrugged. "You were a Light once.

That makes me your queen."

Bran stalked to her, backing her up, and making her trip twice until she met a wall. He held her gaze, silently staring at her for a long minute. "I can kill you right here. One blast of my magic, and everything you've worked so hard for will be wiped away. I won't have anyone, especially a female, telling me what to do ever again. Do you understand me?"

"All you had to do was say that," Usaeil said with a seductive smile as she put her hands on Bran's shoulders.

Bran shoved her arms away and backed up a step. "Remember who has the power."

"That isn't something I'll forget," she answered icily before stalking out of the room.

Cael watched as Bran put his hands on his hips and stared at the wall, deep in his own thoughts. No doubt Bran was trying to come up with another way to take Death's magic, but that vulnerability was a mistake Erith wouldn't make again. She'd correct it once Xaneth got her whatever it was he had taken from Bran.

If Xaneth went to her.

And if Erith or the other Reapers trusted him.

Shite, but this was a mess of epic proportions.

The only thing that made it better was that Death could become the powerful entity that Cael knew she was. That would mean the end of Bran once and for all.

"You think you'll get out of this alive, don't you?" Bran said as he faced Cael. "You won't. I'll make sure of that."

"I've no such illusions."

"That's shite, and you know it. You'd do anything to get back to Death and your Reapers."

There was no use arguing with Bran, especially when he was right. Instead, Cael shifted the conversation. "If I were you, I'd run. There's nowhere far enough you can go that Death won't catch you, but you've got a head start."

Bran suddenly laughed. "Do you think I didn't plan on this happening? You know me better than that, Cael. I have a contingency plan in place that involves Death believing she's won. She'll come with the Reapers, just as I want her to do." Bran paused, his smile widening. "That look you're wearing right there, the despair and fear I see, that's what I've been waiting for. You should've believed me when I said this was the end of the Reapers."

"The supreme art of war is to subdue the enemy without fighting."

-Sun Tzu, *The Art of War*

Chapter Twenty-five

"That's how Bran has done it?" Daire asked, eyeing the folded piece of paper.

Erith looked at it and nodded. She opened it, showing the others the page from her journal. "I wrote and drew this, and I believed I'd destroyed it."

She crumbled the paper in her hand, enjoying the satisfying feeling of destroying what Bran had held over her. Flames erupted from her palm, devouring the sheet until it was nothing more than ash.

Dusting off her hands, Erith looked at the Reapers. It was odd not to see Cael's face, but he wasn't the only one missing. She'd given Kyran permission to make a quick trip to River. If he couldn't get his head straight, he would be useless in battle.

"Somehow, Bran found that paper," she continued. "Reading it gave him power over me, allowing him to take my magic and my life force. But that's over now."

"We hope," Baylon said.

Dubhan nodded. "What if there are more?"

"It's a chance I'll take," she stated.

Eoghan blew out a breath. "It's a big chance."

"I think there was just the one," Xaneth said into the silence that followed. "You should've seen the way Bran kept it near him. It was cloaked right there on his desk."

Erith glanced at the Fae. He stood apart from the others, as though he felt he didn't belong. A few years ago, she would've agreed, but Xaneth was one of the few who had kept the Reapers' secrets. No matter how she looked at it, he was an asset and, more importantly, an ally.

She should've known that one of them would piece together the chance of extra pages, but she'd wanted to keep it to herself for as long as she could. As it turned out, that was a very short period of time.

"I wish I could tell you that Bran had just the one page. I wish I could tell you that I know for certain the others are gone. But I can't," she told them. "When I set the diary on fire, I walked away when I should've remained to make sure it was completely destroyed. So, aye, there's a good possibility that Bran has another page."

Fintan's lips compressed tightly.

Having just returned, Kyran shook his head as he walked up. "That's troubling."

Erith smiled sadly. "Eoghan's Reapers haven't had a run-in with Bran, but they've witnessed his attacks. The rest of you,"—she paused and looked at Xaneth—"each has your own stories to tell about Bran. You know how crafty he is, how sneaky."

"Aye," Baylon murmured.

"But I know more than you," she continued. "I know just how devious he is. I know that it would be just like Bran to suspect that I'd send in a spy to search for what he's using. Then Bran could subtly show where the item was hidden and sit back and wait to see who took the bait."

Xaneth blew out an irritated breath. "You've got to be fekking kidding me."

Erith held Xaneth's gaze a long time before she gave him a reassuring nod. "My guess is that Bran let the page be returned to me for two reasons. One, so he can find out who the spy is, and two, to give me a false sense of security."

"So you'd believe he couldn't take any more of your magic and you'd attack," Aisling said.

Erith smiled. "Exactly. If I didn't know Bran as well as I do, I'd have fallen for that trick. The fact he believes he's smarter than everyone else will be his downfall."

"What's the plan, then?" Bradach asked.

Erith slid her gaze to Eoghan. "We use the ace up our sleeve."

Talin shook his head. "But Usaeil knows about him."

"Does she?" Erith asked with a quirk of a brow and the hint of a grin.

Eoghan smiled knowingly. "I never told her my name."

"She does know you're a Reaper," Xaneth pointed out.

That made Erith grin. "True, and that's what she'll reveal to Bran. It doesn't matter what they do to Cael, he'll never tell them anything."

"It's another gamble, but I'm in," Eoghan stated.

Aisling finished one of the many braids on her head and said, "Me and the boys are as well."

Rordan opened his mouth but hesitated. The guys looked at each other before nodding in agreement. Aisling rolled her eyes and sighed loudly.

"I want to help," Xaneth interjected.

Death looked at him. "Good, because I'd planned on that."

He bowed his head before crossing his arms over his chest as he widened his stance, satisfaction in his gaze.

Erith created a 3-D miniature of the mansion and grounds using magic. She motioned Xaneth over. "Where is Cael being held?"

The Light quickly walked to her side and pointed to the building at the back of the property. "There."

"Bran will have dozens of guards," Talin pointed out.

Xaneth nodded. "There are six sentries, but that's not what you need to worry about. It's the magic. The only way anyone can come and go in that building is if Bran has given them access. And . . ." Xaneth said, drawing out the word when Aisling started to talk. He held her gaze a second before looking to Erith. "As I mentioned before, Cael is being restrained by that same magic."

"I'd hoped we could get to Cael first and get him out, but Bran has made sure we can't." Erith licked her lips as her mind raced with different scenarios. And everything came back to one. "We can't get into the mansion or even onto the grounds without alerting Bran. That means he's going to get what he wants."

"Which is?" Dubhan asked.

Xaneth shook his head ruefully, and his lips twisted briefly. "Exactly what he wanted when Bran tried to get Cael to call for Death—a face-off."

"I'm going to give it to him," Erith said before anyone could say a word.

Fintan shot her a disapproving look. "Have you lost your mind?"

"He wants me," she stated. "Bran wants to drag Cael before me, taunting me with how he's gotten rid of Eoghan and is about to kill Cael."

Neve tapped the blade of one of her knives against her nail. "And with his attention on Erith and the rest of us, Eoghan and his Reapers could come from behind and attack."

"I like the sound of that," Cathal said with a smile.

Erith shook her head. "The only way I kill Bran is if

there's no other way for him to take my magic. I've got to talk to him long enough to see if he'll try to take more."

"And Cael?" Talin asked.

Erith didn't have an answer. She wished she did. She'd searched for one, hoping against hope that she wouldn't fail Cael. But she wasn't so sure.

Baylon jerked back as if her silence had slapped him. "You can't possibly be thinking of allowing Bran to kill Cael."

"Absolutely not," she retorted.

But Baylon continued without hearing her. "I know you want us to survive, but not at the cost of our leader. Cael is our brother, he—"

Erith couldn't take any more. The dam on her anger burst, and she pinned Baylon with a dark look, her voice booming around them like a storm. "If that's what you think, then you know nothing of me. I'm not leaving Cael!"

She drew in a deep breath as silence descended around her. Erith dropped her chin to her chest and closed her eyes that were now flooded with tears at the thought of losing her lover. "I'm not going to let Bran kill him."

"We know that," Eoghan said softly from beside her. "Everyone's emotions are running high."

Her palm itched to feel her sword in her hand. She was

tired of talking, tired of planning. It was time for action.

It was time to save her lover from the madman's hands.

Erith lifted her head, hastily wiping away an errant tear. "I'm going to face Bran alone. Alone," she stated louder when Daire tried to argue. "I want him to believe I'm overconfident and that I feel as if I can take him and his army on my own. The rest of you will be there, but far enough away that Bran can't sense you. And you'll be veiled."

She swallowed, her gaze on the rendering of the mansion. "Bran will insult me and goad me. He'll parade Cael before me, asking me what I'll do to save him. What Bran wants is for me to exchange my life for Cael's."

Erith paused and looked up, meeting Eoghan's gaze. There was something in the Reaper's molten silver eyes that told her he somehow knew about her and Cael.

She ignored it and looked around the group. "No matter what is said, no matter what I do, I won't let Cael die. I won't let any of you die."

"We're prepared for it," Fintan said.

Erith slid her gaze to Neve. "After all the verbal barbs have flown, I'm going to call for my sword. When I do, I want you to appear behind the mansion. The Dark know how much Bran wants you, and you'll draw their attention."

"And the rest of us?" Daire asked.

"Give Neve enough time to lure the majority of the Dark to her, then join her."

Talin's brow was furrowed deeply. "Why? We can't kill the Dark, and they can't kill us."

"Because Bran will know it's a ruse, and he won't look twice at any of it," Erith explained. "That's when Eoghan and the other Reapers will join you."

Xaneth ran a hand down his face. "This is madness. How is this going to work? You will have shown your one trump card."

"That's not my trump card. Not to mention, Bran won't notice or care," she said.

Xaneth shrugged. "All right. That could work. What do you need me to do?"

"Oh, you're going to be a nice surprise. Bran is going to expect you to join me first, but we're going to wait until the perfect time."

"And when will that be?"

Erith smiled. "The same time the Reapers join Neve."

Xaneth threw up his hands in frustration and let them slap against his legs. "You still haven't said how we're going to get Cael or how we'll kill Bran."

"I'm taking Bran's life," Erith said, anger churning within her. "I gave him his second chance. It's mine to take away." She turned her head to Eoghan. "Like I should've done when he killed Theo."

Xaneth's eyes widened, impatience on his face as he waited for more. "And the rest?"

"What's wrong?" Aisling teased the Fae. "Afraid you won't get out of this one alive?"

"Oh, I'm fairly certain I'm going to die," Xaneth muttered.

Eoghan leaned close to Erith and whispered, "You *haven't* said how we're going to get Cael or how you'll kill Bran."

She swiped her hand from one side to the other, wiping away the image of the mansion. "Bran's army will continue to rise each time you kill one until I end Bran's life. Cael will be injured and hurting, but he is a weapon unto himself. If I can give him an opportunity, he'll give me the advantage I need to get to Bran."

"Aye, he will," Baylon replied.

Erith knew Cael would. She just hoped that she would be able to handle seeing him, because she could only imagine what Bran had done to him. Between that and holding her sword again, allowing her past as Mistress of War to merge with who she was now, it might prove to be the final straw that crushed any chance of her controlling the person she'd once been.

"We'll fight for however long you need," Dubhan said.

Eoghan gave a quick nod. "Ready yourselves. We leave in ten minutes."

Eoghan remained beside Erith as the others walked away, each going off by themselves to mentally prepare for what was to come.

"We won't leave until we have Cael," Eoghan promised.

Erith faced him. "If I fall, you still save Cael. Return here. There are doorways leading to other galaxies for each of you to start a new life."

"Cael won't leave. You know that. If Bran takes your life, Cael will fight him."

"Then don't let him."

Eoghan snorted. "The only one who has ever been able to control Cael is you. Right now, I'm more worried about you."

"Me?" she asked in surprise. "Why?"

"Are you going to be able to handle it when you see him?"

Erith searched Eoghan's gaze before she nodded. She didn't even pretend not to know that he was referring to Cael.

"I hope so," he murmured. "I'm glad the two of you finally came together, though it took you both long enough. But you can't let Bran have that knowledge. No matter what."

"I know," she replied softly.

Eoghan walked away, and she turned to find Kyran

waiting for her. She made her way to him. "Did you speak to River?"

Kyran swiped a hand down his face. "Cael warned me there might be repercussions to taking River through magic."

"Is she all right?" Erith asked, worry growing with every second.

He shrugged. "I think so."

"Then what's wrong?"

"She was only three months pregnant. The babe . . . oh, hell," he said and glanced away, trying to get himself under control. "She looks like she's ready to give birth any day now."

Erith had been afraid there might be adverse reactions for River and the babe, but she'd hoped she was wrong. "She's not on my realm alone. Is she in any pain?"

"She says she feels fine," Kyran said with a shake of his head. "But I'm nervous."

"Understandably. Can you stay focused?"

His brows snapped together in a frown. "Of course. I'll not let you, my Reapers, or my wife down."

"Good." Erith smiled as Kyran walked away, but inside, her gut churned. This was just another concern added to the insurmountable ones already there.

Chapter Twenty-six

There was no escaping the agony now. It went through every nerve, every tendon, every muscle of Cael's body. He'd locked his jaw, clamping his teeth together in an effort to keep from releasing the bellow that yearned to escape his lips.

Because once he let it out, he knew he wouldn't be able to stop.

The pain latched on to him, sinking into his skin—into his very soul. It occupied every corner of his mind, giving him nowhere to flee, nowhere to get even a moment or two of peace. While he suffered, he knew the magic causing him such distress was getting joy out of every second.

Bran's words came back to Cael. Bran had warned him that Cael would beg to give any information just to make it stop. Cael had thought he was strong enough to withstand it.

He'd been wrong.

All he'd wanted to do was give Erith a chance to win. Cael could only hope that he had succeeded in that. He knew he wouldn't see Erith again. All those wasted years of yearning for her, dreaming of her.

Of loving her from afar.

He'd waited too long to tell her, to show her how he felt. But even one night with her was better than nothing. Still, he wished he would've told her that he loved her.

"If only you could see yourself."

Cael was in no mood for another confrontation with Bran, but there was no getting away from it. He opened his eyes and glared at his nemesis.

Bran's brows rose on his forehead in mock concern. "Are you in pain? Your body is twitching and jerking as if you're being tortured. And I do think I just heard a tooth crack from the way your jaw is clamped." Bran laughed while rubbing his hands together. "The only thing that would make this better is if I had Eoghan next to you, but knowing he's dead is enough for me."

There were so many replies Cael wanted to voice, but he didn't even try. It was all he could do to hold back the shouts of pain. He knew how badly Bran wanted to hear it, and Cael didn't want to give him the satisfaction.

Bran walked closer. "You thought you'd gotten rid of me. Oh, I saw how furious you and Eoghan were that Death stopped you from killing me. I know if you'd had your way, you would've choked the very life from me. I saw then what you couldn't. Erith will always rule you. *You*," Bran said with a look of disdain, "a man, bending to the whims of a woman."

Cael wondered what Usaeil would think if she could hear him. Then again, she was as mad as a box of frogs. And Bran wasn't far behind her. The two were perfect for each other. One would betray the other quicker than Cael could blink.

"Did you actually think by giving yourself up to save your precious Reapers that you'd somehow survive?" Bran shook his head, confusion lining his face. "I thought you were smarter than that. You've been too long under Death's thumb. All this time, you should've been thinking for yourself, not waiting for her to tell you what to do. You could've ruled the Fae, but you were too trusting. Look what that got you? Betrayed and dead, only to become a Reaper."

If only Cael could make Bran shut up. He couldn't stand the sound of the ex-Reaper's voice. It grated on his nerves worse than the magic boiling through him.

Bran shrugged indifferently. "Your stupidity left the door open for me. Perhaps I should thank you for that. Eoghan, too. If he'd let the past go, he would've given you a run for your money to lead the Reapers. Now that's a fight I would've loved to see. You against Eoghan. I wonder who would've won."

Cael's body went hot, then ice-cold as the pain doubled once again. He squeezed his eyes closed, wishing he could grab his head in a futile effort to stop the stinging that seemed to wrap around his head again and again.

"Oh, you're nearly gone," Bran said softly. "I really wanted Death to see you like this. I wonder if she'd show any emotion. I bet th—"

Cael didn't care why Bran stopped talking, only that he did. It was becoming impossible for Bran's words to register in his mind. And Cael knew he wasn't long for this world.

This time, Erith wouldn't be beside him, touching him as life faded from him. Nor would she be there, offering him another chance at life.

Dying sucked. But Cael would gladly go through it a million times if it saved Erith and the Reapers. Because Bran couldn't be allowed to win.

One minute, he was being held upright against the wall. The next, Cael's face slammed against the floor. The impact radiated the soul-sucking pain through him like undulating waves slamming into a cliff.

A yell formed in his throat and rushed upward, but he clamped his lips tight so that only a low moan was heard.

"Get up!" Bran bellowed as he yanked Cael to his feet.

There was an urgency to Bran's voice that Cael hadn't heard before. As well as a note of unsurpassed glee.

There could only be one reason for that—Erith.

No! The word reverberated in Cael's head as Bran took

hold of his arm and pulled Cael alongside him. The manifestation of the purple orb's magic through his body meant that Cael's muscles were locked, refusing to do as he commanded. He fell three times, planting his face in the grass and then the gravel before two Dark hauled him up and looped his arms around their necks.

His mind was yelling for him to fight, to do *something* to help himself and Erith, but once more, his body betrayed him. He didn't want Erith to see him like this—vulnerable and helpless—no matter the reason.

Cael got his fingers to twitch, and the excruciating pain of those small movements made his knees buckle. Had the Fae not been holding him, he'd surely have fallen once more.

When the Dark followed Bran toward the house, Cael managed to yank his arm away from one. It would have been a triumph of sorts had his vision not gone black at the edges from the agony, causing his muscles to lock and contort again.

The two Fae laughed and grabbed him. Cael fought not to lose consciousness. He needed to see and hear what was going on between Bran and Erith. Maybe, just maybe, if he were really lucky, he might be able to give her an edge over Bran.

He'd take anything over being a burden—or the one who caused Death to lose it all.

Before Cael knew it, they'd passed through the house and were walking toward the front lawn. Bran had been smart picking the location. It was far from any road, with acres of rolling landscape all around.

Bran stopped atop one of those hills, and seconds later, the Fae hauling Cael finally and mercifully halted. Cael's eyes hastily scanned the area until he found Erith standing on top of the next peak, looking radiant and commanding—and every inch the Death that he knew and loved.

Cael didn't know what hurt worse, his body or his heart. He couldn't take his eyes from Erith. Her midnight locks were pulled away from her face in several tiny braids that stopped at the crown of her head so that her beautiful tresses hung down her back.

She had on the boots from Rhi, as well as black pants that looked like a second skin. The black coat she now favored billowed about her legs in the breeze but was buttoned up her front so he couldn't see the rest of her outfit.

He knew the instant her gaze moved to him. There was a subtle stiffening of her body, so slight, others would likely miss it. But he'd been looking for it.

He must look as bad as he felt. He hated that Erith saw him like this. His body wasn't healing, and with what the magic was doing to him, he knew his time was short. If only he could have a moment alone with Erith. He'd finally tell her the words that he'd only dared to whisper in his head.

I love you.

"I knew you'd come," Bran told Erith with a smirk.

Death looked bored, but Cael knew the fire within her. She was furious and hiding it—for the moment. She was smarter than Bran gave her credit for. If she was here, it meant she had a plan. Cael couldn't wait to see it in action.

"You have one of my Reapers."

Bran laughed. "Not just any Reaper. I have your favorite."

"I don't have a favorite," she responded.

Cael had known the words were coming, but hearing them didn't make him feel any better. No matter what, Erith had to get the upper hand with Bran. And that meant that she would say and do whatever was necessary to achieve that.

Bran laughed, the sound cold and hollow. "We both know that's a lie. It was so obvious that you cared about Cael more than any of us. You *let* me kill Theo. Just not Cael."

Erith sneered derisively. "I didn't *let* you do anything, you insane maniac. I've told you countless times that I'm not all-knowing."

"Ah, but you knew the instant Cael and I fought, didn't

you?"

Erith's hesitation made Cael inwardly wince. With that little pause, she gave Bran ammunition to use against her. Cael prepared himself because he suspected what was coming next.

"Ha!" Bran shouted as he pointed at her. "Exactly."

Her narrow shoulders shrugged. "You think because I didn't answer that I gave up some information? How . . . childish of you. Aye, childish is the right word. You're acting like some petulant juvenile who believes he didn't get the attention he deserved."

Cael bit back a smile. Bran's silence that followed had even the Dark holding Cael holding their breath. Cael's gaze searched for any sign of the Reapers, veiled or not. The fact that Erith had come alone wasn't a good sign.

Bran glanced at the ground, one brow cocking briefly. "Your mistake was believing that you couldn't be defeated. Then you made matters worse by sharing your power with us."

"There is no *us*," Erith interrupted him. "You're no longer a Reaper."

Bran slowly nodded several times. "I'm something better now."

"Because you took my magic. That's your mistake." Erith smiled then, but there was nothing kind or soft about it. "You've always wanted what you couldn't have.

You were never content with what you were given. Instead, you stole what isn't yours."

"If you want power, you have to take it," Bran retorted.

With a flick of her hand, Erith unbuttoned her coat and let it fall from her shoulders. Her upper body was encased in a black metal breastplate with silver and gold accents along the edges. A smile pulled at Cael's lips when she turned her hand, and the black sword appeared.

Cael quickly looked at his nemesis to find Bran's lips tightened in a flat line of fury. That only made Cael's smile grow—even as it became more difficult to breathe. He urged his lungs to continue taking in air because he didn't want to miss anything.

"I'm tired of talking," Erith stated.

No sooner had the words left her mouth, than a shout behind the mansion went up. Bran's brows snapped into a deep furrow as a Dark appeared beside him and whispered something.

After a tense exchange, the Fae left, and Bran looked at Erith. "Nice maneuver sending Neve. You know how much I want those females. And I will have them. I don't care how long or how far I have to search. They'll be mine."

"That will *never* happen," Death vowed.

"One Reaper—and a new one at that—can't stand against my army. Neve will be alongside Cael in a matter of minutes."

The Dark army's shouts of happiness shifted to cries of war. Cael didn't need to look to know that the Reapers had arrived. And now he knew Erith's plan.

The skirmish at the back of the manor was a diversion. Knowing Death, Cael would bet his last breath that Eoghan and his Reapers were fighting with the others. But Bran would never know that because he couldn't take his eyes off Erith.

It was a brilliant strategy, but Cael expected nothing less from Death herself. The next part would be up to him, though. He had to give Erith the time she needed to attack Bran. Cael sincerely hoped that she had the strength to do it. Otherwise, they were all dead.

Cael drew in a breath and pushed past the pain while forcing his jaw to relax. Everything was taking twice as long as it should, which had him feeling as if he were trying to extricate himself from a tar pit.

The pain clung to him, reminding him with every movement that it was there, waiting to take the last bit of his life away.

"Not yet," he murmured, his eyes locked on Erith.

He'd once vowed to be her warrior, to follow her every command. But his heart had always been hers—and he would suffer the most horrific agonies if it meant that she would be safe.

"Bran!" Cael bellowed.

"Appear weak when you are strong, and strong when you are weak."

-Sun Tzu, *The Art of War*

Chapter Twenty-seven

Erith wanted to cry at the sight of Cael. The magnificent warrior that he was couldn't—and wouldn't—be diminished by the disfigurement on half of his face and head and on his chest. His pain was visible in the way his body jerked, but still, he fought it.

Just as she'd known, Cael had figured out her plan. Even wracked with agony, Cael could still outsmart everyone. Bran's head snapped to him when Cael shouted the ex-Reaper's name. Erith inwardly wept at the pain that simple word must have caused Cael.

It was all that she could do to remain in her spot and not rush to Cael to heal him and offer whatever comfort she could. His skin had a yellow tint to it, and that couldn't be a good sign.

Bran smiled as he faced Cael. "Finally found your balls, huh? What are you going to do? You can't even stand on your own." Bran glanced at Erith and said, "So much for your famed warrior."

There were many reasons that Bran needed to die, but if there had been even a smidgen of mercy left, it disappeared with those words.

Erith's breath locked in her lungs when Cael shoved the two Dark holding him away and took a halting step toward Bran. Cael was unsteady on his feet, his body swaying as he fought with every last ounce of skill and determination to remain standing.

"Oh, I'm tempted," Bran said as he walked closer to Cael. "So very tempted. The thing is, you're about to die. Erith's timing is perfect. I couldn't have planned it better myself."

Erith's mouth went slack when Cael's chest expanded with a deep breath. His chin dropped to his chest while his arms hung by his sides. A soft purplish glow began to form in his palms, growing stronger and becoming a deep purple.

Cael's head slowly lifted, pinning Bran with a furious look. Tension hung in the air, causing Erith, Bran, and the two Dark to freeze as they all waited to see what Cael would do.

Erith smiled then, recognizing the warrior she'd fallen for so very long ago emerging from the pain-ravaged form. Erith started running toward Bran as Cael threw the two purplish bubbles of magic, landing them squarely in Bran's chest. She didn't know how Cael had managed to use the purple magic, but she was glad that he had.

Erith launched herself over the valley. Her sword suddenly vanished from her hand. She jerked her gaze to Cael, to find that he had the weapon and was attacking Bran with it.

She landed behind Cael and immediately took the life force from the two Dark who were about to attack Cael from behind. Then she whirled around to find Bran holding his stomach with one arm and tossing orb after orb of purple magic at Cael with the other.

Cael used the sword to divert the spheres as he advanced on Bran, one step at a time. Erith teleported behind Bran so she and Cael could attack together. She reared back her hand and formed an orb of magic as she glanced at Cael's face.

Fury contorted his visage. His one good eye was locked on Bran, but with one word, Bran stopped Cael in his tracks.

As Cael toppled to the ground, the sword once more appeared in Erith's hand. She turned, slicing her blade at Bran. Just as her weapon hit the spot where he'd been, Bran teleported away.

"Eoghan!" she shouted, knowing that the Reaper would get himself and the others away.

She rushed to Cael, sliding on her knees beside him. "I'm here. I've got you."

"No," he ground out, pushing her hand away. "Get

away . . . from . . . me."

"Cael, I can help."

His eyes squeezed shut from the pain. "Trap."

"I don't care. I left you once. I'm not doing it again," Erith told him.

Death was afraid to move him, so she erected a dome of magic around them that no one could get through—not even Bran. Then she put her hand on Cael's chest.

He moaned from the pain, lost somewhere between consciousness and sleep. She used her magic to push him deeper into that oblivion to help him get away from the pain. It was a chance she took, because she might not be able to get him back.

When his body relaxed, she let herself search for the magic Bran used. She'd seen many things, but never an orb of purple magic before Bran. Erith wasn't sure how Bran had created it, but she had to find a way to reverse it before it was too late.

"I'm here, Cael," she said again, stroking the intact side of his face.

The fact that his body wasn't healing worried Erith the most. So she searched for the poisonous magic. If she thought it would be difficult to find, she was mistaken. It was everywhere throughout Cael's body. In every bone, every muscle, every vein.

Erith then tried to remove it. She stopped the moment Cael cried out in pain.

The sound of laughter made her jerk her head up. Bran stood about a hundred yards away with his hands behind his back, a smug smile upon his face.

"I promised him that you'd watch him die. I don't go back on my word," Bran stated.

Erith got to her feet and grabbed her sword. "Let's finish this. Unless you want to run away again."

"We will finish it, but not until I see this final part."

She glanced at Cael to see that his chest no longer moved. Bran forgotten, Erith dropped to her knees and put her ear to Cael's chest.

He was still breathing, but barely. If Cael were to die, he would do it with dignity, not with Bran watching.

Erith met Bran's gaze. "Don't make me come hunt you."

"I'll be waiting," he promised.

Erith took Cael's hand and teleported them a dozen different places before she brought him to the isle that led to her realm. To her surprise, the Reapers were waiting for her. She met Eoghan's gaze before she got to her feet and moved back.

Without a word, all thirteen of them lifted Cael and walked through the doorway to her realm. She followed, closing the portal behind her. If Bran had set a trap, he wouldn't be able to get through.

The women were there, but their smiles disappeared when they saw Cael. Erith led the procession into her tower and up to her chamber, where they laid Cael on the bed.

Erith stood looking at Cael, lost in her thoughts, enough that it took her a bit to realize that she wasn't alone. Erith turned her head to find Eoghan.

The Reaper pulled his gaze from Cael. "What do you need from us?"

"Nothing."

"We'll be here." Eoghan started to turn away but then paused. "Where did you send Xaneth?"

Erith frowned, having completely forgotten about the Fae once she reached Bran's, but she hadn't seen him since they returned to Earth. "I didn't send him anywhere. He never did his part of the plan."

"I guess he decided not to help us."

She shook her head. "I don't think he'd do that."

"Then where is he?"

"Send a couple of Reapers to see if they can find out where he's at."

Eoghan's jaw worked as if he wanted to say something but couldn't decide whether to voice it or not. Finally, he said, "I'll tell the others."

Erith watched him leave before she turned back to

Cael. He hadn't uttered a sound since she'd tried to pull Bran's magic from him. When she searched him again, the purple power had bound itself to Cael's magic, making the two almost indiscernible.

"Nay," she whispered when his breathing stopped for several seconds before his lungs filled with air again.

She used her magic to try and pull him back from oblivion. When he didn't wake, she slapped at his face, soft taps at first, before she began to hit him in earnest.

"Wake up! Cael, you have to wake up. Please," she begged.

But there was no denying the truth. He was fading.

The tears she had kept at bay began to fall. She crawled onto the bed beside Cael, resting her head on his shoulder as they'd done after making love.

"Bran was right," she said with a sniff. "You were my favorite. I thought I'd kept it hidden, but obviously, not well enough. You were my favorite because I'm in love with you. I should've told you. We finally get together, only to have you taken from me."

She paused, waiting to feel his chest move. When a full minute passed with no stirring, she closed her eyes as tears poured down her face. She put her hand over his heart.

As Death, she had control over a Fae's soul. But when a Reaper perished, there was no coming back. She didn't know why. She'd spent hours trying the first time a Reaper had died, to no avail. Now, she'd lost the one person she'd thought would always be there.

She squeezed her eyes closed and opened her mouth in a silent scream she didn't dare let free. The pain of losing Cael was worse than she could've imagined. She felt as if she were being ripped apart, torn in every direction. The grief was sharp and keen—and a million times worse than any other emotion she'd ever experienced.

With one blow, she had been rocked to her very foundation.

The tears suddenly stopped as she opened her eyes and gave into the wrath that rose up with the force of a volcanic eruption.

Bran had done this. Bran had taken away the only person she'd ever loved. And he would pay.

Painfully.

But first, Erith would spend more time with Cael. She used to lament the time she had. Now, she wished for even a minute longer with Cael so she could talk to him once more. To hear his voice, see his smile, and look into his silver eyes.

She swallowed as the heartache and anguish returned. Mistress of War waited to attack Bran, but for now, she was still Erith. For Cael.

"I will never forget the first time I saw you on the battlefield," she said through her tears. "You were utterly un-stoppable. Every decision you made led your army closer to victory. And your skill was unmatched against every opponent who came between you and success.

"I would watch you for hours, growing more im-pressed each time. I saw a lot of warriors, but none could compare to you. Then, your gaze met mine that day. I couldn't move, couldn't speak. You were everything. For the first time, I'd found someone I wanted to get to know, someone who made me . . . yearn."

She smiled, sniffing. "I spent more time observing you than I have any other being in the universe. I didn't know what I was feeling at first, but it became clear that it was love. Even when I formed the Reapers, I couldn't stay away from you. You pulled me back like a moth to a flame. And did you ever burn bright.

"There's only one other time I've ever been as furious as I am today, and that's when you were betrayed. You, of all people. I should've realized the jealousy of others. That is one emotion I often forget, and one I should've learned by now. To realize that it is partly what drove Bran to turn on us only makes matters worse."

Erith lifted her face to look at Cael. She could almost pretend he was sleeping. Almost. She rose up on her el-bow and looked down at him, blinking through her tears. Then she placed a kiss on his cheek.

"You will always hold my heart, Cael. There is no other for me. I wish I could've been brave enough to do something about my attraction centuries ago. When I think about what we could've had, I—"

She couldn't finish the sentence. The words stuck in her throat. She rested her forehead against his cheek and allowed herself another few minutes of tears. Then she rose from the bed and wiped her face as she embraced the fury and the past.

That first step was the hardest. Erith wanted to rush back to Cael and hold onto the shell of the body despite the fact that his soul was gone. She'd never fully understood why others did such things.

The wailing, the holding onto a body that was cold and lifeless. Now, she knew the heart-wrenching truth of it. And the pain of it all bore down on her shoulders with the weight of the entire universe.

But she stood tall. For Cael. For herself. For the Reapers and those they loved.

Erith walked from the room and slowly made her way down the staircase that lined the wall of the tower. When she finally reached the bottom, she realized how quiet it was. She walked outside and stood listening, searching for the others.

She was drawn toward the lake. As she made her way through the forest, she spotted the couples off by themselves, holding each other and talking.

Then there were the other Reapers. Aisling perched on one of the thick branches that ran along the ground as she absently ran her hand down the silky fur of a fox that sat beside her. Cathal and Rordan stood together in silence, while Bradach, Dubhan, and Torin were by themselves.

It was Bradach who saw her first. His silver eyes searched hers before he frowned and hung his head. Erith kept walking until she emerged from the forest.

She turned and faced the group that now stared at her expectantly, hoping for good news but bracing themselves for the worst.

Twice she tried to form the words. Finally, she managed two. "He's gone."

Chapter Twenty-eight

The words had been spoken, but Erith still refused to accept that they were true. In her mind, Cael was merely resting until his body could heal.

She would believe that until the end of time.

Her grief was so overwhelming, so devastating that she was crushed under the weight of it. Cael, a warrior unlike any other, had been taken by someone like Bran.

With her sorrow so great, even the birds had stopped singing. The entire realm reflected her emotions. She knew the others were waiting for her to say something, to give them a command, but she couldn't think about anything but Cael.

Of losing him.

Tears burned her eyes, tears that she was determined not to shed. She'd cried as she lay beside Cael. That would have to be enough until she defeated Bran.

But her decision mattered little to the anguish within her. One tear fell, then another and another until she lost count. They streamed down her face to drop from her chin to the ground. She couldn't control the violent, desperate emotions swirling and churning within her, and then she stopped trying.

She let them coalesce, melding together until she could no longer tell grief from anger. They were bound together, wrapping around her like armor.

Erith drew in a shaky breath as the last tear fell. She finally looked at the others. Thirteen Reapers stood before her, stoic and armed, and among them were five women. Their sadness shifted to wrath, for they too had lost a devoted Reaper and friend.

"You're going to need someone to take Cael's place," Cat said as she wiped the tracks of tears from her face. "I ask that you allow me to fill it."

Erith was so used to refusing such requests that it was on the tip of her tongue before she realized it. Then she paused and looked at Fintan. He gave a nod, telling her that he supported his woman's decision.

"We would be honored," Erith told her.

Ettie licked her lips, her eyes red from crying. "We all want to join you."

"This realm is sealed, and I'll seal it again when we leave. But I'd feel better if there was someone here who could defend the others if things go badly," Erith said.

River, looking healthy, rubbed her swollen belly as she cried softly. "I'm a burden."

"Nay," Kyran told her. "This child is a gift. We all want

to protect it, as well as you."

Erith walked to River and laid a hand upon the woman's stomach. The baby kicked her palm as if it knew she was there and was proving that it was fine. Erith gazed into River's pale blue eyes. "I'm not losing any more of you. Do you understand?"

River nodded, her tears coming faster.

"Do you understand?" Erith asked as she looked around the group. "Bran will not win. He's taken Cael, and nearly killed Eoghan. It's time this stops."

Aisling lifted her chin, her lashes spiked from crying. "What about Xaneth?"

"If he's with Bran, I'll strike him down myself," Erith stated. "If he's not, then once Bran is dealt with, we go looking for him."

And she had a pretty good idea of where to start—the Dark Palace.

Thea sighed loudly. "We all know my mother hates Xaneth. She wants him dead. He's the only one who has a claim to the throne."

Erith looked at Fintan. "You and I are going to take a quick trip."

Fintan didn't ask where, just walked to her side and waited.

"We won't be long," Death told Eoghan.

Fintan fell in step beside her as she strode to the doorway. Once they were through it, she took his arm as she teleported them.

When they arrived at their destination, she looked at Fintan as she dropped her hand. "Nothing to say?"

He shrugged as he crossed his arms over his chest. "I had a feeling you'd bring us here."

"Call him."

Fintan held her gaze as he said, "Balladyn."

In a blink, the King of the Dark walked through the double doors of his quarters. He stopped short when he spotted them. "What the fek?"

"I don't have time for pleasantries," Erith told him. "I'm going to put this as succinctly as I can. We're fighting Bran, and there is a good chance he'll win. He's formed an alliance with Usaeil."

Balladyn softly closed the door behind him as he glanced at Fintan before returning his red gaze to Erith. "I can't say I'm surprised. Usaeil always thinks of herself. But why are you coming to me?"

"You know why," Fintan stated.

Balladyn shrugged. "I want to hear it."

Erith was past the point of being insulted. "Bran has forcibly taken your people. He's changing them, giving them additional magic that increases their power. We want you to join us."

"And if I don't, Bran will come for me?" Balladyn

asked, brows raised.

"Don't forget Usaeil." Erith took a step toward him. "Do you know who I am?"

There was a long silence before the king bowed his head.

"Say it," she ordered.

His lips were tight as he said, "Death."

"Bran escaped the prison I sent him to for betraying and killing his fellow Reapers. He is my responsibility. Unfortunately, he got the advantage by syphoning not only my power but my life force, as well."

Balladyn raised a brow. "You look fit to me."

She produced the black sword, which made the king take a step back. "You know this?"

"It belonged to the Mistress of War."

Erith glanced at the weapon. "I've been known by many names. Mistress of War and Death are but a few."

Balladyn's red eyes darted to Fintan, who gave a nod of confirmation. "Why are you telling me all of this?"

"Because I believe Usaeil has taken Xaneth."

"So?"

Fintan dropped his arms. "Xaneth is the queen's nephew."

Balladyn nodded slowly. "He told me. If he's gone, no doubt Usaeil has him."

"He was helping you as well as us when he joined

Bran's army," Erith explained. "We attacked Bran, and Xaneth never showed as he was supposed to. Since Usaeil and Bran are working together, I believe she saw him and took him."

Balladyn ran a hand over his jaw. "So what do you want me to do? Help you fight Bran, or look for Xaneth? I can't do both. And if I know Usaeil, she'll either kill Xaneth quickly, or she'll hold him, torturing him at her leisure."

"I'm banking on the latter. Xaneth helped us a few times. I owe him. But before I can repay that debt, I need to take care of a bigger problem."

"Bran," the king said. His gaze returned to Fintan. "I want the truth from you. You are the infamous assassin, Fintan, aren't you?"

When Fintan's red-rimmed, white eyes met hers, Erith gave him a nod of approval.

Fintan drew in a deep breath. "Aye."

"I knew it," Balladyn said with a grin.

Erith caught the king's gaze. "I know what Usaeil did to you. I know how you fought the darkness for centuries before you became Dark. I know how deeply you love a particular Light Fae. I also know of your partnership with Ulrik. More importantly, I know how badly you want to deliver revenge not just to Usaeil for her betrayal, but to Bran for taking your people. Because, despite being a

Dark Fae, there is still good within you, and you want to protect your people—something no other King of the Dark ever did."

Balladyn turned away to walk to where his library was. "Don't try and make my decisions sound like they were good. I know what I am now. I've accepted it and embraced it. My path with the Light ended the moment Usaeil left me for Taraeth to kill."

"If Taraeth had, I would've offered you a spot with the Reapers."

Balladyn's head jerked to her.

Erith smiled softly. "Every Reaper is a warrior who was betrayed and killed."

Balladyn's eyes moved to Fintan before he nodded slowly. "A part of me wishes I had died that day."

"Your story wasn't finished," Fintan said. "It still isn't."

Balladyn closed one of the books and looked at Erith. "I'll join you."

"You should know that by joining my army, you've now chosen a side. Bran has ignored you, but he'll come straight for you now. His men won't be able to kill you, but he will. Just as I can kill his army."

"I don't understand," Balladyn said.

Fintan motioned the king over. "I'll explain it all."

The three teleported near to Bran's mansion. Fintan kept ahold of Balladyn, keeping him in the Reaper's veil so the king could see who was veiled and who wasn't.

"Eoghan," Erith called when they arrived.

One by one, the Reapers appeared. None seemed surprised to find the King of the Dark with her. Instead, all were anxious to fight.

Erith watched as Balladyn grinned knowingly when he saw Cat walk to Fintan before their fingers intertwined. Then Death looked at each of them.

"We're sixteen to their thousand," she told them. "I suspect Bran has more of my diary pages to take my power, and in order to combat that, I need to feed this," she said as she lifted her sword.

Cathal grinned widely, his red eyes crinkling at the corners. "Yes."

"I'm going straight for Bran's men." Erith then looked at Balladyn. "To kill them."

"I don't want my people to die, but if it saves more from being taken and Bran from gaining control, then do it," Balladyn said.

Erith thought about Cael. She'd believed that he would be standing beside her in this final fight. When the grief threatened to overwhelm her again, she turned toward the fury instead. Only when it was over, and Bran was no longer an issue, would she let herself mourn.

Then, she would give Cael a proper funeral worthy of a great warrior, Reaper, friend, and lover.

Rordan lifted his sword. "For Cael."

"For Cael," the others replied.

Erith touched her sword to the rest and whispered, "For Cael."

Balladyn produced a sword and moved it with the others, nodding to Erith.

She lowered her weapon and stared at the mansion over the undulating landscape and through the branches of the few trees that dotted the grounds. "Xaneth said the main group of men were at the back of the mansion. That's where we'll go. It won't take long for Bran to notice us. He'll try to take my power, and then he'll come for me."

Erith scanned the faces around her and smiled. "I forgot who I was. Eoghan pointed me in the right direction while Cael helped me remember. I feared becoming Mistress of War again, but now, I welcome the fury and bloodlust that used to rule my world. Now, I won't stop until Bran is dead. I will avenge Cael."

Without another word, she teleported right into the middle of a group of Dark. A battle cry roared from her lips as she swung her sword.

The moment the blade tasted the blood of the Dark, it sang for more. Every Fae she encountered had Bran's face, and she hacked each one to bits, working her way through the crowd, satisfaction rising as she grew stronger.

When a dozen or so Dark jumped on her, she slammed her hand upon the ground, sending a blast of magic that took out over a hundred of Bran's men with one blow.

Erith spun as more Dark came at her. Out of the corner of her eye, she saw her Reapers, Cat, and Balladyn fighting. But she was waiting for her target.

And Bran wouldn't be long in coming.

Chapter Twenty-nine

Erith.

It was the first thought that went through Cael's mind when his eyes snapped open. He was ... different. He could feel it in his bones and in his blood. Even in the depths of his soul.

He sat up, recognizing the room immediately. His hand went to the side of his head that had been ravaged by Bran's magic, but instead of mangled flesh, he found himself restored. Same when he checked his chest.

Cael rose from the bed and began searching for Erith. He found Jordyn on the stairway. Her turquoise eyes widened at the sight of him, her jaw going slack.

He waited for several minutes for her to wipe the surprise from her face. Finally, he asked, "Where's Erith."

Instead of answering, Jordyn backed down a few stairs before she turned and raced to the bottom.

Curious about her reaction, Cael went looking for a mirror. He understood when he stared at his reflection. It was him, everything the same—except for his eyes. They were no longer silver but burned a dark purple.

He lifted his arm, looking at his hand as he felt his magic coursing through him. It was stronger than even what he'd had from being a Reaper. Cael also sensed a darkness within the power that hadn't been there before.

And that's when he knew. The magic Bran had used to kill him had somehow melded to his own. Why wasn't he dead, though?

"You're alive."

He turned at the sound of Ettie's voice. She stiffened when she saw his eyes. But he didn't have time for that. "Tell me what happened."

Thea came up behind her and cautiously approached him. "You died."

Confusion and anxiety swarmed him. Cael searched his memories. He thought of fighting Bran, remembered feeling such rage at the fact that his friend had turned on all of them in such a way. And then Cael recalled wanting to fight Bran to save Erith.

He'd used the magic poisoning his body, turning it into a weapon and welcoming it as he went after Bran. And he remembered holding Erith's sword. Then everything had gone dark. He'd comprehended then that he was dying. Still, Erith had tried to help him. Her attempt to remove Bran's magic had been excruciating. Then he'd felt her hand on his face, right before he became unconscious.

That was the last thing he recalled before waking up.

Cael looked around for some sign of Death. When he realized that the only ones he saw were Reapers' wives, a sinking feeling wrapped around his stomach.

He stalked to the women. "Where is Erith?" he yelled.

"She went after Bran," Ettie said.

Cael had to get to her. He wasn't going to let her fight his nemesis alone. Cael belonged beside her. He always had—and he always would.

Cael shoved past the females and jumped over the side of the stairs to land several floors below.

Above him, Thea shouted, "Erith sealed the doorway."

He didn't care if he had to build a new one, nothing was keeping him from going to his woman. It didn't matter how many Reapers were with her, he was supposed to be by her side—and that's exactly where he would be.

He'd worry about how he had come back from the dead later.

When Cael reached the doorway, he put his hand on it and felt the magic ripple beneath his palm. Erith's magic. The portal was sealed, preventing anyone from coming or going. He gave a little push, and the magic opened enough for him to walk through.

Once on the other side, he added his own power to the seal before teleporting to the mansion. He was met by the beautiful sight of the chaos of battle. He smiled, and his fists clenched with the need to join in.

His gaze immediately found Erith as she plowed through dozens of Dark at a time. The dead lay littered at her feet. Cael then found the Reapers but was shocked to not only see Cat alongside Fintan, but Balladyn also joining in the fray.

It looked like Erith had found the unknown Dark Cael had seen in his vision. It had never entered his mind that it might be Balladyn, but it made sense.

Cael spotted Searlas making his way toward Erith, but he didn't worry. She spun elegantly and sliced his head from his body before returning to the four others she battled.

Cael began making his way to her when he did a double-take and found Bran standing off by himself. The ex-Reaper pulled something from the inside pocket of his jacket and opened it.

Cael didn't know what it was, but he instinctively knew that it was how Bran had been stealing Erith's power. He didn't wait around for Bran to begin reading. Cael teleported directly in front of him and grabbed the pages, engulfing them in flames.

"Nooooooo!" Bran bellowed as he staggered back in disbelief. He watched the remnants of the paper float in the air before he looked at Cael, shock reverberating over his face and bearing. "There's no way you're alive. No one could survive what I did to you," he whispered in alarm.

Cael grinned tersely. "I did."

Bran swallowed and gathered himself, his gaze narrowing in determination. He held out his arms, forming two purple orbs of magic. "Perhaps you need another dose."

Cael leaned to the side as one bubble flew past him. He grabbed the second with one hand and, spinning, tossed it back at Bran, who moved before it could hit him. But Cael didn't mind. He had something special planned for Bran.

The ground rumbled beneath Cael's feet. He looked toward Erith to see that she had used a magical explosion that obliterated the Dark around her. She shifted, her gaze landing on him.

The surprise that went through her was evident in the way she jerked at the sight of him. Cael wanted to go to her, to hold her, but he couldn't, not until this business was finished. He returned his attention to Bran and walked toward him.

"This is a trick," Bran exclaimed.

Cael held out his arms. "No trick. This is me."

"Your eyes."

"That's not the only thing changed."

Purple flames leapt from his palms with just a thought. The astonishment on Bran's face was worth every minute of suffering Cael had endured.

Cael sent a wave of magic at Bran. It landed square in his chest and sent him tumbling backwards. But Bran was never one to go down easy. In a blink, he was back on his feet and sending more orbs at Cael.

Despite Cael's attempt to avoid them, one landed on him. The pain he expected didn't come. In fact, he felt ... stronger. He looked down at his thigh where the orb had landed and watched his body heal instantly.

"What did she do to you?" Bran demanded to know.

But Cael knew the answer. Death hadn't done anything. He had. Or rather his love for her had altered his body to accept the poison and turn it into something good, something powerful.

Bran shook his head. "It doesn't matter. All I need is for her to die."

Cael's eyes narrowed. "You'll never get to her."

"Won't I?" Bran asked with a confident smile right before he whispered something.

There was another explosion, one of wood and brick. Cael's head whipped to the side to see a form rush from what was left of the building that had been his prison. Running straight for Erith was none other than Seamus.

"You didn't really think I'd let him just die, did you?" Bran taunted. "You keep forgetting that I have her magic. I can't believe she's had such abilities and not used them.

I can share my power with the living, and I can make my own Reapers. But I don't give them a choice. I make them return."

Cael watched as the movement of Erith's blade hesitated when she spotted Seamus. Every instinct told Cael to go to her, then he remembered that she was Death, she was Mistress of War. She didn't need his help.

He slid his gaze to Bran. "Your mistake is forgetting who she is."

"That's exactly what I'm counting on," Bran boasted.

"The beast within her was dormant. You woke it. What's worse for you is that no matter how much power you took from her, it was never enough to defeat her."

Bran cocked his head to the side. "You talk as if you love her."

"I serve her. That's the difference between you and me. I never coveted her power."

"Because you had her favor!"

"Enough," Cael stated calmly. "You wanted to fight me, well, here I am. Come and get me."

"Gladly."

The two circled each other while Erith made her way through the Dark with the Reapers, Cat, and Balladyn lending their help. Cael wasn't worried about Erith anymore. He'd felt the force within the sword, and with every life she took, she was regaining everything that

Bran had stolen.

Bran was the first to make a move. He rushed Cael, their bodies meeting in a bone-crushing collision. Cael knocked Bran's hands away, but not before two knives found their way into Cael's gut. Bran stepped back and threw two more that landed in Cael's chest.

~

Erith's first thought was that she was seeing things, but there was no denying that it was Cael she saw fighting Bran. Elation—and a little worry—consumed her. She wanted to be there with Cael, but there were so many Dark. And the more she killed, the more the odds turned in her favor.

She used another blast of magic to wipe out those around her. It was a good, easy way to take out several at a time, but it also drained her. Since she had no idea whether Bran could still take her magic, she needed to be cautious and save everything for her coming battle with him.

That is if Cael didn't kill him first.

Each time she glanced their way, it looked as if Cael were winning. As strong a warrior as he was, he couldn't equal the magic that now ran through Bran. Erith frowned as she saw the two Fae locked in combat. Or at least Cael *shouldn't* be able to hold his own with Bran. Yet, somehow her lover was doing just that.

A board slammed into Erith from behind an instant after she heard a loud explosion. She turned and saw something—or someone—running straight for her. Instinct had her readying herself, her sword on a downward arc.

Then, she saw the face. Her arm halted as she recognized what was left of Seamus. His face and body bore the same types of marks that Cael's had, and she realized quickly that the kindhearted Dark she had come to trust was no longer there.

Seamus crashed into her, knocking her breath from her as he slammed her into the ground. His fist came at her face, and Erith managed to turn her head at the last minute.

The ground shook from the hit. She calmly slammed her knee into him, sending Seamus over her head. But he grabbed hold of her and flipped her with him. Now, she was on top and able to land a few blows to his face.

"Seamus, stop!" she ordered.

But the creature she battled was something other than Seamus. Whatever thoughts she had of trying to save him vanished. The only way to stop him was to kill him.

Erith flipped her sword in the air and caught it by the pommel as she plunged it downward. Instead of landing in Seamus's chest, it sank into the ground.

That fact barely registered before she was yanked backwards by her hair. The sword dropped from her hand, and when a Dark tried to pick it up, the weapon vanished.

Erith would've smiled if she didn't have Seamus pummeling her in the side of the face with his fist. She reached back and latched on to his calf where she poured magic into him, splintering his bones.

His cry of pain loosened his hold, which gave her the chance she needed to get free. She called for her sword and spun before she lunged, pushing her blade into the spot where Seamus's heart was.

She winced as her sword found its mark. The life drained from Seamus, and she saw a spark of the Dark she'd known. He smiled at her, relief clear on his face before he fell over.

Her heart hurt for what she'd just had to do. She slowly pulled her sword from him and watched the blood drip from the end onto the grass. Erith looked at her allies, who each still battled the Dark. Not once did they stop, not once did they give up. As many times as the Fae came at them, they fought back.

Balladyn gripped a Dark's head and yanked it clean off before tossing it away. He wasn't the only one. Fintan kept close to Cat, but with her magic, the Dark couldn't get near her to do any damage.

And Death's Reapers . . . they were a fighting force that should terrify anyone who thought to go up against them. She'd never been prouder of the Fae she had asked to join her.

Erith swung her head toward Bran just as Cael pulled one of the four knives from his body. It was time to take down the one who had begun it all.

Chapter Thirty

Cael's gaze moved from the blade in his hand to Bran. He felt his wound heal, the skin and muscle meshing together without so much as a mark to show that anything had marred him.

"That should've killed you," Bran said, backing up a step.

Cael merely smiled and withdrew another of the knives. "You mistake me for what I was. I'm something . . . more . . . now."

Bran was so intent on Cael that he never noticed that Erith was now behind him. Cael wanted to look at her, to peer into her lavender eyes and tell her that he'd returned for her, but he kept his gaze on Bran. No matter what he wanted, no matter how badly he hungered for Erith, Bran's reign of terror would end, now.

"No," Bran said with a shake of his head. "This can't be happening. I planned this out perfectly."

Cael pulled the third and fourth knives from himself, dropping them to the ground as he advanced on Bran. He had no need of the weapons. The magic within him had always been potent—even before he became a Reaper—but now, now it was a hundred times stronger.

And he wanted to unleash it on Bran.

Yet he held off. This was Erith's kill. She needed to extinguish Bran so that it could erase what she believed were her past mistakes.

"Did you honestly believe you could triumph over Death?" Cael asked.

Bran's nostrils flared as his shock morphed to anger regarding Erith. "She had the ability to rule the universe, and she didn't take it."

"Everyone has a role. Hers is more important than subjecting every being to a regime. You'd know that had you understood her at all. Instead, you were too wrapped up in the power being a Reaper gave you."

"Power?" Bran replied with a bark of laughter. "There was no power in our position. She told us what to do, and you, like Eoghan and Theo, hurried to carry out all her little duties, simply because she didn't want to dirty her hands."

Cael watched Erith in his peripheral and found her smiling, her gaze on him. It was everything he could do not to shove Bran aside and yank her against him, devour her mouth in a kiss that showed her exactly how much he loved her.

"You could've been the best of us," Cael told Bran.

"You could've done so much. Instead, you sought to take advantage of your influence over others. You coveted what wasn't yours. And you betrayed your family."

"You were never my family!" Bran bellowed. "I left mine behind when I was killed."

Cael crooked an eyebrow. "Do you think you are the only one who had a good life before they were betrayed?"

Bran shook his head. "It doesn't matter what I say. You'll always have some kind of answer that supports Death and her views. I'm tired of talking."

"Finally, something we can agree on."

The words weren't even completely out of Cael's mouth before Bran attacked. Cael saw it all in slow motion. Bran's rage contorting his face, the orbs of magic in each hand as he reared back his arms, and then the spheres flying through the air at him.

Cael leaned first one way and then the other, letting both bubbles slam into him. He smiled at Bran's fury of having forgotten that his magic made Cael more powerful.

It wasn't until Bran stepped back in utter astonishment and ran into Erith that he realized that someone was behind him. Cael slid his gaze over and met lavender eyes that had haunted him for thousands of years.

Erith could've killed Bran at any time while he and Cael spoke, but whether she was Death or the Mistress of War, Erith didn't stoop to something so cowardly. It's what set her apart from the others. What made her special, superior.

Unexpected.

Astonishing.

Bran slowly turned and came face-to-face with Death.

"Hello, Bran," Erith said calmly.

Bran shifted to keep both Cael and Erith in his line of sight. Then he glared at Death. "What did you do to Cael? How did you save him? I always knew he was your favorite, and this proves it."

"I did nothing," she replied.

Cael took a step toward Bran. "She didn't. You gave me the ingredients. Then, you put me in a situation of your making. That gave me all I needed to mold them into what I needed."

Cael didn't realize the truth of the words until they were spoken. Because that's exactly what had happened. His drive, his love for Erith had pushed him past the point of death to continue to fight for her, to love her—leaving him to become whatever he was now.

"It's over," Erith told Bran.

Bran snorted loudly and raked his gaze angrily down her body. "It'll only be over when I breathe my last, and that's not going to happen."

"A fool, as always," Cael stated.

Bran looked from one to the other, his eyes narrowing. "You're lovers!"

Cael glanced at Erith as he smiled, thinking of the joy he felt when he held her. "Aye."

"If only I'd pieced that together sooner," Bran said more to himself than anyone else.

Erith's sword burst into gold and silver-tipped onyx flames that danced along the curved blade. "You took my magic. You took my life force. You took Cael. There wasn't anything you didn't take from me."

Bran sneered. "You forgot Eoghan."

"Nay, she didn't," Cael said and pointed to where Eoghan fought with the others.

A trace of dread filled Bran, seeming to knock some of the wind out of his sails as he turned and looked over his shoulder to see not only Eoghan but another six Reapers.

Cael shrugged, his lips twisting. "We might have forgotten to let you know that Eoghan returned and that he's now leader of a second group of Reapers."

Bran's head snapped to Death. "Another group?"

"I never said there was only one," Erith replied.

"This isn't how this was supposed to happen!" Bran bellowed in outrage.

~

Whatever hope Erith had that Bran would realize he was beaten and surrender died with his yell. She'd seen his betrayal, sat by him as he died, and welcomed him into the Reapers. No one was perfect, and that included her. Bran had made poor choices that had led to his betrayal, but she'd seen that sliver of good in him.

The problem was that it was just a smidgen of good with darkness all around it, suffocating the light inside him until it was no more. And Bran welcomed the darkness. That was the difference between him and everyone else who battled it.

The strength Bran had gained by being a Reaper had led to him desiring more. He was never content to be in the shadows, hiding what he was—or carrying out Death's commands.

She'd seen his discontent growing, but she'd thought he would see the futility of his ambition and settle into being a Reaper. None of the others had the aspirations Bran did, and she hadn't known how to handle it.

Ignoring the problem and thinking it would work itself out had been the wrong course of action. Her decision had cost the lives of four Reapers. She hadn't wanted to lose another—whether by Eoghan's and Cael's hands, or her own.

Yet she'd made another wrong choice by tossing Bran into the Netherworld. The prison realm had only stirred his anger and revenge. Now, here she was, back in the same place she'd been before she threw Bran into the Netherworld.

A part of her wanted to give him the option of imprisonment, but that was a mistake she wouldn't repeat. Enough lives had been disrupted and taken as a result of that choice.

The moment she passed judgment on Bran, the flames on the sword leapt higher. It was another side of her new self, and she quite liked it. Though she wasn't going to enjoy taking Bran's life.

"You think I'm going to go down easy?" he taunted her.

She gave a shake of her head. "I would expect nothing less of you."

Erith didn't need to ask Cael to stay out of the fight. She knew he would by the way he stood, watchful and ready. There was much she wanted to say to Cael, but she couldn't stop looking at his eyes that had gone from silver to the darkest purple she'd ever seen.

Cael had always had a presence about him, but there was something different now. Something more commanding, fiercer—if that was possible. And it made her stomach quiver with delight.

Erith focused on Bran. Despite his egotistical, narcissistic nature, Bran was a formidable opponent. And even with the majority of her power returned, she didn't take her victory for granted.

They came together in a clash that sent sparks flying through the air. His magic met her sword as they came face-to-face, and she saw the determination in Bran's eyes. He would never relent or give up. If she were going to win, she needed to take his life.

"You don't have the stomach to kill me," Bran stated with a laugh.

Erith shoved him away, bending backwards when an orb came at her face. She watched it fly over her, narrowly missing her.

She landed on her back and kicked up to her feet before she spun, swinging her blade down toward Bran. Erith gritted her teeth and kept advancing, sending Bran stumbling backwards as her swings grew stronger and harder each time.

Memories of her past life as Mistress of War returned with a vengeance. The battlefields, the cries of the dying, shouts of anger, and the air heavy with blood and death.

But it didn't overwhelm her. She took control before the bloodlust consumed her. For the first time, she truly realized who she was.

She was the Mistress of War.

She was Death.

She was both—stronger, wiser.

And accepting of both halves of herself.

She released a battle cry as she leapt into the air, grabbing the pommel of her sword with both hands as she plunged it into Bran's chest on her descent.

The world went quiet. The Reapers and Dark Fae ceased fighting. The only sound was Bran's ragged breaths. Erith belatedly noticed that his hands gripped her arm.

Her gaze followed her arm to the black blade that had pierced his heart. She looked into Bran's face then, hating the misery swelling within her.

"You have been judged," she stated.

Bran coughed as his legs crumpled. He fell back, taking her with him. Cael was beside her in an instant as she rose up on her knees. A moment later, the Reapers—along with Balladyn and Cat—surrounded them.

"You won," Bran said with a little laugh.

Erith drew in a breath as Cael's hand rested on her shoulder. "There's no joy in taking your life. I will admit, you were a formidable enemy."

"I nearly bested you." Bran smiled, blood filling his mouth.

"You were one of my Reapers, Bran. You were family. This was the last thing I wanted."

He swallowed, his breathing becoming shallower. "But

it had to be done."

"I hope you find peace, wherever your soul goes."

Bran held out his hand. Erith didn't hesitate to take it. When Bran died, she would be beside him, but she wouldn't offer him new life. This time, he would be gone forever.

He smiled, a tear leaking from the corner of one eye and falling into his black hair. "Don't ever let anyone else get that close to killing you."

"I won't," she promised.

Tears gathered in her eyes when his lids closed for the final time. Then, he disintegrated to ash and floated away on the breeze. Erith watched it for a moment. Then she gasped in shocked surprise as all the magic Bran had stolen from her returned.

She felt alive, renewed. And formidable. She lifted her face to look at the others.

After so much anger between Bran and herself as well as the Reapers, she had expected his death to be many things. She hadn't been prepared for the anguish she felt over having to kill him. And by the look on everyone else's face, neither had they.

Erith climbed to her feet and faced Cael. The tears that fell down her face were ones of relief at finding him alive, tears she hadn't allowed herself when she was in battle.

Erith moved closer to him, peering up into his dark

purple eyes. "You came back."

"For you." He reached up and gently caught one of her tears on his thumb.

"Good."

His smile was slow as it widened across his face. Then his arms reached for her, pulling her close before his mouth was on hers, kissing her as if he hadn't tasted her in forty lifetimes.

She melted against him, no longer caring who saw them or who knew about their relationship. Because she loved Cael.

And the world needed to know it.

Chapter Thirty-one

A new chapter was beginning. Cael knew it without the words having to be spoken. Bran was vanquished, and everything could go back to what it had been for the Reapers.

Or could it?

He didn't want to be relegated to someone Death communicated with simply because he led the Reapers. He wanted her. *All* of her.

Cael cracked open an eye to find everyone around him wearing shocked expressions, except for Balladyn, Eoghan, and Fintan. Balladyn, for his part, had no idea of the inner workings of the Reapers, nor did Cael know why the King of the Dark was with them.

As for Eoghan, the smile on his friend's face said it all. And Fintan also seemed pleased.

Cael reluctantly ended the kiss. He and Erith stared at each other, smiling for a long time in silence. It was on the tip of his tongue to tell her of his love, but he'd rather do it in private instead of with everyone watching.

Erith's gaze dropped and slid to the side as she too became aware that they weren't alone. "There is much we need to discuss," she whispered.

He nodded.

Then, with a sigh, she moved to his side. In an unexpected change, she slid her fingers against his. He curled his hand around hers and shot her a grin. Together, they faced the others, but there were only smiles and nods of agreement.

"I didn't see that coming," Cathal stated.

Rordan grunted. "You wouldn't see a mountain coming at you."

"I, for one, am happy," Baylon said.

Daire couldn't stop smiling, while Neve was nearly bouncing, she was so happy. Kyran gave them a wink, and Fintan bowed his head, though there was a twinkle in his eyes. Cat clapped her hands together softly, also smiling. Talin let out a loud whoop, and soon, everyone was cheering.

Eoghan walked to them. "It's about damn time. Now, want to tell me how the hell you're alive and why your eyes are purple?"

"Aye," Dubhan agreed. "I'd like to know that, as well."

In the next heartbeat, the cheering halted as they all looked expectantly at Cael—Erith included.

Cael shrugged, unsure where to begin. He turned his head and locked gazes with Erith. "I knew how badly

Bran wanted me, and I counted on that when I handed myself over in exchange for him letting Talin and Neve go. I knew he'd want to use me to get to you."

Erith's hand tightened on his.

"I don't know what kind of magic he used or how he was able to call it forward, but I've never felt pain like that before," Cael continued. "He told me it would slowly get worse, and it did. At the end, when you came, I couldn't even stand on my own. Breathing hurt so badly, I held my breath to ease it."

He paused and glanced at the others. "I knew when Erith showed up that there was some kind of plan. As soon as I heard the battle at the back of the mansion, I assumed you hoped I'd give you a way to get to Bran."

Erith's smile was watery as she nodded. "I knew you'd figure it out."

"I didn't have much time left before the magic Bran used killed me. I was prepared to give my life for you to succeed." He turned his attention to the others. "All of you."

Torin frowned irritably. "And?"

Cael's gaze lowered to the ground as the painful, furious events returned to his mind. "I used the last of my strength to get free of the Dark holding me. Then there was nothing but anger." He slid his gaze to Erith. "And love. I couldn't fail you or the Reapers. I wouldn't. Somehow, I took the magic that had been killing me and used it to help myself. It meshed with my own power, and that's what allowed me to get to Bran."

"But you fell," Erith said. "Bran said something to you, and you fell over."

"He tried to call the magic back to him, and it was enough that it halted me. That gave him the time to see you beside me as I lay dying."

Erith faced him. "I tried to take his magic from you. That caused you to cry out in pain, so I brought you to my realm. Where you died."

He cupped her face, rubbing his thumb across her cheek. "When I woke up, I felt . . . different."

"With the purple eyes, I'd say you are," Neve said.

Aisling's head tilted to the side. "Bran syphoned Death's power then used it on Cael, who then managed to shift and change it to meld with his own. Am I the only one who sees the purple eyes as a part of Death?"

"I'll be damned," Eoghan murmured.

Cael frowned when he looked at Erith. "Is that true?"

She put her hand on his chest and closed her eyes. A second later, they flew open as she gaped at him. "Yes."

"Equals," Bradach said into the silence that followed.

Cael and Erith shared a smile. Movement out of the corner of Cael's eye caught his attention. He lifted his head in time to see Balladyn take two steps away from the others before he teleported away.

"We need to get this place cleaned up before any mortals come," Eoghan said.

Cael couldn't believe that he'd forgotten about the Dark that remained. The magic Bran had shared with them was gone, but they knew who the Reapers were. And that meant they needed to die.

Erith's face was grim as she stepped away from him to retrieve her sword that was lying in the grass. Cael moved in front of her when she straightened.

"They can't know of us," she said.

Eoghan quickly said, "Xaneth did and didn't speak. Balladyn knows."

While everyone looked around for the King of the Dark, Cael caught Erith's gaze. "Enough have died today."

"I agree, but do you know what will happen if others know who you are?"

"Aye," he said with a nod.

"Then you understand why those who have survived need to die."

Cael turned to look at what was left of the army. "They've not run away. Do you know why? Because they fear you. Us. They know we can find them."

"They can still tell others about all of this," she argued.

"That's a possibility. But what if they couldn't?"

Her brows snapped together. "What do you mean?"

"It's a wild idea I'm taking from the Dragon Kings. What if we erase their memories of everything having to do with Reapers?"

Erith's lips parted as her gaze moved between him and the Dark. "I don't know if I can do that."

"I can."

Lavender eyes slid to him as her lips turned up at the corners. "What are you now? I feel the strength of your magic. It matches mine."

"I'm the one who is going to help you solve this problem."

They strode hand in hand to the army. Erith stood beside him as Cael used his magic to wipe the Darks' minds of anything having to do with Reapers or Death before sending them on their way.

When the last Fae left, Cael and Erith returned to the others. When Kyran commented on Balladyn's disappearance, Erith waved away his words.

"I'll be visiting Balladyn soon," she said. "But there is something I want to say first. I kept the two groups separate for many reasons. I was lucky that it all worked out in the end and we were able to work as a team."

"Family," Daire corrected.

Cael liked the grin that pulled at Erith's lips. She was happy. Truly happy. And that elated him.

She pressed her lips together. "For too long now, I've

been alone on my realm. It's a vast place, and quite honestly, the most perfect realm there is. But I realized that it's also the ideal spot for all Reapers to live."

Cael was as astonished as the rest of the group. He raised a brow when Erith looked at him, but she just winked, a sparkle in her eyes that he'd not seen before.

"No one can get into my realm that I don't want," she continued. "The Halflings who have found love with the Reapers will be safe there."

"You mean . . . for all of us?" Kyran asked.

Death smiled. "Your child will grow up safe from the Dark, Kyran."

To Cael's shock, Kyran pressed the pad of his finger against the corner of his eye as he ducked his head, obviously overcome with emotion.

"Go to River," Cael told Kyran.

Erith nodded. "Aye, and Eoghan, take your Reapers to their new home. All of you go and rest. You deserve it."

In seconds, they were alone.

Cael wanted to reach for her, but he was suddenly nervous. So much had changed, especially himself. It blew his mind that he was equal in power to Death. It wasn't something he'd wanted, but now that he had it, he found he liked it. A lot.

She took a few steps away before she faced him. "My heart was ripped out of my chest when I thought you'd died."

"Don't you understand? I'd die a million times for you."

A tear fell down her cheek. "The only reason I didn't crumble into a thousand pieces was because I intended to make Bran pay for taking you away from me. I spent thousands of years hiding what I felt for you."

"And what do you feel?" he pressed, hope nearly bursting from his chest.

She stared at him for a long moment. "I love you. Don't you know that?"

His legs ate up the ground between them as he rushed to her, pulling her against him. "You've had my heart from the first moment I saw you. I became a Reaper just to be near you, just to be able to see you. I never, in my wildest dreams, imagined you'd be mine. I love you for everything you are—and everything you'll be."

"Cael," she whispered before bringing his head down to meet hers.

The kiss was explosive, fiery. He couldn't stop kissing her. After believing he'd never hold her again, he never wanted to let her go. She felt right in his arms, and in his heart.

"You can't be a Reaper," she said between kisses.

He pulled his head back and gawked at her. "What?"

She laughed and smoothed her hands over his face.

"First, I want you with me. We are going to be together, right?"

"Of course."

"Then you can't lead them."

He hadn't thought of that, but still. Not be a Reaper? He'd been one far longer than he'd lived as a Fae.

"And," Erith said, pulling his thoughts back to her. "There's the little thing of your new magic."

He grinned. "I'm still getting used to it."

"I don't understand how it happened."

"Are you upset by it?"

It was her turn to be taken aback. "Never! Finally, I have someone who matches me in every way. I'm overjoyed by it."

"Good," he said and tried to kiss her again.

But she put a finger between them so that he kissed that instead of her mouth.

He frowned in frustration, his lips twisting. "What? I want to kiss you."

"I'd like to do much more than that, but before we get to that—because we both know it'll be days before we come up for air—we need to talk."

"Isn't that what we're doing?" he asked with a grin.

She eyed him. "In a manner."

"Can we do it now? Because I can't stop thinking of stripping you out of your clothes and having my way with you."

"Fair enough," she murmured seductively. "Are you going to be okay giving up being part of the Reapers?"

"I'll have you, which is what I really want."

She quirked a brow. "That won't be enough after a while, and you know that."

Damn the woman for always being right. "I suppose you have an idea."

"I do."

"Care to share it?"

"Later," she replied slyly.

Cael held her tighter. "I've been yours to command since I saw you that first time. I'll always stand beside you."

"Take me home and make love to me."

He didn't have to be told twice.

Chapter Thirty-two

DARK PALACE

Something was different. Balladyn couldn't quite figure out what it was, but it was definitely . . . *something*.

He hadn't hesitated in helping the Reapers, though he couldn't quite figure out why that had brought him such joy. No doubt it had something to do with dealing a swift and decisive blow to both Bran and Usaeil.

Balladyn's hatred of the Light Queen ran deep. Not just because of what she'd done to him, but because of what she continued to do to Rhi. And her aligning with Bran couldn't go by without some sort of reaction.

He quite liked how the Reapers responded—and that he was involved.

But why had they asked him? More importantly, what did that mean for him? Especially now that he not only knew their faces but also Death's.

He slowly walked through his chambers to his bookshelves. Balladyn halted by the table and stared down at the books laid out that had any mention whatsoever of the Reapers.

It was Rhi's question about them that had sent him delving into the tomes and researching the mysterious group and all the different stories involving them.

Balladyn closed a book and left his hand on top of the cover. He had so many questions, but in all honesty, he was a little afraid to ask them. After all, he'd seen with his own eyes just what Death could do. And it far surpassed his own power as king or even what Usaeil could muster.

There was a part of him that wondered if it was a good sign that Death had visited him. Did it mean that he might become a Reaper?

He gave a shake of his head. Balladyn knew well what he was—and all that he'd done. He wouldn't allow himself to think that something so grand could be within his grasp. Maybe once. But not now.

A stirring in the air around him caused him to stiffen. "I expected I'd get a visit," he said and lifted his head only to meet the red-rimmed, white eyes of Fintan.

The Fae lifted a brow. "Did you now?"

"Aye. Just not from you."

"Oh, I've no doubt Death will want to have a little chat."

It had taken one betrayal to make Balladyn wary of everyone, including Fintan. "Then why are you here?"

"To tell you that I'm glad you joined us."

That took Balladyn aback. "I wasn't expecting gratitude."

"We asked for your help, and you granted it. Of course, we're thankful," Fintan said with a confused frown. "You've been mired too long in deceit and treachery to recall what it's like to be a part of something good."

"I remember." That was the appalling part of it all.

Fintan eyed Balladyn for a long, silent moment. "Aye. I think you do. Why did you leave the battle?"

"The words exchanged by Death and Cael were private. Or, at the very least, for other Reapers. It seemed an intrusion to stay."

"You should've remained. You helped us win, and you should be part of the celebration."

Balladyn shook his head. "Thank you, but I have other duties."

Fintan glanced down as he sighed. "I saw you watching Death and Cael. You long for such a relationship. With Rhi."

He didn't bother asking the Reaper how he knew such a thing. There were no doubt many things the Reapers knew about him. "It has always been her. There is no other for me."

"Then hold onto her." Fintan looked around, taking in the entire upper floor of the palace. "I see a big difference between you and Taraeth." He turned his head to Balladyn. "You care about the Dark. Taraeth never would've joined us. He would've sent you in his stead, just to be sure he wasn't killed."

Balladyn nodded slowly. "That's true. So, Death would've asked Taraeth to join her?"

"Nay," Fintan stated implicitly.

That made Balladyn smile. "I didn't think so."

"Death's decision to come to you wasn't done lightly. You need to understand that. Everything she does is done after careful thought and consideration. She weighs every variable, thinks through all the different outcomes."

Balladyn wasn't sure what to say to such a statement. He stared at Fintan as the Reaper's words sank in. "Do you like being a Reaper?"

"Very much. It isn't an easy job, but I've found somewhere I belong with others who have become my family."

Balladyn came around the table to stand opposite Fintan. "What happens to me now? In all my research on the Reapers, I never found any definitive answers. Now, I not only know you, but I've seen firsthand just how powerful each of you is."

"I wish I could tell you what Death has planned, but I didn't ask. Our rule is that any Fae who knows of us must die. It's why Bran betrayed the Reapers. He told a female he was in love with, breaking our rules. Death killed her."

Balladyn swallowed, unsurprised by Fintan's revelation. He'd hoped to lead the Dark for thousands of years, but it looked like his reign would be one of the shortest in Dark history.

"But," Fintan continued, "Death could make an exception since she came to you, revealing herself and us in order to ask for your help."

"I'm ready to die."

Fintan's brows snapped together. "I'm surprised by your words."

"You shouldn't be. I never wanted to become Dark. I was happy as a Light, and enjoyed leading the Queen's Guard. I hoped to marry and have children with Rhi. Then Usaeil betrayed me, and I ended up with Taraeth. It would've been kinder had he killed me as he was supposed to. Instead, I've become this."

He stopped, thinking of how he'd captured Rhi and hurt her. How she had forgiven him, he'd never know. He didn't deserve it, that was for sure.

"So you'll give up?" Fintan asked with a snort.

Balladyn moved past him to the full-length windows staring out over the vivid green landscape of Ireland. He'd never thought to love a place more than he did the Fae realm, but he'd actually come to adore Ireland.

The silence drew him back to the present, reminding him that Fintan was waiting for an answer. "Give up? I don't really think I'd have a choice with Death."

"It sounds as if you want to die."

"Die? No," he replied. "But I'm a realist. I may love Rhi with all that I am, but I can never have her. Not only am I Dark, but no matter how I've tried to ignore it, her heart was given to another long ago. And whatever affection she held for me, I recently ripped to shreds."

Fintan came to stand beside him, his gaze out the window. "We all make mistakes. Talk to Rhi. Explain."

"It will only prolong what I know is coming. I've seen what she hasn't. Her Dragon King is once more dominating her world. I love her enough to let her go because I know she could never love me as she does him." Balladyn turned his head to Fintan. "Perhaps that makes me pathetic, but I have enough dignity to want someone who loves only me."

The Reaper smiled as he looked at Balladyn. "You were a great Light Fae, and I think you can be an even greater Dark. Remember all the things about Taraeth and Usaeil you knew were wrong and make sure you never do them."

"I'll probably make new mistakes."

"That's called living."

Balladyn held out his arm to Fintan. They grasped forearms as he looked into the Reaper's eyes. "I liked you the moment I saw you on the streets of Galway. Thank you for coming to see me."

"The color of your eyes doesn't define you. Remember that, King," Fintan said as he released Balladyn's arm.

With one last smile, the Reaper was gone.

Balladyn felt a kinship with Fintan. Maybe it was because they'd both been betrayed by those they served, or perhaps it was because they'd held the same position within the Dark. Either way, Balladyn considered him a friend.

It wasn't something he'd had in a very long time. Once a Dark, he hadn't trusted another, let alone opened up to anyone enough to become friends. The closest thing he had was Rhi, and even their relationship was tenuous at best.

He missed Fintan almost as soon as the Reaper left. The frank talk, the open and honest discussion was new to Balladyn. Or rather, a reminder of how his life had once been when he was Light.

It made him think of what his life could've been like had Usaeil not held such jealousy for Rhi and taken it out on anyone who loved Rhi. Balladyn turned his gaze back out the window, but it wasn't the rolling green hills he saw.

Instead, it was an existence with Rhi as his wife with their children running around them. It could've been an amazing life full of love, laughter, and the occasional argument so they could make up again.

Balladyn closed his eyes as they burned with emotions. That life was the one he'd dreamed of while Rhi was falling for her Dragon King. Balladyn had kept a tight hold of it, which was the only way he'd gotten through those days.

But it was as fictional as thinking that he and Rhi could rule the Light and Dark together. And that's what hurt the most.

Everything he'd wanted, everything he'd loved and held dear was gone, stripped away by a world bent on vengeance and ruin. He was King of the Dark, and yet he craved to reverse time and return to being a Light—even if he couldn't have Rhi.

But he couldn't do that. All he had was what was within his grasp now. Being a Dark—and King of the Dark—meant that he couldn't trust anyone. There would never be a time when he could take a wife and climb into bed with her at night, telling her of his day and all that had gone wrong. There would never be a friend he could talk through his decisions with.

And there would never be children.

Fintan had said he'd given up. Perhaps. But he was disheartened with everything and so lonely that it was unbearable. Having the all too brief moment with the Reapers and then Fintan's visit had only made Balladyn long for all the things he could never have.

He'd hated everything Taraeth was, but he knew he would end up just like the previous king. Everyone who led the Dark did because there was no way around it.

Balladyn thought about stepping aside and letting someone else become king. He thought of Ulrik and their pact to take down Usaeil. Would Ulrik still trust him now that he was safely ensconced back at Dreagan with the other Dragon Kings?

More importantly, did Balladyn even want to try? It had taken a lot to trust Ulrik, and now that he did, he didn't think he could handle it if the Dragon King turned his back on him.

Balladyn opened his eyes once he had his emotions tightly leashed once again. He was tired of fighting with himself, weary of living in the past, and exhausted from wanting a woman who could never be his. He wanted it all to end.

It was time.

He turned away from the windows and glanced at the table of books. The one on the far corner caught his attention. The cover changed colors in different light, and it made him think of Xaneth.

If there was one thing he could do before Death found him, it was to find—and maybe even rescue—the Light Fae from Usaeil. The queen was a vindictive bitch, and since her alliance with Bran was now finished, she would take her anger out on her nephew.

Balladyn was aware that it might already be too late for Xaneth, but he had to try. For himself and the honorable, loyal Fae he'd once been.

He hurried to the table and moved aside the books so he could use his magic to search for any sightings of Usaeil continuing her masquerade as a movie star. She loved the attention too much to give it up, and if he could locate her, then Xaneth would no doubt be close by.

The hope that Balladyn had as he began his search dried up faster than water in a desert. Usaeil had seemingly vanished from the human world. There wasn't a single picture or mention of her on any social media.

That only meant that Balladyn would have to find her the hard way.

Chapter Thirty-three

Erith couldn't stop smiling as she looked out the window of her tower to watch the sunrise. She wasn't naïve enough to believe that it would be smooth sailing from here on out, but she no longer felt as if a storm raged around her constantly.

Because she had Cael.

"Seeing the unabashed delight on your face is going to make me vain," Cael murmured as he came up behind her and moved her hair.

She sighed as he placed kisses along her neck, causing her to tilt her head sideways to give him better access. "You've had many reasons to be conceited, and yet you never acted it."

"Perhaps. Then again, I never had you in my arms," he whispered into her ear.

Erith turned to face Cael, looping her arms around his neck. "It's been three days since we returned and holed up here in the tower."

Cael leaned back as he shook his head. "If you say it's time to go outside, I'm going to have to toss you onto the bed and remind you why that simply isn't possible."

She laughed. She couldn't help it. She had laughed more in the last three days than in her entire life—which was a really long time.

He lifted her and spun, falling back on the bed as he held her against him. Then he rolled, pinning her beneath his hard body. "Why would you want to leave the tower?"

"Because we must." She put her hand on his cheek and smiled. "We can't stay in here and ignore our duties."

"Your duties," he corrected.

She shook her head. "*Our* duties."

He rose up on his elbow and quirked a brow. "You really want to include me in that? Because I'm fine with standing behind you and letting you do all the work."

"Nice try. I know you. You couldn't do *nothing* even if your life depended upon it. The Fates deemed that you harness the magic that Bran used against you. For better or worse, you have as much as I do now."

"I can feel the others trembling where they stand," he said with a chuckle.

But she didn't laugh. "You don't understand the changes within you yet, but you will. Shall I show you how to judge the Fae?"

"If you want me to stand beside you, then I will. But you're Death. That is your duty. I'll find something else, *mo shíorghrá.*"

My eternal love. That made her smile. "I'm excited to find you something to call your own."

"But," he said with a sigh, "we still have to leave the tower."

"The others are waiting for us."

Cael grinned as he shook his head. "Trust me, all of my Reapers are in bed with their women. Same with Eoghan. As for the others, I'm sure they're off having fun. Downtime is good."

"I know that," Erith said, taking offense that he thought she didn't. But then she had to admit, she hadn't been thinking about any of them—only her duty.

He raised a brow, and she rolled her eyes. "Fine. I concede that I was thinking they were waiting for me to get back to work."

"After all we've been through, I think everyone deserves a holiday."

She alone knew just how perilously close they had come to being destroyed by Bran. She would share those facts with Cael soon, but not now. Now was for their newfound love and the future ahead of them. But there would be no secrets between them. That was a surefire way to a division so deep that no couple could come back from it. She'd seen it countless times before.

Erith pulled Cael down for a kiss, but he drew back, his brow furrowed. "What is it?"

His lips flattened. "Xaneth."

Her heart stopped in her chest as shame fell over her. "I've been so wrapped up in you, in us, that I forgot about him."

"We both did." Cael jumped up and held out his hand for her, pulling her up beside him. "We can't leave him to Usaeil—if the queen does have him."

"It has to be Usaeil. Xaneth was intent on joining us. He wouldn't desert us," Erith said.

"Agreed."

Together, they walked from the tower. Once she had opened her realm to the Reapers, they had spread out, exploring the world to find places to erect their homes.

She and Cael found Eoghan and Thea first, simply because they heard Thea playing her violin. Erith wasn't surprised that the couple sat atop a bluff with a grand view of the mountains.

"I didn't expect to see either of you so soon," Eoghan said when he saw them.

Thea set aside her violin as Erith and Cael approached. "This place is so...." She smiled at Erith. "I have no words to describe the beauty."

Erith tried to return the woman's smile, but her stomach was knotted at the thought of Xaneth suffering at Usaeil's hands. The more she thought about the time she'd wasted in not looking for him, the more horrible she felt.

It was Cael who said, "We're here because we're going to begin looking for Xaneth."

"My group is already on that," Eoghan said. "They wanted something to do, so I sent them out, hoping they could pick up some kind of trail."

That made Erith feel a little better. "I'd still like to start searching myself. Can you alert the others, Eoghan? I'm going to return to the tower and see if I can find him."

"I'll do that," Cael said. "I need to see just how powerful my magic is."

This time, the smile came easily to Erith.

Cael frowned suddenly. "Kyran just called for me."

"And me," Eoghan added.

Together, the four of them teleported to Kyran to find him hovering over River, who sat on the ground. Kyran tried to get her to stand, and she slapped his hand away.

"What is it?" Cael asked.

Kyran looked up, relief on his face. "The baby is coming."

River leaned back on one hand, the other resting on her swollen belly. "I've been in labor for the last three hours."

"What?" Kyran yelled, running a hand nervously through his long hair. "Why didn't you tell me?"

"Because these things take time," Erith said, stepping in. She squatted down beside River as she noticed the lines of strain around the Halfling's mouth. "Cael, take Kyran back to the tower and set up the room on the second floor for River."

"Wait," Kyran said. "I want to be with my wife."

Erith looked at Kyran. "We're counting on you to get the room set up for her and the babe."

"Right," he murmured and looked helplessly at Cael and Eoghan. "How do I do that?"

"We'll help," Eoghan said.

Cael winked at Erith before they left.

With the men gone, Erith turned to River. "How bad is the pain?"

"It's been uncomfortable, but I had a bad contraction and couldn't stop the moan," River admitted with a twist of her lips.

Thea moved to River's other side to help support her. "You were going to have to let Kyran know sooner or later."

"He's been a nervous wreck ever since the baby grew so rapidly after we came through the doorway. It's gotten worse over the last few days, as if he's kn—" Her words halted as a contraction hit. River pressed her lips together and moaned low through the pain. "As if he's known," she finished a few moments later.

Erith nodded to Thea to hold onto River, and then she teleported all of them to the tower. Kyran was instantly by River's side. He lifted his wife gently into his arms and carried her to the bed.

"I've got you, my love," Kyran whispered as he laid her down and kissed her forehead. "I'll be right here beside you."

River's pale blue eyes met his as she smiled. "I know."

There was a sound behind them. Erith turned and found the others behind her. She didn't ask how they knew what was going on. Their little family was a constant surprise.

"I've got this," Neve said as she shouldered through them. She stopped beside Erith. "Unless you want to deliver the baby?"

Erith moved aside. "I don't know the first thing about it. Please."

Neve walked to the bed and began to talk in low tones to River and Kyran. Erith turned and walked from the tower to give them some privacy. Everyone followed except for Talin, who remained to lend Neve a hand.

"You know, I was thinking just the other day how quiet everything was," Erith said, reaching for Cael's hand.

Fintan laughed. "It's about to be anything but."

"I can't wait to hold the babe," Cat said wistfully.

Jordyn nodded eagerly. "And go shopping for clothes."

Everyone seemed to realize at once that there was nothing in the realm for either mother or babe.

"They don't have a house," Baylon stated.

Erith waved away his words. "They can remain here until they've decided on the right place."

"What all does a baby need?" Daire asked worriedly.

Ettie grinned. "That, I know."

It took less than thirty minutes going through Ettie's list for Erith, Cael, Cat, and the Reapers to conjure with magic everything that was needed.

Then they waited. Hours stretched as River's labor continued. It was well into the night before they finally heard the loud, shaky wail of the infant.

Everyone rushed into the tower, but Erith hung back. Cael paused and looked at her.

"What is it?" he asked.

"I've never held a baby before."

He looked at her askance. "Never?"

"I don't think I've been around many children."

Cael chuckled as he drew her into his arms. "All that's about to change."

"I like that."

"Come on. Let's go see the newest addition to our family," he urged and took her hand.

Erith let him lead her into the tower and through the doorway into the bedroom. She felt like an intruder as she spied River staring down at the newborn, her love shining like a beacon, her hair stuck to her sweat-soaked face, while Kyran had a smile so bright, it could rival the sun as he sat beside River on the bed.

As one, the group slowly crossed the room to gaze with helpless reverence at the tiny life nestled in River's arms.

"It's a boy," Kyran said proudly, tears in his red eyes.

The joy, love, and happiness that filled the room choked Erith. She hadn't realized until that moment that she had needed the Reapers more than they ever needed her. She'd tried to keep her distance from them, but it had all been because she was afraid that if they knew how much she wanted to be with them, they'd leave.

Erith slowly backed out of the room and returned outside to walk among her plants. A bat flew through the trees, gobbling up insects, while a wolf howled in the distance.

"You left," Cael said as he came up behind her, wrapping his arms around her.

"I never had a family," she said, looking up at the night sky. "I was just born. I never had anyone to hold me or teach me as I grew. I learned from watching other beings."

Cael walked around her, cupping her face in his hands. "I can't imagine how utterly alone you were, but somehow, you were brought to me. And I'll be forever grateful for that."

"Did you ever want children or a family?"

"I didn't really think about it," he said with a shrug. "I was a soldier. I assumed I'd get to that someday, but not until the war was finished. What about you?"

She licked her lips. "I never thought I deserved one after everything that I've done. So, I hand-picked my family from each of you."

"Who says Death can't have children?" he asked with a grin.

Erith smiled, her heart fuller than it had ever been. "No one."

"Then I guess we'll find out."

He leaned down and took her mouth in a long, slow kiss.

Epilogue

Cael walked beside Erith as they made their way down the streets of Belfast. For weeks, they had searched for any sign of Usaeil or Xaneth, without any luck.

Somehow, the Light Queen was masking herself from Death, and that was a very bad thing. Erith might not be too upset by it, but Cael was furious. After everything they had just gone through with Bran, to now have Usaeil using magic that far surpassed her own? It was upsetting, to say the least.

"Stop worrying," Erith told him.

He glanced her way, shooting her a dubious look. Both were using glamour to hide their eyes. To any human looking their way, he and Erith were no different than anyone else on the street.

"I wish you'd be a little more worried," he said.

Death chuckled and leaned her shoulder against him. "Are you concerned for me?"

Her teasing tone brought a smile to his face, even

though he was very worried. He lifted their joined hands and kissed the back of hers. "You know I am."

"I'm not."

The previous night, Erith had told him all she knew about Usaeil—including what she suspected was about to happen between the queen and Rhi. He'd been adamant about going after Usaeil themselves, but listening to Erith speak, he knew that the coming confrontation between Rhi and Usaeil was one they couldn't interfere in.

No matter how much he might wish it were not so.

There had been no word or sign of Xaneth, which only made things worse. All of the Reapers felt some measure of guilt for not being able to locate the Fae.

The only way for Erith to do it was to judge him and send a Reaper for his soul. Since she didn't want to do that, they had turned to Cael. While he felt the potent energy of his magic, learning all he could do with it was an agonizingly slow process.

Still, he had managed to find a location at least—Belfast.

"You're gloating again," Erith said without looking at him.

He grinned. "Perhaps, a little."

"A lot. Conceited, I believe is what Daire called you."

Cael turned down a narrow alley and had Erith up

against a building in a heartbeat, his body pressed against hers as he looked down at her, a wicked gleam in his eyes. "Conceited, aye?"

Her hands caressed up his sides before moving to his chest. "Hmm."

"Well, I suppose I have been." He wasn't too worried about it. While he'd promised Erith that she would never need to turn into the Mistress of War again, she had vowed to help him learn to control his newfound magic.

Suddenly, she sighed and rested her head against his chest. Frowning, he gently grasped her face with his hands and tilted her head back so he could look into her eyes.

"What is it?"

"The longer we go without finding Xaneth, the more worried I become. I should've been looking for Usaeil when we attacked Bran."

Cael kissed her forehead and pulled her into his arms. "You can't be everywhere or think of everything. Xaneth is strong and smart."

"But he doesn't know we're looking for him."

They clasped hands again and moved back onto the street. They hadn't gone even two blocks when they turned the corner and came face-to-face with none other than the King of the Dark.

Balladyn quickly hid the surprise on his face. "Have

you finally come for me?"

Erith's brows snapped together. "I have meant to come and speak with you, but we've been looking for Xaneth."

Cael studied the Dark. "You think Death is here to judge you."

Balladyn's eyes slid from Erith to Cael. "Aye."

"I came to you," Erith said. "I told you who we were. I did that not just because we needed your help, but because I believe you'll keep our secret."

The king frowned. "So . . . you're allowing me to live?"

By his tone, Cael suspected that Balladyn didn't want to be given such a reprieve.

Erith released Cael's hand and walked to Balladyn. She stared up at him for a long moment. "You are the best thing for the Dark. Lead them like you used to lead your Light army."

Balladyn looked away, obviously uncomfortable.

"What are you doing here?" Cael asked him.

Balladyn's head snapped to him. "Looking for Xaneth."

"Why?" Erith asked him.

"I felt as if I should," the king said with a shrug.

Erith smiled. "And that's why I've let you live."

"Besides," Cael said, "we know where to find you if any secrets do get out."

Balladyn held his gaze, not backing down. The king removed his glamour for just a second, letting his red eyes flash. Cael grinned, liking the audacity that was inherently Balladyn. The king didn't know that it was that boldness, that fearlessness that had made him such a brave Light—or such a powerful Dark.

"Have you seen Usaeil?" Erith asked Balladyn.

The Dark shook his head. "I found a post on Twitter from someone thinking they saw her here. I suppose we should thank Usaeil for pretending to be a movie star. Otherwise, no one would know what she looked like."

"We didn't think to look for that," Cael admitted.

Erith moved out of the way for others to pass and returned to Cael's side. "She knows we're coming for her."

"Rhi will be pissed she's not getting a piece of Usaeil," Balladyn said.

"Oh, she will," Erith said and looked over her shoulder.

Cael shrugged when Balladyn raised a brow and turned his attention to him, hoping Cael might elaborate. If Erith wanted Balladyn to know, she'd tell him. It wasn't Cael's place.

"I suppose I should leave you to it," Balladyn said and began to turn away.

"If you hear anything about Xaneth or Usaeil, will you let us know?" Erith asked.

The king looked at her and bowed his head. "You have my word."

They watched Balladyn walk away. Once the Dark

turned the corner, Cael looked at Erith and asked, "Was it wise to allow him his life?"

"You think he'll betray us? He's had a month to do it."

Cael shook his head in disbelief. "You gave him this time to see what he'd do."

She smiled and lifted one shoulder. "He proved his worth. It's also nice to have an ally if we ever need one again. Besides, Rhi knows of us and also hasn't said anything—not even to Balladyn."

They continued walking. Each of the Reapers had a grid of the city to search for any sign of Usaeil, but so far, no one had found anything.

"She wouldn't be out in the open," Cael said.

Erith snorted. "It's Usaeil. She'll believe she's safe."

"We better find her soon. I don't have a good feeling about Xaneth's survival."

"Me either," Erith whispered.

~

No matter how fast he ran, he wasn't quick enough. Xaneth jumped over a log as the sounds of approaching Trackers reached him. His lungs burned, and sweat dripped into his eyes. He didn't know what Usaeil had done to him—or even where he was—but the one thing he did know was that his magic was gone.

If he still had it, he'd be facing the Trackers head-on instead of running for his life.

He tripped on a hidden root and went face-first to the ground. Dazed, he tried to get to his feet by pushing up on his hands. The leaves beneath his palms slipped on the ground, and the next thing he knew, he was rolling downhill, slamming into various items before he finally crashed to a halt.

Xaneth didn't move. His entire body ached, and he was fairly certain that several bones were broken. Was this how he would die?

The one thing he'd vowed was that his life wouldn't end with him cowering. Whether he faced a Tracker, Usaeil, or Death herself, Xaneth would do it with his chin held high.

All that hiding, all the deals made between the Light and Dark, straddling both worlds had gotten him exactly nothing. He'd done the right thing and had gone to Death with what Bran was using to drain her powers. He'd expected to die on the battlefield with the Reapers—not be taken by Usaeil.

His bitch of an aunt had been waiting for him. She'd somehow known that he would be at the mansion. The moment he lowered his veil, she was there.

He hadn't even had time to call out to any of the Reapers. Not that he expected them to do anything. They all despised him—especially Aisling.

Xaneth closed his eyes. He was tired of running, tired of hiding. With no magic or weapons to fight the Trackers, he didn't stand a chance in Hell. But he was part of a royal line of great Fae, and he would do them proud.

He struggled to get to his feet, ignoring the pain that ran through him. Then he waited for the Trackers to find him. The minutes ticked by with nothing.

Finally, his legs gave out, and he fell to his knees before slumping over as exhaustion filled him. He would sleep for just a little before he fashioned weapons to stand his ground.

Read on for a sneak peek of the next thrilling
Dark Kings novel
IGNITE
Available May 2019

Chapter One

Dreagan

Things weren't going good, and they didn't look to be improving anytime soon.

V ran a hand down his face wearily. All he wanted was to go to his mountain and figure out why his sword wouldn't work. But he couldn't. If he did, every Dragon King at Dreagan would know something was wrong.

Eons after having his sword stolen and then hidden from him, it was now back in his grasp. But it did no good. Every King was counting on him to use it in order to check on the dragons.

He paced his room inside the manor, wondering if it was somehow his fault that his weapon wouldn't respond to him anymore. Had he done something to . . . ? That couldn't be it. The sword was his, part of him. All Dragon

Kings had a sword that only they could use.

So if it wasn't him, then what was it? What kept him from being able to use his sword to check on the dragons? Ever since the Kings forced the dragons to leave during the war with the humans, they had no idea if their clans were alive or not. The Kings didn't even know where the dragons were.

The dragon bridge was manifested from the combined magic of all the Kings, and it was the one and only time they had ever used such a bridge.

V couldn't stay in his chamber anymore. He stalked from his room and made his way downstairs. As he walked across the vast expanse of Dreagan—staying far from the Visitor's Center at the distillery where people lined up to take tours—he was glad he didn't run into any of his brethren.

Only Cináed knew about his conundrum. If this continued, V would have no choice but to tell the rest of the Kings. After all he and Roman gone through in Iceland just to find his stolen sword, it wasn't right that he couldn't make it work properly.

V kept walking. He didn't care where he went. He just needed to burn off some of the anger and anxiety that churned like a raging storm within him. His first choice would be shifting into his true form and taking to the skies, but that wasn't something they could do during the day. The fact they were hiding from the humans prevented that.

V could use his power. Every Dragon King was granted a special type of magic. For him, it was being able to disguise his dragon form when he shifted. He was so tempted to do that, but he didn't. It wouldn't be fair for him to take to the skies while others could not.

He had no idea how much time passed before he found himself walking along a paved road. V paused and looked up to get his bearings. He was no longer on Dreagan, and with their land encompassing sixty thousand acres that meant he had walked quite a ways.

V heard the roar of an approaching engine. He grimaced when he recognized the unmistakable sound of the Maseratti GranTurismo MC Stradale that belonged to none other than Constantine, King of Dragon Kings.

He watched as the bright blue sports car came into view. And just as expected, Con slowed when he spotted V. The Dragon Kings were the most powerful of beings on the realm, but even they had someone to answer to. That someone was Constantine.

Con rolled down his window, his black eyes locking on V's face. He was attired in his usual—a suit, starched shirt, gold dragon head cufflinks, and no tie. "Everything all right?" he asked.

V nodded. "Just walking."

A blond brow shot up on Con's forehead. "Toward the

village?"

"I needed to stretch my legs."

"And you couldn't do that on Dreagan? Or was it that you didn't want to run into any Kings?"

V blew out a breath and looked over the top of the car to the opposite side of the road where sheep grazed on the steep hills.

"I see," Con said after a moment. "You know you can talk to me about whatever is troubling you."

"I know." V met Con's black gaze. "I just need some time. Finally having my sword back after so many millions of years without it is taking some getting used to."

Con blinked, his expression devoid of any emotion, but V knew him well enough to know that Con was trying to discover what it was V was hiding. It was one of the many reasons Con was King of Kings.

"You know where to find me," Con replied.

V gave a nod. Con stared at him a moment longer before he drove off. The last thing anyone at Dreagan needed was the knowledge that something was wrong with his sword. With all he and Roman had discovered in the mountain on Iceland in regards to the Others, there was much the Kings had to do.

The Others.

The mere thought of them made V want to retaliate. The mysterious group was a mix of good and evil Druids as well as Dark and Light Fae. Why such an alliance would come together still confused the Kings.

Worse, the Others seemed to be after the Dragon Kings. And they had waited thousands of years before taking action. No one knew why the Others had been so patient.

Or what they were after.

V waited until he saw the taillights of Con's car disappear over a hill before he turned and resumed his walk. He couldn't think about the Others right now. He had to focus on his sword. Yet the two were connected.

It was the Others who had initially tried to get his sword. Fortunately, a group of humans that V once protected discovered the Others' plan. The humans used their skills to steal the weapon from V and hide it before the Others could lay claim to it.

He wished the gypsies would have told him their plan, but he knew he wouldn't have listened to them had they tried. He would've told them he could take care of things himself. The truth, however, was that he would've underestimated the Others. And the gypsies had not.

It was the Others who spelled V so he lost his memories about when and how his sword was stolen. But he now had them returned. His memories gave him little insight into the group, however. What they did show him were the lengths some mortals would go to in order to help the Dragon Kings.

That was in direct opposition to what the majority of humans had done to the Kings, which began the war between them. V still couldn't believe that the Dragon Kings, the strongest, greatest beings on the realm, had given up everything to the mortals.

That was a road he didn't need to wander down. His mind returned to the Others. Despite the attempt by the gypsies, the Others found the man who had taken his sword. The gypsies made sure that the Others couldn't touch it. Instead, the nefarious group put other traps in place throughout the mountain in Iceland to hinder anyone trying to retrieve the weapon.

It was through great difficulty and the help of friends that V and Roman were able to escape the mountain not only with their lives, but with the sword as well.

This wasn't the first time the Others had set ruses and deceptions for the Kings. Perhaps it was because of the tricks the Others used that made V apprehensive. First, it was the wooden dragon carved as a replica of Con. One touch to that figurine caused chaos to erupt.

There was also the incident in New York with the black dagger and a fellow King, Dorian.

And now this.

At least, those were the only ones he knew of. There could be more. That in itself made his worry double.

Read all of the Dark Kings Novels
Darkest Flame (Volume 1)
Fire Rising (Volume 2)
Burning Desire (Volume 3)
Hot Blooded (Volume 4)
Night's Blaze (Volume 5)
Soul Scorched (Volume 6)
Passion Ignites (Volume 7)
Smoldering Hunger (Volume 8)
Smoke and Fire (Volume 9)
Firestorm (Volume 10)
Blaze (Volume 11)
Heat (Volume 12)
Torched (Volume 13)
Dragonfire (Volume 14)

The Dark Warriors Series
Midnight's Master (Volume 1)
Midnight's Lover (Volume 2)
Midnight's Seduction (Volume 3)
Midnight's Warrior (Volume 4)
Midnight's Kiss (Volume 5)
Midnight's Captive (Volume 6)
Midnight's Temptation (Volume 7)
Midnight's Promise (Volume 8)
Midnight's Surrender (Volume 8.5)

About the Author

New York Times and *USA Today* bestselling author **Donna Grant** has penned ninety novels, novelettes, novellas, and short stories spanning multiple genres of romance including the exhilarating Dark Kings and Reaper paranormal series, the romantic suspense Sons of Texas series, the historical paranormal Kindred series, and the contemporary Heart of Texas series. She lives with her two children, a dog, and three cats in Texas.